Colonel Smythe's Daughter

By

Keith Armstrong

I hope you are not too traumatised by this

Keith

xx

First published in Ireland, in 2014,

By

Fairbairn Publishing, Fairbairn House,

Drumgora, Stradone, County Cavan,

Republic of Ireland

www.keith-armstrong.com

Dedication

To

Amie, Zoe, Ruby

About the Author

Keith Armstrong was born in Lancashire, England, and emigrated to Ireland in 1967. He lives with his wife Rosemary in Drumgora, County Cavan. Since his semi-retirement from international textile design and engraving, he has devoted a lot more time to writing. "A Day at the Races" was his first novel published in March 2013. His second novel "Sand Dollar Logistics" was published in December 2013.

Colonel Smythe's Daughter is his latest novel.

Chapter 1

My name is Luke Clemson, I'll be 33 years old next birthday, although, I feel considerably older now. I'm sat in a confined space, not much bigger than 8' by 6' and the light is not very good, making notes about what's happened in my life over the past number of years, trying to make sense of the life changing events that have occurred.

It must be almost 20 years ago, since I first saw Megan Offington-Smythe, at the county fair in Bishop's Bluff. She was visiting her cousin along with four other friends. I suppose she would've been about 14 or 15 at the time. She stood out from the rest of the group, because of her stunning good looks, with her Mediterranean-like appearance, raven black hair, piercing blue eyes, and a lovely olive complexion. When she smiled, she revealed perfectly formed dazzling white teeth.

My friends and I looked at her in awe, she had such jaw dropping beauty however, being realistic, she was untouchable, way outside of our league, and was surely destined for stardom. We found out she came from a wealthy family, so that was even more reason why she wouldn't be looking in our direction.

I later learned she'd an older brother called Tyrone, who'd been in trouble with the police. He'd been caught drug dealing after a lengthy surveillance operation. The chief constable at that time was a friend of his father, Colonel Offington-Smythe. He told him they wouldn't press charges if they could get him away from the area.

Apparently, the family had a tea plantation and sheep farm in Hobart, Tasmania, so as in days of old, he was to be packed off to 'Van Diemen's Land.'

His father told him this was his only chance. It was up to him to make a success of running these operations, because this was all he was going to get out of the estate.

The story goes, Smythe senior was so incensed that he'd brought the family's name into disrepute, everything else was being willed to his daughter. This caused huge resentment between him and Megan, because as the eldest child he expected to inherit the bulk of the estate, so he vowed never to speak to her or his father again.

I saw her several more times that year when she was visiting her cousin Sarah in the village, each time she had the same effect on me.

However, when Sarah moved away from the area, Megan had no reason to visit so I never saw her again.

I left school that summer after finding a job with a specialist cabinet making company. They crafted an amazing array of furniture, also carried restoration of timber in period and listed buildings. I was apprenticed to a master craftsman called, Bob Barron, who taught me everything I know. How to use the different tools without receiving injury, but more importantly, how to make the most beautiful furniture. He was my mentor for six years, until I completed my apprenticeship.

During this time, apart from making period furniture, we'd also go to carry out restoration work on old properties. One week it could be a church or an abbey, another week it would be a stately home or some other listed building. I could be carving a gargoyle or restoring an oak front door. The work was wonderful, and varied. I just loved it, soaking up all the training and instruction from Bob's vast wealth of experience like a sponge. Nothing, was too much trouble for him, he explained everything in such easy to understand detail. Crafts had always interested me, woodwork especially, it was one of my favourite subjects at school, although I was never that gifted academically, I knew I was good with my hands.

When Bob retired, he gave me all of his tools that had been made especially for him over the years. He said I was welcome to them, all he asked, was that I put them to good use. Bob had worked on way beyond his retirement age. I know he did it just so that he could see me finish my apprenticeship. However, towards the end he'd severe arthritis in his hands and fingers, every day duties became a major task for him. When he retired I missed him terribly, however, the cycle moves on. I now had my own apprentice to pass on all my knowledge and try to train him, just as Bob had passed on his skills to me.

Sadly, about six months after retiring, Bob passed away after a brief illness. Hundreds of people attended the funeral to pay their respects to him and his grieving widow Dorothy.

It was a sad time for me, Bob was the nicest man I've ever known, he was such a caring person, and he would always go out of his way to help people. He'd such amazing skills and could almost make wood talk.

I now had Bob's old clients to look after, and I saw a number of them when I visited some of the stately homes that he'd carried out restoration work on over the years.

One of them was Wigglesworth Manor, built in the Gothic style. He'd done some repair work there, ten years previously after they'd suffered a serious damage caused by woodworm. The owner, Colonel Roderick Offington-Smythe, had been in touch with my company and asked that someone pay him a visit.

It was a lovely sunny day, as I turned off the main road, through the impressive entrance with its ornate metal gates, then up the long winding driveway that led all the way up to the beautiful Wigglesworth Manor.

The gardens were truly spectacular and were a riot of colour. When I got out of my car, the scent from all the blooms filled the air. Several staff, were tending to the neat manicured lawns, topiary shrubs were being trimming and shaped like a barber trims a client.

As I took my tools out of my car, Colonel Offington-Smythe came out to greet me. He was a huge man with rosy red cheeks, a moustache and looked every bit a military man, so much so, I almost felt I should salute him.

"Mr Clemson, I assume, I am Offington-Smythe, thank you very much for coming so promptly. I understand you have taken over from Mr Barron, he was a lovely man, did some outstanding work for me a good few years ago?"

"Yes, he was, I must say I miss him a lot. He taught me everything I know."

"If you follow me, I will show you the problem that I have discovered."

He led me into his beautiful Gothic home, in through the great hall with its wonderful vaulted ceiling. What appeared to be family portraits, depicting the colonel's ancestral history, hung on the walls. At one end of the room there was an incredible marble fireplace, over it hung a large, impressive oil painting, of what I assumed was the Battle of Waterloo.

As we walked out of this breathtaking room, we came to the foot of the most incredible carved wooden staircase I'd ever seen. I could appreciate the workmanship that had gone in to crafting this magnificent work of art, it must've taken an age to produce it.

"I think we have a serious case of woodworm at the lower part of the staircase. As a precaution, we had the pest control people in just last week, that is the awful pungent overpowering odour you can probably detect. They sprayed chemical everywhere, in fact, probably drowned the little buggers because they poured in so much of the stuff.

"I did not realise we had a problem, until my foot went through the bottom step. I have placed a piece of plywood over it to stop anyone else from falling through.

"They are almost as bad as termites, when I was a child we lived in India when my father was a Brigadier in the British Indian Lancers. I recall that the house that we lived in had serious damage with these little blighters. You do not realise they are actively eating the wood until it is too damned late, apparently, it is the cellulose that they are after.

"One day I remember, a door fell off its hinges and when it hit the ground it just disintegrated into dust, all that was left were the hinges and the handles. When my father realised what had happened, he started to investigate. Most of the timber at first glance seemed unaffected, however, it was just an outer-shell that remained. All the inside had been eaten away with these little sods and you could just push your finger through what was left of the wood no problem. We had to vacate the house as it was in danger of falling down.

"I hope we do not have a similar situation here. What do you think, can it be repaired?"

"I'll take a look."

I checked over the staircase thoroughly. I spent over an hour, examining the stairs from top to bottom with a magnifying glass, looking for any signs of active woodworm.

"I think you've been lucky, you probably caught it just in time, it seems that only the bottom four steps and risers have been affected, as well as the Newel posts, also the gargoyle heads will have to be re-carved.

"I'll take a couple of photographs for reference, and make accurate measurements off each of the sections that need replacing. When I get back to the factory, I'll prepare a detailed quotation for you then let you know how much it'll cost, before we start manufacturing up any of the parts. It'll take us two to three weeks to make them up then suitably age them so they'll blend with the existing staircase."

"Very well, I will leave you to it, thanks very much for your help, I look forward to hearing from you. Can you find your own way out?"

"Yes, I think so."

I took several pictures of the damaged pieces, and was on my knees looking up the stairs, when I saw a tall figure approaching. Although, strong sunlight coming through the ornate stained glass window on the landing, shining directly into my eyes, made it difficult to see, who it was.

As the person descended the steps and got closer, I could see it was a young woman wearing riding breeches. She wore black leather boots and had a crop in her hand. As she turned her head to the side, I could see her hair was tied in a neat bun at the back.

"You don't have to genuflect on my behalf young man," she said, giggling as she strode out through the great hall.

My heart raced, had I just seen an apparition, or was it really her, Megan Offington-Smythe? Surely, there weren't two women blessed with the same beauty on this planet. It'd been over seven years since I'd last seen her in Bishop's Bluff.

Oh, what joy I just couldn't believe it, after all these years to see this woman again. Calm yourself Luke, I thought, you're acting like a love struck teenager. I was on a high as I gathered my stuff to head back to the factory. It never dawned on me that this was where she lived, or that she was connected to this particular family.

For years after first seeing her, she'd been in my thoughts constantly, beautiful women have that effect on me. Megan knew she was mesmeric, the old adage, if you've got it flaunt it, certainly applied in her case, as she turned heads everywhere she went.

After I'd come down from a high, and started to act as a mature adult, I made detailed drawings of all the pieces that had to be remade and costed the whole job, including fitting them in place. I passed the total cost of the project onto Colonel Offington-Smythe, and he gave me the go-ahead to start producing the parts.

Alastair, my apprentice and I worked on them after selecting suitable pieces of oak from the timber store. The gargoyles and newel posts took two weeks to carve, but I was happy that they were very close to the original. The treads and the risers had been completed, then, they were suitably aged with the help of a blowtorch, steel wool, several coats of linseed oil and beeswax. They'd a lovely patina, and when I offered them up to the original, they matched in perfectly.

We carefully removed the treads and risers one at a time, then fitted in the new pieces. It took a long time to do this, so I arranged to return, to fit the newel posts and their caps.

The next day after I'd fitted the last of the gargoyles, I was standing back admiring our work, thinking what a good job we'd done, when I became aware of someone standing behind me. As I turned, I saw it was Megan.

"Would you care for some tea, Luke?" she said with a smile on her face.

I felt weak at the knees as I gazed mesmerised at her beauty. She had a low-cut, pink top on that showed her ample cleavage, she was wearing shorts exposing her long, sun-tanned legs.

"Thanks ma'am, that would be lovely," I blurted out.

"It's Megan not ma'am, you make me sound like some old fuddy-duddy. Come along, follow me," she said in an authoritative voice.

I followed her like a love-struck puppy, through the great hall, down a long corridor into the kitchen.

"Take a seat, Luke," she said as she poured out the tea, "help yourself to sugar if you take it. There's also some of cook's sponge cake. It's her award winning speciality, so feel free to dig in."

I helped myself to some of the cake, while I looked intently at Megan, God she was so beautiful.

"I must say, you've done a great job with the stairs, Daddy will be thrilled when he sees it, and he's due back from London later tonight."

"I hope he'll be satisfied with our efforts, we've put a lot of work into it to get the wood to match the original."

"He'll be delighted with the repair. I know it, you're obviously very talented and not just a pretty face."

"Not sure which of those two comments I appreciate the most. Don't often get compliments in my line of work."

"Oh I can't believe that, you're an extremely handsome young man, I'm sure the girls fall over themselves to meet you."

I could feel myself blushing, I was quite embarrassed that she would be so forward to make such a comment.

"I'm afraid I don't have much luck in that department, in fact, I've never had a steady girlfriend," I stammered.

"I can see we're going to have to change that," she said with a wicked grin on her face, "how would you like to come to the hunt ball on Saturday, it's being held at the Rochford Arms Hotel? It will be a super event, they usually are, and there'll be lots of nice young girls there, most of them unattached! What do you say?"

"I don't think it would be my scene, I would be well outside my comfort zone."

"Nonsense, you'll really enjoy it, I won't take no for an answer, I'll send Charles our driver around to pick you up on Saturday night at seven thirty, all you'll need to do is to wear an evening suit. Just write your address on this piece of paper so he knows where to collect you from."

That was how it all started, after this, my life would never be the same again.

Chapter 2

How could I have married Luke Clemson, he was just too nice and innocent, like a lamb to the slaughter?

When I first saw him, I was attracted to his athletic figure, wavy jet-black hair and handsome face. His smouldering grey eyes took my breath away. To put it simply, he was an adorable hunk and didn't deserve the kind of treatment that I subjected him to.

My father was totally against our union, he felt I was marrying beneath my station, but I was determined. I said I loved him and as usual, I got my way in the end.

We were married in the chapel on the Wigglesworth estate. It was a grand affair with over 1000 guests in attendance. I remember well, the day of the wedding was beautiful, warm and sunny, all the flowers were in full bloom, as if they'd been commanded to be their very best on this special day. The reception was held in our grounds in several marquees that'd been erected especially for the occasion, the wedding was the highlight of the local social calendar. Afterwards, we left for our honeymoon on the beautiful island of Bermuda.

When we returned a month later, we took up residence in one of Daddy's cottages on the estate. Luke continued in his line of work and because of his ability, he gained status in the trade as a master craftsman.

The first two years we were deliriously happy and tried unsuccessfully to have children. Perhaps if we have had, the outcome would probably have been a lot different. Some responsibility may well have changed my outlook on life. Sadly, one of us was firing blanks. It wasn't for the want of trying, we were at it like rabbits, night and day, and I'm surprised Luke had the energy to go to work some days.

However, we failed to have any children and that's one of the things that helped wreck our marriage.

I'd no real qualifications to speak of. Academically I was only average, early on it was felt I wasn't university material. Modelling was an option I'd thought of, a couple of agencies that I'd been in touch with, felt that with my looks obtaining work wouldn't be a problem. However, when Daddy found out what I was planning, he nearly had a heart attack and wouldn't hear of it, so I was packed off to finishing school in Switzerland.

When I returned three months later, I joined one of his companies as an advertising executive.

The idea was, that I'd learn everything about the business from the ground up, then one day, takeover. However, after working there for just under a year, I decided enough was enough, work wasn't for me I'd become a lady of leisure.

After this and prior to marrying Luke, life was just one big social event, and I certainly played the field. However, even this can become tiresome after a while, so I felt it was time I settled down. When I met Luke, I felt he was the one for me.

However, after a couple of years I started to get restless and bored with married life, eventually I began a string of affairs. That's just me, that's the way I am, totally selfish, spoiled beyond what's reasonable, I don't care who I hurt in the process.

Luke was doing some restoration work in an old abbey in Northumberland, it was too far to travel back each evening so he stayed over, this went on for a couple of weeks. It was during this time that I met Clive Harlow, a real estate broker with a loveless marriage, or so he told me. Anyway, after several wonderful nights of passion, his wife showed up at the cottage one day, she threatened to 'cut my tits off' if I so much as looked at her husband again. I think Clive was more afraid of his wife than I was, so it came to an abrupt end.

That was the start of it, every time Luke had to travel to do some restoration and had to stay over, I played around. I just went from affair to affair. I don't know if Luke knew about these early relationships, but to be honest, I just didn't care. My father certainly knew about them, he came to see me and threatened to cut off my allowance if I didn't stop. He told me everyone was talking about it, that I was becoming an embarrassment.

I stopped for a while and became the dutiful wife, that is, until I met Jason Wimpole, God he was such a dish. Unfortunately, Luke came home early one day and found us in a compromising position. It was all very awkward, Jason got dressed as quickly as he could and beat a hasty retreat. Luke didn't say anything, it was almost as if he was prepared to put up with it just to keep me happy. Perhaps if he'd have gone ballistic, I may've changed my ways.

After this, I spent the next several weeks helping Daddy with his election campaign. He was standing as a Tory candidate, it was felt he'd more than a good chance of being elected to Westminster.

"Luke, we're going out to dinner on Saturday, Daddy is hosting a party at the Firkin Arms to thank all those who've helped him in his election campaign. It should be a great night."

"I always feel out of my depth at these events?"

"This is very important to him, he'll be offended if you don't put in an appearance."

"Very well, seeing as you put it like that, I'll go."

It was a fantastic night, Daddy thanked everyone who'd helped with his campaign. However, as the night progressed, one or two of them got the worse for wear through drink. One of my earlier conquests, Basil Thornwood, decided he'd inflict some ridicule on Luke.

"Well, well, if it isn't Joseph the carpenter, how's your wife the Virgin Mary, sorry, Megan doing?"

"Surprised you're asking, you probably see more of her than I do."

"Bitchy, who rattled your cage?"

I could hear Basil mouthing off, realising there could be a problem, I quickly walked over to them to calm things down. Luke stared at him then decided it was best not to make a scene and moved away, although, Basil continued to pour scorn on him.

"Basil, why don't you grow up, you deserve to get a kick in the balls for those comments? Consider yourself lucky that Luke was the bigger man and decided to walk away."

"Anytime he wants to try, Megan, let him bring it on."

With that, he fell backwards and collapsed in a drunken heap, then his friends carried him outside in the fresh air to revive him.

When we got home later that night, Luke didn't mention the incident with Basil, although he was very quiet. It had obviously upset him.

A few days later, Basil showed up and apologised to me for his behaviour, and wanted to be friends, he'd always be there if I needed him. Never at any stage did Luke discuss my behaviour or affairs with other men, so I'd no idea what his thoughts were.

Daddy was elected to Westminster, over the coming weeks, and months, there were a number of celebrations where I was introduced to a lot more potential lovers.

After this, there was a string of different men, including Basil, who was never very far away from the action. All the time Luke was a loving husband, he never once mentioned any of my extramarital episodes.

I loved Megan, but I felt I was reaching the end of my tether. The situation couldn't carry on indefinitely I'd have to do something about it.

She'd hurt me in so many ways on numerous occasions, and still continued to rub my nose in it.

Initially she'd gone behind my back, but later on, she didn't even attempt to hide the fact that she was cheating on me. There's only so much a man can take, of deceit and lies. She was offering her body out like a common slut, yet I'd been denied any of her favours in the bedroom for several months.

I came home from work early one day and heard her talking on the telephone to Basil Thornwood that was the last straw, I knew I'd to act and find out conclusively what she was up to. I hated this arrogant individual, with his snide comments and pompous attitude. He never missed an opportunity to offer verbal abuse, calling me a commoner on a number of occasions, and a sad case of working class ineptitude.

She'd arranged to go over to his house at 8 o'clock that night. He lived only a short distance away, less than a mile as the crow flies, although by road, nearer to three miles.

As soon as she left the cottage, I raced out of the back of our property, through the fields then climbed the wall that ran all the way around the Wigglesworth estate, down the lane towards Thornwood's house.

Megan had already arrived when I got there. I could hear the sound of raised voices coming from inside his home.

A neighbour in the cottage opposite had come outside to investigate. She was staring intently at the property as she smoked a cigarette, then walked over to Thornwood's house and peered in the window. She stood there for several minutes, observing what was taking place, before returning to her own cottage. As soon as she went back inside, I approached his house from the rear.

Eventually, the shouting stopped, as I got closer and looked through a kitchen window, I could see them clearly. They were kissing passionately, Thornwood then pulled up her skirt, removed her pants and placed his hand in her crotch. After several minutes, he pushed her back onto the kitchen table and they proceeded to have sex.

For me to witness this was sickening, I found it hard to keep my emotions in check, in fact, I was ready to explode.

I knew that she'd been deceiving me for years, I suppose subconsciously I was hoping it was all in my mind that there was an innocent explanation, but now there was no doubt. To witness what they were doing was just too much for me to bear. I couldn't watch it anymore, I walked away and started being physically sick. How could she do this to me, did I mean so little to her that she could just act like a bitch in heat?

After about an hour had passed, Megan came out of the house. On her way out she knocked over several garden tools that had been standing up against the rear wall of his property. She bent down, picked them up placed them back against the wall then, got into her car and drove off.

I sat there for several minutes without the will to live. Thornwood had made my life a misery. He never missed a chance to ridicule and abuse me, and here he was still doing it.

Eventually, I mustered the strength to get to my feet and make my way out of his grounds. I walked down the lane, climbed over the wall back into the estate across the fields to our cottage.

There was no sign of Megan. I poured myself a large Scotch, sank into an armchair to try to come to terms with what I'd just witnessed. It was like my worst nightmare come true, how could she behave like that?

Megan didn't return home until 2.30 in the morning, she climbed into bed without comment and assumed I was asleep.

Chapter 3

I was in my office when the desk sergeant put a call through to me.

"Chief Inspector Hyde, just had a hysterical woman on the phone, she says her boss, Basil Thornwood, has been murdered. She's the cleaning lady, over at the Glebe house, in Kilmington. Her name is Eva Bartok. When she turned up to perform her cleaning duties this morning, she found him dead on the kitchen floor. He has a pitchfork stuck into his back, and there's blood everywhere.

"I've directed a patrol car to the house and instructed the forensic team to head out there straight away."

"Thanks, Frank, I'll go over there just as soon as I finish collating all the evidence in the Malone case."

Glebe house was set in magnificent grounds, with beautiful maintained gardens, no shortage of money here I thought.

As I pulled into the courtyard, I could see several reporters present, some from the local rag. They raced over as soon as they spotted me.

"Chief Inspector Hyde, have you any comment?"

"Yes, clear off and let me investigate, you can see I've only just arrived? When we've completed our investigation there'll be a statement, until then, keep well away from the scene, otherwise I'll have you arrested."

Whoever was tipping these rats off had to be found, every time there was an incident they arrived before I did.

My men had erected tape surrounding the property. It was now a secure crime scene. I donned a coverall suit, shoe covers, rubber gloves and went inside.

He was dead for sure, he'd multiple wounds in his back. With the final blow, the pitchfork had been rammed in with such force it'd gone through the body and anchored it to the wooden floor of the kitchen.

"Jesus, whoever did this meant business, any idea how long he's been dead, Tony?"

"Walter Everette the pathologist, estimated the time of death was between six and ten p.m last night. I've lifted several prints off the handle of the pitchfork but they are not that clear. I've taken prints off the deceased to eliminate them, I'll start to process them as soon as I get back to the lab."

"Have you spoken with the cleaning lady yet?"

"Yes, although I didn't get much more out of her than what we already know. She found him when she opened the house up at eight thirty this morning to start her cleaning duties. She's with detective Masters at the moment and has agreed to come down to station to give us a sample of her fingerprints as soon as she feels well enough."

"Thanks, I'll go and knock on a few doors to see if anyone saw or heard anything."

I discarded my fashion accessories, and walked across the courtyard to the mews cottages on the other side. I gave the large brass knocker a couple of taps.

The door was opened by a tall, dark-haired female, she was thin with a very weathered appearance, probably the next time she'd see 40, and would be on someone's front door.

"Good morning, sorry to bother you, I'm Detective Chief Inspector Tyler Hyde, can I ask you a few questions?"

"Certainly, please come inside, I'm Vera Maddox?"

I was shown into her lounge. There was a predominance of pink in the room, something that Barbara Cartland would probably have enjoyed. I was directed to a large armchair, as I sat into it, I sank down several floors, all the way to the basement. I knew I'd need help in getting out of it.

"Did you see or hear any disturbance, between six and ten last night?"

"Yes I did, just after eight o'clock across the courtyard over at Glebe house, I heard a couple rowing it went on for some time and sounded serious. They were both shouting and hurling abusive insults at one another. Anyway, after about twenty minutes things quietened down, not long after the woman came out, got into her silver Mercedes sports car and drove off."

"Do you have any idea who it was?"

"Yes, it was that Clemson woman, she's always around there. Married of course to someone else, been carrying on with him for some time, apparently, she's a bit of a one."

"Did you hear exactly what was said?"

"Yes, things like 'stupid bastard' and 'common slut' and 'I'll kill you' the kind of everyday lovers talk," she said with a smirk on her face.

"What's happened, has someone been hurt?"

"I'm afraid it's worse than that, someone has been killed or to be more precise, murdered."

"Oh my god, was it Mr Thornwood?"

"I'm afraid it was, but that's all I can tell you at the moment.

"Do you have any idea where Mrs Clemson lives?"

By this time she was sobbing uncontrollably, eventually after several minutes she gained some composure.

"Yes, she lives in a cottage over on the Wigglesworth estate, she's the daughter of Colonel Smythe he owns the place, he's also a Tory MP."

"Thanks for your help Ms Maddox, one of my officers will stop by shortly, I'd appreciate it if you could give him a written statement covering the events as you've described them to me. Here's my card, if you think of anything else don't hesitate to ring me, goodbye."

I extracted myself from the depths of the armchair, damaging several vertebrae in the process, then left the cottage.

I tried unsuccessfully to reach Miss Clemson on the telephone, I knew I'd have to visit her home.

It was after 6.00 p.m when I drove into the Wigglesworth estate and located her cottage.

"Good evening, I'm sorry to bother you, I'm Detective Chief Inspector Tyler Hyde, are you Megan Clemson?"

"Yes I am."

"Would you mind if I asked you a few questions?"

"Not at all, would you please come inside, inspector?"

I was shown into the lounge and asked to take a seat.

"Could you tell me where you were, at approximately eight p.m last night?"

"Yes, she was here with me all night, I'm her husband, Luke. Has something happened?"

I looked at Megan Clemson, she was a strikingly beautiful-looking woman in her late twenties early thirties, tall, dark-haired, with a figure most women would die for. She'd a worried look on her face.

"There was an incident last night at Glebe House, apparently your car was in the vicinity, and you were seen to leave the property at approximately nine p.m. A Mr Basil Thornwood was murdered, I understand that you knew him?"

"Oh my God, Basil dead, how can this be, how did it happen?"

"I'm afraid he was stabbed to death with a pitchfork in a frenzied attack. His body was discovered by his housekeeper early this morning."

At this point Mrs Clemson had descended into hysterics, her face buried into her hands, sobbing uncontrollably as her husband held her and tried to comfort her. This went on for some considerable time.

"Are you sure you didn't visit Mr Thornwood last night?"

"Like I told you, she was here with me all night, never left the house."

"I'd prefer it if she could speak for herself, if you don't mind."

Eventually when she had calmed down, she answered me.

"Like my husband said, I was here all evening, never left the house."

"Very well, I'd appreciate it if you'd come down to the station, either later tonight or tomorrow morning to give a statement. I can see you are visibly upset, so as soon as you feel you're able to do so, I'd appreciate it if you'd pay us a visit. Sorry to be the bearer of such bad news, I'll bid you goodnight." With that I got up from my seat and left the house.

"Why the hell did you say I was here with you all evening, it looks like I'd something to hide?"

"As soon as I saw him and he announced who he was, I knew it was trouble, so I was just doing my best to protect you. As it turned out I probably helped you by saying that, after all, you weren't here last night, he said your car was seen in the vicinity and you were spotted leaving the house. So my actions have given you an alibi as to where you were last night."

"I'm so sorry, Luke, it's difficult to get my head around the fact that Basil's dead, I know you were only trying to help. You don't think I'd anything to do with it, do you? I did see him last night, we just talked about Daddy's successful election campaign that's all, but he was alive when I left him, I promise."

I looked at her, even now she couldn't tell the truth.

"If you stick to your story they'll find it difficult to prove you were at Glebe house, it's our word against theirs. I know you couldn't do such a thing, but there are probably a lot of irate husbands out there, who would've loved the chance to dispose of that philandering piece of shit."

I didn't for one minute believe their story that she hadn't left the house the previous night that was just her husband covering for her.

Mrs Clemson appeared at the station later along with the family solicitor, Claude Thompson. He was someone who I'd crossed swords with on a number of occasions. She denied she'd seen Basil Thornwood on that fateful night, or that it was her car that'd been seen near his house. Whoever had reported this, they were mistaken.

During the course of the interview, her father the Right Honourable Roderick Offington-Smythe MP, called the chief constable. He made known his outrage that his daughter had been taken in for questioning, in regard to this vicious murder.

She denied any involvement, and reluctantly because of this outside pressure, we had to let her go. However, my forensic team were actively involved gathering whatever evidence they could.

In the course of our investigation, it became clear that Megan Clemson, was indeed, in the words of Vera Maddox, 'a bit of a one.' Several dozen males were identified as possible suspects, although, because of their marital status they were reluctant to be interviewed. Shame, we interviewed them anyway. No doubt the divorce rate was set to climb as a result of our investigation.

Tony from forensics had managed to eliminate Thornwood's prints from those taken from the murder weapon. However, other prints needed to be identified and eliminated.

Chief Constable Atkinson, advised me to tread cautiously regarding Megan Clemson, he didn't think it would be a good idea to bring her in for fingerprinting.

Politicians, damned interfering assholes, let us get on with doing our job, and let them stick to making a balls up of running the country.

Megan had been spending a lot of time with her father since the murder of Basil Thornwood, and I'd barely seen her. To be honest, after witnessing firsthand what she was doing with him, I couldn't bring myself to talk to her. She obviously felt that Daddy, would be the one to help, after all, she could hardly turn to me, not without disclosing everything she'd been up to.

I had compiled a list of all her lovers, or at least, the ones that I knew of. It was a sickening catalogue of deceit and infidelity. Seeing it put down on paper, made me wonder, how the hell had I put up with this for so long? How could a woman be so devious and hurtful, without a second thought for the person she was cheating on?

I was in the station reviewing the Thornwood case, when the morning mail was placed on my desk. In it was an envelope that contained a list of names, stating they were past lovers of, Megan Clemson, it'd been posted anonymously.

Jesus, she had been putting it around, when I added it to the list I already had, it made over 50 people who'd been sampling her wares. Was it a jealous lover who had killed Thornwood, or was it the husband of one of the women that he'd been having an illicit relationship with, from our detailed investigations, there appeared to have been many? They all seemed incapable of a monogamous relationship, I put it down to inbreeding, it was either that, or something in the water supply.

Several names on the list were high profile businessmen, married to some of the socialites in the area. Plus, members of the judiciary seemed to have been dipping their wicks, she wasn't choosy, it was like she was on a one-woman mission, to shag as many men as possible.

This investigation had the possibility of causing mayhem to a number of marriages when all was revealed, it was only a matter of time before it would be, then the shit would really hit the fan.

"Daddy, I know I've been very foolish cheating on Luke the way I have, I suppose I'm not capable of being faithful, now I'm paying the price as I'm the number one suspect in a murder case."

"Do not worry pumpkin, I will think of something. The only evidence they seem to have is the sighting of you and your car outside Basil's house. Who do you think it was that passed this information on to the police?"

"It could only be that nosy cow, Vera Maddox, she lives in the mews cottage right opposite Basil's house. The other property is unoccupied at the moment, so she has to be the one.

"She could've easily have seen me, she's always standing outside watching, smoking a joint, never takes her eyes off the place. She could never get a man. Basil said she threw herself at him on more than one occasion, but he was never that desperate."

"Inspector, it's Frank on the front desk, one of our patrols have found the body of a middle-aged women in Ashcombe Copse, just outside Kilmington. She's partially clothed and it looks like she's being strangled. Tony from forensics is already on his way, I've dispatched another unit to help with securing the site."

"Thanks, Frank, I've just finished giving evidence in the Malone case, I should be able to leave court in about ten minutes, then I'll head straight over there."

By the time I got over to Kilmington, the press had been tipped off, and there were the usual pack of pain in the arses looking for information.

"Keep out of the way gentlemen, there'll be a statement in due course."

I walked over to forensics officer, Tony Morehouse, who was talking to the state pathologist, Walter Everette.

"What've we got, Walter, have you established the cause of death?"

"Due to the fact the body has started to decompose it's not so easy to tell, but it's a white female, about five feet ten inches in height and middle aged. It looks like she's been garrotted with that garden twine that is wrapped around her neck, with a serious number of blows to the head and face for good measure, making a positive visual ID impossible.

"However, something's not quite right. With the blunt trauma to the face, there's very little evidence of blood. Judging by the dark discolouration in her lower legs that would indicate to me all the blood had settled there and the facial injuries were inflicted sometime after the initial death, but I need to get the body back to the morgue to do a full autopsy to establish which came first."

"Is there any ID on her?"

"Constable Pierce has just found a handbag in the bushes over there, if it belongs to her, a driving licence indicates it could be, Vera Maddox," said Morehouse.

"Bloody hell, she's our only eyewitness in the Thornwood murder case. I interviewed her only last week. That's seriously bad news. Don't give any information to those news shites over there, let the bastards wait."

I looked at the body but it was impossible to say if it was her or not, due to the serious nature of her injuries. My gut feeling told me something wasn't quite right about this. Why batter someone's face making it impossible to identify them, then, leave their handbag with their documents in it close by?

I drove straight over to the mews cottage belonging to Vera Maddox, but there was no sign of her, maybe it was her body after all. I couldn't gain access through the front so I went around to the rear of the property.

The kitchen door was unlocked so I went inside. A strong smell of marijuana hit me the minute I went into the house. Several things caught my attention. There was what appeared to be dried blood on the kitchen floor, although not a serious amount, there was also a length of rope hanging over the back of a chair. Upstairs, her bed was unmade, several of her clothes were scattered on the floor, something odd, when in the rest of the house everything was obsessively neat and tidy.

I contacted forensics and asked them get over to the cottage as soon as they had finished at the murder site. I completed my investigation then headed back to the office to figure out what the hell was going on.

"Hello, Tyler, its Walter, just got the body of Vera Maddox up on the slab, something's not right about it. In fact, there are a number of things that don't add up.

"This person appeared to have been married, there's an indentation in the ring finger where a wedding band had been worn for many years. My understanding is that Vera Maddox had never been married.

"I'd also say that this body, could have been deceased for several days, before she was battered beyond recognition. But the main thing is, she wasn't garrotted or battered to death, she died from a heart attack and has undergone valve replacement surgery in the past. I don't think this is Vera Maddox.

"The only similarity is the age, probably within one to two years. I've taken x-rays of her skull and jaw and I think we'll have to contact the dental community, to see if we can get a positive ID from her teeth work. I'm sending the x-rays straight across to your office, you should have them within the next half hour."

"Thanks Walter, so Burke and Hare are alive and kicking? I was thinking to myself it was a bit suspect, how come there was no evidence of a post-mortem?"

"I don't know Tyler, is the honest answer to that, we may never know."

"It would appear, Walter, someone is trying to mislead us but who, but more importantly why?"

As soon as we'd the x-rays in our possession, we made contact with a number of dental surgeries. After several phone calls, we found one that had done work on Vera Maddox.

I headed straight over to the Kilmington dental clinic to meet Shahid Nazeer.

He compared the dental x-rays, with those of Vera Maddox. They didn't match. He imported a copy of our x-rays into his system he said he'd search his records to see if he could find a match. However, due to the high number involved, it would take some time.

We now had two problems, who was this woman and where had she come from, but more importantly, where was our main witness, Vera Maddox?

Over the coming days, all dental practices in the area were contacted, but none of them could find a match for our x-rays.

The clothes taken from the body were upmarket not supermarket brand, so we decided to check with some of the boutiques around Kilmington to see if these had been sold to Vera Maddox.

The end of the second day of searching, we found a boutique called 'Flaunt It' that sold the brand of clothing found on the body. They remembered having sold the skirt to a person called Vera Maddox about a month previously.

Someone was obviously trying to convince us this was her body.

Chapter 4

"Daddy, there are some awful stories being printed about me, I don't know where they're getting their information from, it's like someone is out to destroy me. They're just pure lies a total fabrication, plus they're also linking me now to the disappearance of Vera Maddox.

"I know I may have played around a bit, but nothing like the rubbish they are printing about me. I feel so ashamed, I'm afraid to step outside, there seem to be photographers hiding behind every bush."

"Not to worry, pumpkin, I am in the process of issuing legal proceedings for libel and defamation of character against the Kilmington Gazette, I have also pulled all our advertising from this rag. I do not see why we should support them when they are printing this kind of crap. I have also secured the services of 'Baseball Bat Security' they will make sure none of the paparazzi, if you can call them that, get anywhere near Wigglesworth.

"Have you spoken with Luke recently?"

"Yes, I spoke with him yesterday, apparently the press are hounding him everywhere he goes, every time he leaves the cottage they follow him, it's not very pleasant for him either in a number of ways, why do you ask?"

"You do not suppose he had anything to do with the murders do you?"

"Absolutely no way, Daddy, Luke wouldn't be capable of doing something like this, he's so kind and gentle, it's out of the question."

Megan was spending more and more time with her father just a short distance away at Wigglesworth Manor. Contact with me, had been reduced to the odd phone call. This didn't concern me too much, after all, our marriage was over, all that remained, was how it would all end up and how many more people would be destroyed in the process.

I'd been subjected to a certain amount of interest from the press when the news first broke, mostly they felt sympathy for me, the wronged husband of this adulterous woman, but this had now more or less finished, they were now concentrating their efforts on Megan.

When I studied the list of her lovers, several of them caught my eye who I felt perhaps should get a bit more attention. Neil Derek was one of them, a successful builder responsible for many of the new housing developments just outside Kilmington. He was a close friend of Roddy Smythe in his mid 30's. His wife had left him and moved out of their mansion because of his philandering ways.

I'd met him on a number of occasions, had even done some detailed restoration of woodcarvings on his property, which was a grand listed building. I didn't like him, I thought he was a slick individual, I wouldn't have done the work, only he was a friend of Megan's father and he insisted I help him.

At the time, I didn't realise he'd been one of her conquests or it would have been a different story. I found out afterwards he was a sexual pervert, not only had he had an affair with Megan over a number of months, but also, with several of his close friends' wives, in fact, as somebody else put it, 'anything that had a pulse'.

Several weeks had gone by, but we were no further to solving the mysteries that seemed to be occurring on a regular basis. We'd no idea who the person was found in Ashcombe Copse. Several missing persons were investigated, but none of them matched our body.

I was coming under more and more pressure from the Chief Constable, to move the enquiry along and come up with some answers. I'd a team of five detectives working with me, but we didn't seem to be getting anywhere. All the associates of Megan Clemson, and Colonel Offington-Smythe were a very close-knit community, reluctant to give any kind of useful information.

Our star witness had disappeared without a trace. Could it get any worse? Apparently, yes, because not long after, a report came in that a body had been found on a building site just outside Kilmington. Scenes of Crime officers were already there when I got to the location.

"Hi Tony, I understand we've another body, do we have any idea who it is?"

"Yes, it's the developer for this project, a guy called Neil Derek, he's through here."

The body was lying face down, there was a pickaxe embedded into the top of his skull.

"Jesus Christ, that's enough to bring tears to your eyes, any idea how long he's been dead?"

"Not long, the body is still warm, rigor mortis hasn't set in yet. I've managed to lift a lot of prints off the handle, I'll take the deceased prints to eliminate them. It's very similar to the Thornwood murder, this pickaxe has been driven in with such force it's gone straight through the top of his skull and has come out just above his top lip."

"That would give him a bit of a lisp, who found the body?"

"The site foreman, a guy called Jacob Landsea, he's in shock at the moment, could be for some time. Detective Rick Masters is with him trying to piece together exactly what happened."

"Three bodies in as many weeks, this is becoming a bit like Brian Rix farce, there has to be a common denominator in all of this, we need to find it urgently."

The spot where the body was found had been made secure, and all staff on the building site taken in for questioning. No one had seen anything or anybody out of the ordinary.

The site foreman had discovered the body not long after starting work at eight-thirty a.m and had immediately called the police. Whoever had done this, had to have committed this crime possibly, between six or eight a.m. Detailed statements, were taken from all the staff on site, as well as their fingerprints. However, when all the prints were processed, none of them matched the ones taken from the murder weapon.

"Megan, prepare yourself for a shock, I have just heard Neil Derek has been murdered, his body was found on one of his building sites earlier today. Found with a pickaxe through the back of his skull."

"Oh my god, Daddy, that's shocking, I can't believe it, Neil was such a good friend to all of us, who'd do such a thing?"

"Well, it could be any number of irate husbands, because as you know, life to him was one long continuous affair. But he did not deserve to be butchered like that. I gather his wife, Delia, has gone back to the family home, apparently she is absolutely distraught, it is possible she could be a suspect."

"What's happening to us, it's just more bad news on top of more bad news, the police don't seem to be doing anything? The only people that are active are the newspaper reporters, and they are becoming a pain in the arse.

"The minute I step outside of the estate, there's someone flashing a camera or sticking a damned microphone in my face, I'm bloody sick of it."

"Well Megan, there is every likelihood that this will increase because this is far from being over. The coverage is also having an adverse affect on my new political life, even the PM is asking questions."

"I'm sorry Daddy, it would seem it's all my fault, I should've kept my legs closed."

"Too late to worry about it now, pumpkin, we just have to dig in and hope it passes over soon enough."

I discovered that Alan Walters was also someone who'd availed of Megan's services for over three months. He was a car dealer, selling upmarket cars like Ferrari, Mercedes and Porsche.

He was in his early thirties, unmarried, and felt he'd the God-given right to seduce every woman he came in contact with, assuming they caught his eye of course. He was good-looking, tall, with an athletic figure, and a regular squash player. He was so accomplished at the game he often gave lessons in the local squash club.

A number of married women had taken up the sport and he was only too willing to offer his services. The president of the club called him in after he'd received complaints from some of the husbands, who didn't take kindly to the kind of tuition that he was giving.

Obviously, he met Megan when she bought her Mercedes sports car from him, and the affair started then. He came to our house on several occasions afterwards, just to make sure she was happy with the service. I have since discovered the kind of service he was giving her.

It was just over four weeks after the first murder, when we got a breakthrough regarding the body found on waste ground outside Kilmington.

It was discovered that a new grave had been opened and a body taken from it, at a cemetery in Rochdale, in the north of England.

The body was that of Jane Mills, she was a 43-year-old teacher, who'd died suddenly from a heart attack whilst at school. She'd a history of coronary problems and had undergone valve replacement surgery some years previously.

Apparently, before her sudden demise, she was going through a messy divorce, her parents became convinced that somehow her husband could be implicated in her death because of her hastily arranged funeral. They insisted the body was exhumed and an autopsy performed.

When their concerns were taken onboard and the application was finally granted, they opened the grave. It was then they discovered her remains had been removed.

That's when the hunt for the body began, seeing as details of our mysterious woman had been circulated to stations around the country, it didn't take long to figure out who she was, and eventually, she was positively identified from her dental records.

Someone had gone to a lot of trouble and made a very amateurish attempt to mislead us into thinking it was the body of Vera Maddox, but why? But more importantly who?

The evidence was pointing towards Megan Clemson. Our witness was sure she'd seen her leave the victim's house that night, so if our main witness was eliminated, bang goes our case. However, when I interviewed her, my gut feeling was she didn't do it. But, I've been wrong before.

Chapter 5

As I raced out of Wigglesworth Manor, I almost ran over one stupid clown as he leaped in front of my Mercedes to take a photograph of me. These scum, why don't they get proper jobs? I've had about as much as I can take of them.

I drove up Fetlock Lane, parked outside of the Masons Arms, and went in for lunch. I hoped that some of my friends would be there. However, the place was deserted so I tried contacting some of them by phone, but they all seemed to be otherwise engaged.

At mid-afternoon, I left the pub, then drove into Walters Autos to see Alan, but only caught a glimpse of him hurrying out of the showroom. I know he'd seen me, what the hell was his problem?

His secretary said he'd an urgent appointment in town, and he'd gone for the day. If I didn't know any better, I'd say he was trying to avoid me. I tried his mobile phone several more times in the course of the day, but he didn't answer.

The next person on my hit list was Jeff Landers, who owned a pub called the 'Vomiting Dog' in a place called Ringwood. Jeff was someone who I'd been involved with some years earlier.

"Hello, Jeff, nice to see you again, how've you been keeping?"

"Fine, Megan, what can I get you?"

I thought he sounded a bit curt, "Give me a large glass of Chardonnay please. Any of the old crowd, been in lately?"

"Can't say I've seen anyone, but I'm not here all the time, bought another pub, 'The Cock and Bottle' over in the town of Freckleston, spend most of my time over there now."

"Good to see you're expanding. Daddy always said you were a go getter."

"Cut the crap, Megan, why are you really here?"

"Same old Jeff, blunt and to the point, it's one of your more endearing charms. But you don't have to be so dammed rude, after all, we did have something going for over three months."

"Look, if you'd kept your knickers on, I might still have had a marriage, instead, I'm divorced, most of my money has gone in a settlement, now I've to start all over, borrowing to move on. Something I shouldn't be doing at this stage of my life."

"It might have escaped your attention, Jeff, or you're suffering an acute case of amnesia, but you pursued me at the time, bombarding me with phone calls, never missing a chance to corner me when I came into the pub. Anyway, it's history I regret it just as much as you do, I'm sorry it has ended badly. Linda was a lovely woman, probably the first time I felt any kind of guilt when we went behind her back."

"Don't concern yourself with her, she's come out of this a wealthy woman and has already moved on with a younger model, plus my kids treat me like a leper now, so my humiliation is complete, perhaps you can understand why I'm bitter."

"Hindsight is a great thing, Jeff, we should never have become involved it was utter madness. But the reason I'm here is, I'm just wondered why most of my male friends seem to be avoiding me."

"Have you not seen the Kilmington Gazette today?"

"No, we don't purchase that rag anymore, they couldn't print the truth if it came from the Archbishop of Canterbury himself."

He reached behind the counter, picked up a copy, and handed it to me.

The headline read:

'Male friends of Madam Clemson running for cover.'

"That's fucking libellous, Daddy will close that rag down."

When I read what the front page said, I understood why no one would speak to me.

Their reporter, Kelvin Smith, had been supplied anonymously with a list of men's names and spoken with a number of them who, he described as, my past acquaintances. They were all very frightened, and felt they could be the next target. He couldn't name them for legal reasons. No, but it was Ok to name me, the bastard. I took the paper, left the pub immediately, and drove back to Daddy.

"They have gone too far this time pumpkin, I will get our legal people onto this straight away. They wont get away with this, it is bloody character assassination."

I felt awful, am I really that bad news that people have to hide and avoid me? I thought I'd go and see how Luke was.

I walked the short distance from the Manor to our cottage, he was just arriving home as I got there, so I followed him inside.

"Hi, Luke, just wondered how you are coping with all that's going on at the moment."

"Oh, I feel wonderful, I'm getting used to seeing the inside of a police station. I'm only just getting home after three hours of interrogation over the death of Neil Derek.

"Hauled in over the demise of another one of your conquests, and quite frankly, getting a bit pissed off being the number one suspect in all this lunacy."

"I'm sorry, Luke, what happened?"

"We'd been doing restoration work at Cannock Hall near Salisbury, had only just got back to the factory when I got a visit from Detective Tyler Hyde who asked me to go down to the station. He wanted to know my whereabouts in the early hours of July sixth. I didn't realise that Derek was dead, I haven't had chance to pick up a newspaper the last week, as Alastair and myself have been working flat out on the property for the National Trust. Anyway, I'd a cast iron alibi, Alastair, and the staff of Flagship Hotel confirmed I was staying there on the day he was killed. There would be no way that I could be in two places at once, plus it's over forty-five miles away from the murder scene.

"That detective, is like a dog with a bone, he kept picking away at my alibi, and he also said he didn't believe our story that you didn't leave the house the night that Thornwood was killed. But I was adamant we were together all night I just kept to the story, so there's not a lot he can do.

"I asked him that if any more of your lovers gets bumped off, would I automatically be the number one suspect and taken in for questioning, because if that was the case, I might as well move my bed into the police station to save him time."

"That's not very nice, Luke, that makes me sound like a real tramp."

"If the cap fits, wear it. What did you expect, you've treated me like shit the past number of years. My only fault was that I loved you too much."

"You've changed, Luke, this isn't like you, it's very hurtful, I'm leaving."

"Want to know what hurt feels like, try being on the end of deceit and adultery for over six years?"

With that, she stormed out of the cottage.

It was just after 3.00 a.m on September 5th, when a fire started in Walters Autos. The blaze had started in the workshop, within seconds highly inflammable paint thinners ignited and engulfed that whole section, before spreading into the showrooms, setting numerous high value cars alight.

By the time the emergency services got there, the unit was well on fire and it took six appliances to bring it under control, but by this time the building was totally destroyed.

As soon as the area had cooled down, the forensic people were able to move in to begin their investigation. It soon became apparent, that this was no accident as they found several points of ignition.

It was estimated that the value of the cars alone that were destroyed, was in excess of a million pounds. It was late in the day when they prised open the boot of a Mercedes sports car and discovered a body inside. Although the body had been kept away from the direct flames, it had been severely barbecued making a positive visual ID impossible.

I raced over there as soon as I was made aware they'd found a body.

"Any idea who it is, Tony?"

"Not at this point, but it appears to be a male, well done, in his late twenties early thirties, with what looks like, the remains of a squash racket rammed up his arse. But we need to get the body out and let Walter do a full autopsy, to see what killed him. But this fire was no accident, as it was started in the workshop in several places, before it spread into the showrooms. It would appear that we've another murder on our hands."

Detective Tyler Hyde had phoned me and asked me to come down to the station to answer a few questions.

"Sorry I can't, I'm in East Lothian at the moment doing some restoration work on a Hislop Castle for the Scottish National Trust. We've to finish it by the end of tomorrow because the house opens to the public the following day. I'll start to head home just as soon as our work here is complete. Can you tell me what it's about? No, on second thoughts don't, let me guess, another murder victim. Like I said before, I could become a regular feature in your station. Meanwhile the person who is really responsible will carry on. Perhaps you should just lock me up for a few months and see if anymore lecherous people are eliminated?"

"Don't tempt me, Mr Clemson, just make sure you call into the station the minute you get back."

By now the press were all over me like a bad rash.

'What was the investigating officer doing after another murder victim had been found?'

The Chief Constable was on my case, life was becoming difficult for all my team. We'd three murders, one grave robbery, a witness that had disappeared and about 50 possible suspects, or maybe even more. We just didn't have any real idea how many adulterous people were involved, or whether it was male or female that was responsible for these crimes.

The body that we found in the trunk of the burnt out Mercedes, we eventually identified by his dental records. It was confirmed to be that of the owner of the business, Alan Walters. Cause of death, internal bleeding caused by a squash racket being inserted with such violent force into his anus it had ruptured several internal organs. The pathologist felt he was probably still alive when he was locked in the Mercedes, as a result, died an excruciating death. Our murderer was very original, of that there was no doubt.

Luke Clemson paid me a visit as soon as he returned from Scotland, but he'd a cast iron alibi. I'd already checked his story and he was indeed doing restoration work at Hislop Castle at the time of the fire so I could rule him out as a suspect.

Chapter 6

It was time for some direct action. My team and I were coming under increased pressure, not only from the Chief Constable but also from the press. I pulled off the main road into the Wigglesworth estate, and was immediately stopped at the entrance by several shaven, bald-headed men who denied me access. They looked intimidating, like clones, with cauliflower ears and flattened noses, with faces only a mother could love.

"What do you want?"

"I'm here to see Megan Clemson, it's official business."

"Suggest you get your arse out of here pronto, we've had enough of you press, so turn your car around and piss off."

I then produced my warrant card, and informed him he was obstructing police business, so if he didn't move his 'arse and piss off' I'd investigate how legitimate they were. Reluctantly, they moved to one side then I started up the long driveway to the manor.

I'd never seen the main house close up before in the daytime, it was certainly an impressive pile. I gave the large metal doorknocker a couple of thumps, eventually after what seemed an age, the door was opened by a doddering old fart, I assumed was the butler.

"I'm Detective Chief Inspector Tyler Hyde, I wonder if I may have a word with Mrs Clemson please?"

"You can wait in here, I'll see if she's available."

Eventually she appeared in her riding attire.

"Can't stop now, I'm just about to exercise my horse."

"This is important, I need to speak with you urgently."

"Sorry, no can do, make an appointment like everyone else has to do."

With that, she swaggered off to the stables with her head in the air.

"Just make sure you come down to the station before the end of today, otherwise if you don't, I'll send the uniformed people out and arrest you, the choice is yours."

No doubt that will piss Daddy off, but who cares, who do these people think they are?

It was late afternoon when the station sergeant advised me that Mrs Clemson was in reception with her solicitor.

"Thank you for coming, please take a seat."

I could see she was very annoyed. In fact she looked ready to explode. She'd her hands in a clasped position, nervously spinning her wedding ring.

"Can you tell me where you were between the hours of seven p.m last Tuesday and three a.m on the following morning?"

"Of course, at home in bed at Wigglesworth Manor."

"Can anyone confirm this?"

"Certainly, Daddy can."

"Why, do you two sleep together?"

She rose to her feet ready for battle with fists clenched.

"Don't be so fucking insolent you stupid man."

"I'm sorry, it's just that the house is so vast and there must be numerous entrances in and out of the place, someone could easily come and go without being seen."

"Think what you want you cretin, I was at home all night, in bed on my own. How dare you make such an outrageous suggestion, who do you think you are?"

"Just someone who is trying to do their job, but not getting a lot of help from people that are involved directly or indirectly. It would appear that the truth is stranger than fiction."

At this point, she broke down completely and the tears started to flow in abundance. Her solicitor asked could she have a glass of water and this was duly supplied, she then swallowed a number of pills. Eventually, when she'd calmed down, he advised her not to say anything further, then he told me that the interview was over.

"Once again inspector, you show your immense ability to piss people off, resulting in the utmost cooperation, when will you ever learn?"

"You never stop learning in this job, there's always something to test your powers of understanding."

"You'll be hearing from my MP, who happens to be my father, you nasty little man."

"My client was at home at the time as she has already stated, so unless you can come up with something that can prove otherwise, this discussion is finished."

As soon as they'd left the room, I took the glass she'd used, carefully placing it into an evidence bag, then, took it straight up to Tony in forensics.

"The prints on that glass belong to Megan Clemson, see if they match any of those taken from the murder weapons."

"How did you manage that?"

"Let's just say, it's years of being able to piss people off."

Within the hour, Tony confirmed that he'd found a thumb, fore and middle prints on the glass that matched those taken from both weapons. Success at last!

We headed out to Wigglesworth Manor, this time I was waved through by the ugly brothers and drove straight up to the main house.

"I need to speak with Megan Clemson, urgently."

"What do you want with my daughter?"

"I'm here to arrest her in relation to the murders of Basil Thornwood, and Neil Derek, we have conclusive evidence that she was involved with both murders."

"That is preposterous, there is no way my daughter had anything to do with those murders, they were very close friends of hers."

"So were half the male population of Wiltshire, by all accounts, now can you get her here, or do we have to perform a search of the house to find her?"

"Do you know who you are talking to?"

"I'm well aware who you are, I'm afraid your position doesn't cut any ice with me, now we're playing by my rules, so get her down here before I lose my patience totally."

Eventually, she appeared and reluctantly came with us to the station. She was detained for questioning in the presence of her solicitor, although she protested her innocence throughout the interview. She said her husband was with her the whole time the first murder was committed and that was a fact. And she was at the manor in bed when the second murder took place.

"Can you explain to me then, how come your fingerprints were found on both murder weapons used in the killing of Basil Thornwood, and Neil Derek?"

"No idea, I never gave you my fingerprints, how did you get them?"

"We took them from the glass you used in the interview room."

She looked at her lawyer, "Is that allowed, they took them without my permission?"

"Well I have to say it seems most irregular what you've done, not standard procedure."

"Sorry if you don't like it, but tough, I'm investigating a series of murders and I'm afraid when you come up against poor cooperation, you resort to whatever you have to do. I'll ask you again, how did your prints find their way onto the murder weapons?"

She thought about it for a while.

"I've absolutely no idea how my prints could've got there, I don't believe they're mine, I think you're just trying to pin something on me, because you don't agree with how I conduct my life."

"The prints are yours whatever you say. It's a fact, pure and simple, I'm afraid there's enough evidence to charge you with these murders."

At this point, she broke down completely, so I left them in the interview room whilst I put the details to my superiors.

The Crown Prosecution Service felt there was more than enough evidence to charge her with the two murders.

She appeared at the local magistrates court shortly afterwards and pleaded not guilty, was then remanded on bail to appear later in the year at the crown court.

The prosecution pushed for a custodial remand, but her father had hired a top lawyer. As a result, she was granted bail with the condition she surrendered her passport, as well as reporting to our station once a week.

Her alibi was a major stumbling block for us, so I thought I'd pay a visit to her husband.

I drove out to their cottage and found Luke Clemson just about to leave.

"May I have a quick word with you before dash off?"

"If you must, but I can't spare much time I've things to do."

"This won't take long, I'm sure you've heard by now we've arrested and charged your wife with two murders.

"When I interviewed her the day after the first killing, you confirmed that she was in your company the whole night. I'm giving you the opportunity to come clean and tell me the truth.

"When this goes to the Crown Court and it will, your testimony under oath, assuming it stays the same, will be perjury. This is a very serious offence, punishable by incarceration. I'll ask you again, if you tell me the truth I'll forget you told me lies the first time around, was she with you all evening?"

"She was with me the whole night, and that's the truth. You've charged the wrong person. She wouldn't kill anyone. And neither would I, and to be perfectly honest, I'm getting pissed off being hauled into your station, every time another one of her conquests gets bumped off, it's getting a little boring."

He had a point, we needed to expand our investigation but this clique stuck together like shit to a blanket, truth wasn't in their vocabulary. However, the Crown Prosecution Service felt that there was overwhelming evidence to charge his wife with the first two murders, despite their alibis.

"Very well, but don't say I didn't warn you."

With that, I returned to the station.

Jason Wimpole, had received a parcel in the mail, he noticed it had been posted from Scotland. He knew he hadn't ordered anything and was a little unsure what to do. He placed it on the floor and periodically looked at it.

Eventually, he couldn't resist it any longer, the curiosity was killing him, and placing the parcel on the kitchen table, he proceeded to open it. He removed the outer wrapper then used a knife to slit through the top of the carton, carefully opening the flaps. He leapt back when he saw what was inside.

The word 'BANG' was written on the bottom in large letters, there was an envelope inside. Written on it was 'next time you won't be so lucky.'

He appeared at the station not long after, in an agitated state.

"Leave it with us, Mr Wimpole, we'll see if we can obtain any prints off it, would you leave us a sample of yours so that we can eliminate them from the carton, if you don't mind?"

He went with one of my staff and duly supplied them with a set of his prints.

I was just about to leave my office when Tony from forensics called me.

"Inspector, I've got a match for the prints. You're not going to believe this, but do you remember the squash racket that we extricated out of the rear end of Alan Walters? Parts of the handle had been protected from the fire. After I had managed to remove and carefully clean it, I recovered a number of prints. A lot of them match the ones just supplied by Jason Wimpole."

"Well, well that's a turn up, let's get him back in."

One of my men contacted Wimpole, and invited him to return to the station.

"Mr Wimpole, thanks for coming in. You may recall that recently there was a fire over at Walters Autos, the principal of this company was found murdered in one of his cars. A squash racket had been inserted where the sun doesn't shine, and guess what, we've matched a number of your prints you've just supplied, to those found on the murder weapon that was used on Alan Walters, any idea how that could've happened?"

He sat there shaking like a leaf, by now, probably regretting he'd been in to report the previous incident. He was ringing his hands and seemed to be really wound up, eventually he replied.

"My sports bag was stolen from the locker room at the squash club, I'm not sure about the date, but I reported it to the management at the time and the police were called and they did attend. I'm sure you'll find a record of it, if you bother to check."

Smart little prick. I thought I'd got him banged-to-rights, but his explanation if confirmed would raise some doubt. A couple of phone calls verified what he'd told us, so we reluctantly we'd to let him go, for now at least, once again the waters had become muddied.

Chapter 7

I was in my office reviewing the murder cases, in an effort to move forward. Constant pressure from above, was causing me stress, I was ticking off the days to my retirement when I could leave it to someone else. In the past, I've known senior investigating officers who've had a regret if they retired before they solved a particular crime. Not in my case, I was so frustrated with these lecherous people who didn't know fact from fiction, and all seemed to have the morals of a tomcat. The sooner I could leave it to someone else, and retire to my bolthole in Spain, the better.

We'd charged Mrs Clemson with two murders, but I'd this nagging doubt about her guilt. The murderer of Alan Walters was still at large, our prime suspect, Wimpole, had a plausible explanation as to how his prints had been found on the murder weapon. Also, we'd to find the whereabouts of Vera Maddox, and who'd robbed the body of Jane Mills from the grave in Rochdale. The main common denominator in all this was Megan Clemson. The three murdered men had all been her lovers at different times, the obvious conclusion was that her husband was responsible but he'd got alibis and besides, it was just too convenient. Was someone trying to fit him up?

I was mulling over what we could do and what direction our investigation should head in, when the Police in West Yorkshire contacted us. They'd found a middle-aged woman wandering in a distressed condition on the A684 just outside Bainbridge. She'd been taken to the Airedale General Hospital for treatment. Her name was Vera Maddox from Kilmington, she told the police she'd been kidnapped but managed to escape from a farmhouse she'd been held captive in. She'd run miles over moorland country until she found her way onto the main road.

"Did she give you any hint as to who had held her captive, Inspector Halliwell?"

"No, she was very upset and distraught, just give her a little time I'm sure it'll all come out in due course."

"Well thank God she's been found alive, she's a vital witness in a murder case, is there any chance you could post someone on duty to make sure there's no attempt on her life?"

"We already have a constable on the door to keep an eye on things."

"That's perfect, we'll leave now hopefully, be there just after lunch. Many thanks for all your help, Inspector."

Myself, and Detective Rick Masters headed off to interview Vera Maddox.

It was a pleasant trip as we headed north into Yorkshire. We decided to take the scenic route to give her a bit more time to recover, so we drove through the Dales.

The views were spectacular with all the dry-stone walls that divided the fields into different sections. Magnificent old stone farmhouses were dotted around, some of them advertising afternoon tea and scones with clotted cream and jam. We stopped briefly, to sample the gourmet delights of this beautiful county, then continued on to the Airedale General hospital.

It was after 4.00 p.m when we arrived there, we were taken through to a private ward where she was resting.

"Have there been any visitors, Constable?"

"No sir, apart from the doctors and the catering staff."

"Good, please keep a close eye on her she's a vital witness in a murder case."

Vera was sat up in bed and greeted us with a smile as we entered the ward.

"How are you feeling, Vera?"

"Hello inspector, much better now that I'm free, but absolutely scared to death during the whole time from the minute they kidnapped me, to the time I managed to escape."

"If you're up to it, I'd like you tell me what occurred, because the sooner we find out who was behind this kidnapping, the sooner we can arrest them."

"I'm fine now, ask away."

"Just tell me in your own words, what exactly happened the day that you were abducted."

"I suppose it was about eight-thirty on that Wednesday morning when two people appeared at the back of my property.

"I'd only just got out of bed and had gone downstairs to make some tea. They knocked on the back door and asked had I noticed the smell of gas because someone had reported a possible leak. I immediately felt they weren't genuine, because one of them was wearing an ill-fitting wig that kept slipping to one side, the other one had a moustache that looked twisted. They seemed very nervous, that made me nervous, so I started to close the door. It was at this point they just pushed it open and rushed past me. I was dragged from behind, one of them had his hand over my mouth to prevent me from screaming, they gave me a couple of slaps to my face, burst my nose and blood was everywhere. I was terrified I thought they were going to rape and kill me.

"They tied my hands behind my back then placed a rag into my mouth and bound tape around it. They placed a bag over my head, it was fabric of some kind, then I was taken outside and thrown into the back of a vehicle, a van I think."

"Do you think you'd recognise either of them again?"

"If they'd similar wigs and disguises, yes I would."

"Please carry on."

"We drove for what seemed an age, I'd estimate at least three hours, then we turned off the main road and it got very bumpy, I think this lasted about half an hour."

"Did they say anything that might indicate who they were?"

"Initially, they didn't say anything, not for the first few days, they'd just say "food" then it was placed on a table. I was locked in a secure room, a basement with running water. Unfortunately, most of it was down the walls. It'd a single bed in it, and I'd a bucket to pee in. If I needed to do anything further, they placed the hood on my head and I was taken up stairs to the toilet there. It was all very primitive.

"They always wore woollen ski masks, but I don't think they were the same people who'd taken me from Glebe Mews. After a week they said the odd word, I heard one of them say "Roddy had been on the phone" that was all, but he sounded like he'd an Irish accent.

"They fed me three times a day on a diet of bacon and eggs, sometimes beans on toast, the odd time, hamburgers from McDonalds, although by the time I got it, it was stone cold.

"Every time they left the room, I heard them turn the key in the lock because it made a very distinctive noise. I got used to that pattern of sound each time, when you've nothing else to do, little things like that register in your brain, they become familiar. Anyway, when they left last night I didn't hear that distinct sound when they closed the door, I think they just forgot to turn the key. I don't think they lived there all the time, because I'd hear a vehicle drive up in the morning and then leave in the evening. There was a narrow window high up near the ceiling and I would see their legs as they walked past.

"I waited until late at night, then when I heard the vehicle leave, I checked the door. I turned the handle slowly and found it was unlocked, so I climbed the stairs into the kitchen as quietly as I could.

"I still wasn't sure if there'd be someone there. Everywhere was in darkness, apart from a faint light coming from the moon shining in through the window. I was reluctant to switch on a light. I felt my way across the kitchen to the back door but it was locked. There was a window over the sink, so I climbed up and undid the latch and pushed it open, although it was small, I managed to squeeze my way through and dropped onto the ground.

"As soon as I was outside I ran like hell, although I'd no idea where I was going. I fell numerous times, climbing over dry-stone walls slipping every few feet, but I was determined to get as far away as possible before they discovered I'd escaped. I kept going all night, until the police picked me up on the main road.

"I kept asking myself, why the hell would they abduct me? Was it something to do with the murder of Basil Thornwood, because I can't think of anything else?"

"We think that's probably the reason, Vera. There'll be a policeman outside your room for the whole time you're here. We'll also send a car to collect you as soon as they say you can be discharged, which I understand from the staff nurse, will be sometime tomorrow.

"Do you have any idea where this farm was, or did they give any indication of its location?"

"Absolutely no idea, other than they told me, it was probably in the Yorkshire Dales. I would recognise the inside of the farm if I ever saw it again though."

"We will ensure you are safe until we capture whoever is behind this, for whatever reason.

"Get some more rest, one of my staff will collect you from here and when we get you back to Kilmington, we'll post police outside of your house, we'll make sure you are looked after. Take care, Vera."

On the way back I kept thinking about what she'd said.

"Do you remember when she said she heard them talking and one of them said "Roddy had been on the phone" I wonder if he could be Roderick Offington-Smythe?"

"Aren't you grasping at straws on that one sir, it could be anyone?"

"Maybe, but I think we should explore the possibility that he's somehow involved."

Nothing further was said on the way back to the station.

Chapter 8

It was time to move out of our cottage on the Wigglesworth estate, I'd the feeling I was no longer welcome, so I rented a small house in the village. It was convenient for work only about 15 minutes drive and I wouldn't have to pass the press every single day, plus contact from Megan had almost ceased.

Every day there were more and more revelations in the papers, Megan, was getting such notoriety it'd become an embarrassment to be associated with her. I know her father was getting wound up with all the press attention, and had issued several writs in the hope he could get them to back off and stop damaging his fledgling political career.

"Chief Inspector, it's Luke Clemson, just wanted to let you know I've moved out of our cottage on the Wigglesworth estate. No doubt I'll be called in again for questioning so to make your life easier to contact me, I've moved into 'Rosedale Cottage' on Fetlock Lane, just by the Old Forge restaurant."

"Thanks for letting me know. Whilst I have you on the phone, can you answer me a question? Do you know of a chap called Clive Harlow, apparently he's in the real estate business? His wife has reported him missing. He went to show a client some property and just never returned."

"Don't know him personally, have you checked with Megan, she may be able to enlighten you as to where he is? Another one down just another few hundred to go."

"That's not funny, Mr Clemson, this is a serious matter, I assume you can account for your whereabouts on Monday the twenty seventh September?"

"Absolutely, in the factory all day making a new front door for Grimbold Manor, in fact, Harold Nesbit the estate manager was with me the whole time if you care to check with him."

"Don't worry, I will."

A car was sent up to Yorkshire to collect Vera Maddox and make sure she was ensconced back in Glebe Mews. A police officer was posted on duty outside her home to ensure no further kidnap attempts were made.

I'd given a lot of thought to what Vera had heard that 'Roddy had been on the phone.'

I decided we should investigate property owners in the Yorkshire Dales. It was a long shot and probably wouldn't bear any fruit, but I needed a break of some kind.

We started with the spot where she was found and worked in a ten-mile radius but it took in a lot of property. It would be a huge task so I put two of my officers on it to check with the Land Registry and other agencies to see if anything of interest turned up.

When I got to the cottage to see Luke, I got a shock. There was a note informing me he'd decided to move out to save embarrassment all round. He'd taken all his clothes and the finality of it hurt me deeply, after all, we'd been married a long time. He shouldn't have done it because it was his home as much as mine. On the other hand I couldn't blame him, he'd been exposed to the most vicious treatment at the hands of the press. Daddy seemed to think that because of his weakness he'd compounded my situation. Of course, my adulterous ways hadn't helped and I know I hurt him deeply, but because of his love for me, he'd put up with it. I suppose one man can only take so much and he'd reached the end of his tether.

I buried my head into my work to try and block out was taking place in my private life.

The Company that I worked for, was owned by two lifelong friends Tom Wilson, and Archie McGoldrick, who were both reaching retirement age.

They each had children coming up through the ranks in the business, and were beginning to excerpt some influence as to what direction they wanted things to go. The emphasis seemed to be moving from a high quality craft organisation producing superb bespoke furniture on a limited basis, to churning out pieces at a much faster rate. It was all about increasing turnover and profits, or at least that's what they told me.

The company had been attending a number of furniture exhibitions in Europe. As a result, orders were starting to come in at a much faster pace. In an effort to boost production, the size of the factory had almost doubled over the previous year, also new and more efficient machinery had been installed.

I didn't particularly like the direction the company was going in, it'd changed dramatically from that environment I was used to. None of the young team had my experience they were basically salesmen, who in their words were trying to bring the company into the present century. I was asked to accompany them to a couple of exhibitions to be on hand to cover any technical questions that may arise.

Despite my initial reservations, I quite enjoyed it, being away from my current situation.

It was decided that they'd attend the High Point Furniture exhibition in North Carolina, a show that is held twice a year. I was asked would I like to go. Never having been to the US before I quite fancied the idea so I said yes, and made sure all my travel documents were in order.

A number of items of furniture had been made then shipped over to a small warehouse they rented temporarily in Salem, North Carolina, in preparation for the event.

The show was a great success with a large volume of orders taken for 'New antique furniture.' God what are they like?

The last day we sold most of the furniture at knock down prices to avoid having to ship it back home.

During the course of the show, I got quite friendly with the woman on the next stand, a beautiful looking lady called Stephanie who lived in South Carolina, at a place called Myrtle Beach.

She was an all-American girl, tall, blonde with an athletic body and she'd an infectious smile, revealing an abundance of snow-white teeth. Her twin brother Chuck, was also tall, blonde, and judging by the amount of beautiful women who constantly seemed to be on their stand, he'd great appeal to the opposite sex.

She asked me, "When are you going back to the UK, Luke?"

"Not until Friday, although the rest of the team are going back later tonight."

"What are you doing for the remainder of the time you are here?"

"Nothing planned, when I've made sure all our furniture orders are correct and packed all our promotional materials away, and shipped back home the remaining items of furniture, I suppose I'll take a drive out somewhere, just to pass the time."

"Would you like to go sailing, we've a thirty-five-foot yacht that sleeps six? Chuck and I are taking a few days off to relax and unwind. The past weeks have been hectic to say the least. We'll be going out tomorrow, probably sail down the coast to St Augustine in Florida. Don't worry, we'll have you back in plenty of time to catch your return flight."

I thought about it for a while, "Yes, I think I'd like that very much."

The past week had been so different, it seemed like another world, a million miles away from my experiences of the past number of months.

"We'll pick you up at your hotel at eight a.m. Just pack a toothbrush, some shorts and tee shirt we've everything else you'll need on board."

"I look forward to it, thank you for the invite."

I was just in the middle of making love to Julia Roberts for the fourth time, when I was roused from my sleep by the station Sergeant.

"Chief Inspector, I realise it's early, but I thought you should know. There's a pub over in Freckleston called the 'The Cock & Bottle' well it's like this, it caught fire during the night in highly suspicious circumstances. The owner who lived above the pub has been found dead inside, he was a chap called Jeff Landers, and wait for it, a friend of Megan Clemson."

"Oh, Christ, here we go again, send a car over and pull her husband in for questioning as soon as possible. He's living at Rosedale cottage over on Fetlock Lane, if he's not there, try his place of work, Heritage Craft Fine Furniture on Bridge Street."

I was preparing myself for another onslaught from those knob heads at the Gazette, as I got ready to head over to the crime scene, when the Chief Constable stormed into my office.

"What the hell's going on, Tyler?

"Another murder on your watch. We're becoming the laughing stock of the Met, they say we're like the hit comedy films 'Police Academy' I've been christened 'Commandant Eric Lassard' and you are known as 'Inspector Balls Up' and your whole team have become the butt of everyone's jokes."

If only he knew, Commandant Eric Lassard, is the least offensive nickname I've heard him called, normally it's 'bollock brains' or 'knob head' to name a couple.

"It has to stop, unless you make some progress within the next seven days, I'll pull you and your men off this case."

"I hope that's a promise and not a threat, I'll gladly hand over the reins and good luck to them, because whoever takes over, no doubt they'll find the same reluctance as I've found in getting any kind of truth from these bed hopping assholes."

He stood there pointing his finger at me. I felt like a scolded child, who'd pissed in his bed and had been found out.

The fucking nerve of him, 20 years in the job coming up through the ranks to be talked to like some raw recruit fresh from police training college. Roll on retirement.

Chapter 9

Deciding to seek out Clemson myself, I drove over to his place of work and spoke with the girl in reception.

"I'm Detective Chief Inspector Tyler Hyde, can I speak with Luke Clemson please?"

"I'm sorry, he's not here. He's in America."

"Since when?"

"He left yesterday, we are doing a show in North Carolina, he's gone until a week next Friday or Saturday, I think."

"Can I speak with a senior member of staff please?"

She showed me into the waiting room whilst she contacted someone.

"Hello Inspector, Archie McGoldrick's my name, how can I help you?"

"Would you've any idea where Luke Clemson would've been at about three am this morning?"

"Probably, somewhere over the Atlantic, he left for the US yesterday with the rest of the team. They took the late flight from London Heathrow to Raleigh Durham, in North Carolina, I think it departed at ten p.m last night."

"Are you sure he was on it?"

"Yes, he was, I got a message through just a short while ago, they all arrived safely and are busy putting finishing touches to our stand ready for the opening day at High Point, a show we are exhibiting in."

I didn't want to hear this. We'd definitely have to rule him out of the equation. Thanking him for the information, I made my way back to the station.

It wasn't long before my men at the scene of the fire at the Cock and Bottle put in a report.

The pub had dated back to 1670 and had been in its original state, with oak beams and a thatched roof. The building was of such historic importance it had a preservation order on it.

However, it'd been completely destroyed in the fire. The burning thatch had created such intense heat that all Cob walls had collapsed, the only thing recognisable, was a single chimney rising up from the ashes. It would take several more days to cool down, before they could access the whole site, to ensure there were no more bodies buried in the debris.

As we sailed south towards Florida, the weather improved and got noticeably warmer. Stephanie and Chuck were very experienced yachtsmen, they told me they'd been sailing all their lives, Chuck had even represented their country in the America's Cup, on two occasions.

We tied up the yacht in the Cat's Paw Marina, St.Augustine, afterwards went to a nearby restaurant for dinner.

"Lobster is the speciality here Luke, if you like shellfish, or if you prefer meat, they do a lovely prime rib. What about you sis, your usual?"

"Fisherman's platter I think, I'm feeling ravenous, the sea air always does that for me."

"Yes, I think I'll have the same, but please, the meal is on me, you two are killing me with kindness, at least let me buy you dinner."

After the meal, and several bottles of wine later, we went for walk into the old city.

"Luke, this is the oldest, continuously occupied European origin port in the continental United States. It was founded in fifteen sixty-five by Spanish admiral, Pedro Menendez de Aviles. It was the capital of Florida until it was changed to Tallahassee in eighteen twenty four."

Chuck reeled off the facts like a tour guide, but it was interesting to hear everything about this beautiful old city. It was full of historic buildings and sported the oldest stone fort in the US. As we walked around, I felt totally at ease and relaxed with Stephanie and her brother, not looking forward to returning home, I could get used to this lifestyle.

Daddy had just told me about Jeff Landers, dying in the most horrendous manner, I knew I'd be getting a visit from inspector balls up in the near future.

I hadn't seen Luke for almost a month and had no idea where he was. Press attention had waned recently, but I knew that as soon as the trial date was announced, they'd be back with a vengeance, scurrying around like rats, looking for every morsel of food. I wish the police would get moving and find whoever was responsible, instead of continuously pointing the finger at Luke and me.

The two detectives that I'd assigned to search land records, were still trawling through all the data relating to the properties in the Yorkshire Dales.

"Sir, I think we might've found something, do you want to come through to our office whilst we still have it up on screen?"

I hurried straight down, anxious to see what they'd discovered.

"We've found two farms in Yorkshire, apparently owned by the Mervy Syntax Corporation of Belize. Further enquiries show one of the two is rented out to a tenant farmer going by the name of Colin Bradbury, it would appear that the other property is vacant, although the records might not be that up to date. However, the highly significant thing is, we've traced this corporation to Mugford Joyce Investments, with a registered office in Brighton. One of the directors of this shell that is registered with the Companies Office is, wait for it! Roderick Offington-Smythe."

"That's bloody brilliant boys, so my suspicions were right. I think the next step is maybe try and get a look inside, but have Vera Maddox with us, so that she can confirm it's the same property that she was held captive in. If we go in all guns blazing looking for a warrant, he'll sweep the place clean, that's the last thing we want. Excellent work guys that's the first real break that we've had."

The next step was to talk to Vera to see would she be prepared to help us, my gut feeling was there wouldn't be a problem, but you never can tell. I took a drive over to her mews property.

"Hello Vera, after much searching we've located two properties in the Yorkshire Dales, we think that one of them could be the farm that you were held captive in. Would you consider taking a drive with us to Yorkshire to see if that's where you were held prisoner?"

"Not a problem, whenever suits you just let me know, I'd be glad to help."

"What about if we collect you at eight a.m tomorrow?"

"That's fine by me, I'll be ready."

"Stephanie, Chuck, it has been an absolute pleasure, I've had such a wonderful time, it's been the most amazing experience for me, never having been on a sailing boat before, it's something I'll never forget. Thank you also for your kind job offer, I'll give it every consideration. I'll definitely keep in touch, thanks very much for all your hospitality, goodbye, and take care."

Stephanie gave me a warm hug and Chuck shook my hand.

With that, I headed down to the gate for my long flight back to London.

On the way back home, I'd plenty of time to think what I'd be going back to. It didn't exactly fill me with the joys of spring. Back to the sniggering and finger pointing, the constant interrogation from that master sleuth, inspector balls up.

I kept thinking about what Stephanie and Chuck had offered me, a place in their organisation doing what I love most, using my hands to craft fine pieces of furniture.

Within their small company, inherited after their father passed away, they had four master craftsmen with a wealth of experience between them, my kind of people. They'd gained a reputation for their ability to make and repair, period pieces of furniture also to do restoration work on heritage buildings.

There is an abundance of old colonial properties in the south. From the Carolina's down through Georgia and Alabama to Northern Florida and they'd worked on a number of them. To me this was mouth-watering work, being able to work on something that was straight out of 'Gone with the Wind' was so appealing.

The first thing I did when I got home was to buy the Gazette to see what those intrepid reporters had managed to ferret out.

One thing, that immediately caught my eye, was the recent fire at the 'Cock & Bottle.' And the unfortunate death of Jeff Landers, pity I thought, another one bites the dust.

Myself, and Detective Rick Master's, had arranged to take Vera Maddox up to Yorkshire, to look at the two properties linked to Offington-Smythe.

When we arrived at her mews cottage she came out to the car, dressed up to the nines, mutton dressed as lamb, sprang to mind.

"Morning Vera, how are you feeling now?"

"On top of the world, I'm looking forward to my day out."

The constable we'd placed on duty guarding her property, looked at me and raised his hands in prayer, he mouthed 'thank you' the relief on his face was evident. The poor sod, apparently she'd invited him in for numerous cups of tea, he kept thinking any minute she'd dive on him, and have her wicked way with him. At least he'd escaped that fate for one more day.

It was late morning when we arrived in the Dales and drove to the first property.

It was quite large farm, with several stone outbuildings. As we got out of the car and walked into the cobbled yard, the farmer approached us.

"You lost?"

"Don't think so, are you Colin Bradbury?"

"Yes, what can I do for you?"

I showed him my warrant card, "I'm Detective Chief Inspector Tyler Hyde, we're investigating a kidnapping that occurred recently, when this woman was abducted and held at a location in the dales."

"You bloody serious, it certainly wasn't here?"

"Would you mind if we had a look around, she would recognise where she was held if she saw it?"

He stood there assessing what I'd just said.

"Not a problem, where do you want to start?"

"The main farm if that's Ok with you?"

"Follow me."

Vera followed him into the farm, she checked out the kitchen and all the rooms on the ground floor, but a shake of her head told me we'd have to look elsewhere. We investigated all the outbuildings, but she was sure this wasn't the location.

I thanked the farmer for his help, and we moved on to the next search area.

"Lower Crag Farm is our next stop, it should be up this dirt track."

I could see Vera's expression change, as we drove up the bumpy road, lined on either side by high dry-stone walls. After about twenty minutes we drove through into a cobbled area and parked up. I walked across the yard and banged on the front door but no one answered. We then walked round to the rear of the property and peered in through a window into a kitchen.

"This looks promising, this small window here I think, is where I escaped from, but I can't be one hundred per cent sure. But if I saw the cellar I would be convinced."

The kitchen door was locked, but soon gave way under the pressure from Detective Masters considerable weight and we moved inside. There was a door at one end that led down to a cellar, we threw a light switch and went down the steps. At the bottom was another substantial door with a key still in the lock. Turning it there was a distinct sound as the key rotated in the lock, Vera smiled.

"That's the sound I told you about, this is definitely it."

We moved inside, there was a strong damp smell, the walls in places had water running down them, and there was green moss growing everywhere.

"This is it, even the bed is still here, and look, my personal en suite, that rusty old bucket."

"No expense spared here then, this'd put the Ritz to shame. You're sure this is it Vera?"

"Absolutely, Inspector, no doubt whatsoever, this is it."

I immediately called inspector Halliwell of the West Yorkshire police, asking for assistance both technical and to secure the crime scene. Within half an hour, backup arrived, the farm was sealed off and the forensics team started their work to recover any available evidence. We left them to it and by late afternoon we started our journey back home to Kilmington.

Chapter 10

I found it very difficult to settle back into a normal routine after my experience in the US. I constantly thought about Stephanie and the offer that she and her brother had made to me. Megan wanted to see me but I kept putting it off as long as possible. Eventually, she turned up at the factory just as I was leaving for the day.

"Luke, can I speak with you?"

"Don't think there's anything further that we can say, it's best we both move on."

"That's exactly it, Luke, I don't want to move on, I'm still in love with you. I want us to get back together where we should be."

"Until you meet someone else and you won't be able to help yourself and you'll cheat on me again. You've a problem, Megan, and I'm not the one to solve it. I've been hurt in more ways than you can imagine I've no intention of repeating the experience. People are still meeting unexplained and untimely deaths, fingers are still being pointed at me, and my life has been a nightmare the past year. Every time one of your conquests goes missing or is murdered, I get called in for questioning. It's all very stressful to say the least. You've your murder trial coming up soon. I think you should concentrate on preparing for that, because you could be in trouble."

"I'm not responsible for any of these murders. The jury will know that and they don't send innocent people to jail because we live in a civilised society. Plus Daddy's got the best lawyer in the country to defend me. He says all the evidence against me is circumstantial."

With that I walked away and got into my car. She was in tears as I left her. I'm not a cruel person, I did feel a twinge of regret and thought maybe we should give it one more try. Then, common sense took over and told me, move on, you've been hurt enough.

Forensics had been able to collect a mass of evidence from the farm in the Dales, including cups and a number of items they were able to get fingerprints off as well as DNA samples.

Armed with the trail of evidence including the records that showed the true owners of the farm in Yorkshire, I thought it was time I paid a visit to our local MP.

As I turned off the main road into the entrance to Wigglesworth Manor, several of God's beautiful children stepped forward to block our entrance. They had the standard uniform, baseball bat, and shaven head. When the leader of this group of Neanderthals realised who I was, he stepped to one side, knuckles dragging on the ground, then signalled to the others to let me through.

I was sure that by the time I had got to the big house, they'd have tipped off Offington-Smythe.

"I wonder if I could speak with my MP please?"

After several minutes, I was shown into a small room and advised he would be down shortly.

"Inspector, sorry for keeping you waiting, I am afraid since I was elected to parliament, time is not my own, what can I do for you?"

"I understand you own several properties in the Yorkshire Dales"

"Where did you hear that?"

"Is it true or not?"

"To be honest, we have a number of property investments up and down the country, I can not remember where they all are."

"Let me refresh your memory, we've located a company in Belize, Central America, called the Mervy Syntax Corporation, which in turn is owned by a company in Brighton, that goes under the name of, Mugford Joyce Investments. You're listed as a director of this company."

He looked stunned, nervously hopping from one foot to the other.

"However, there's no harm in you being involved with these companies or the property that they own. But, when we discover that a recent kidnap victim was held in captivity in one of your properties, namely Lower Crag Farm, in the Yorkshire Dales, then it becomes our business."

"What are you suggesting, that I have been involved in kidnapping, that is insane?"

"Let me tell you the significance of this. Some time ago, a Basil Thornwood was murdered and a neighbour witnessed your daughter, Megan Clemson, at the property at that time. You're aware that we've charged your daughter with this and one other murder. The witness was abducted from her home and held captive in one of your properties. I'd say that's highly suspicious, wouldn't you?"

"Suspicious or not, it has absolutely nothing to do with me, this discussion is over I am not answering anymore questions unless my solicitor is present."

"Contact him by all means, because you are coming with me down to station for further questioning."

He was about ready to explode, the veins in his forehead standing out, pulsing like beacons.

"Do you know who I am?"

"You asked me that once before, let me repeat myself, I'm well aware who you are but it doesn't make any difference, you'll be treated the same as any other citizen, politician or not."

He was taken down to the station and interrogated for several hours. He denied any involvement in the abduction. We knew we needed to get the people who'd been at the farm to tie him in directly to this crime. Reluctantly we'd to let him go but we would continue our investigations.

I'd just got back to my office when Detective Masters informed me they'd identified a print found at the farm. It belonged to a petty criminal, a guy called Thomas Clarke who'd a number of convictions for burglary, theft and handling stolen property.

"Get someone over to his last known address and pick him up."

A squad car was despatched immediately, but by the time they got there he'd vacated the building. It looked like he'd left in a hurry, a fire was still burning in the grate, there was a kettle on the stove and the water in it was still warm. My men had missed him by only a few minutes no doubt he'd been tipped off by Offington-Smythe.

His mug shot was circulated to forces around the country, we would have to hope he could be located and be picked up. Clarke was originally from Waterford so the Gardai in the Republic of Ireland were contacted and his photo sent across. Airports and seaports were alerted in case he fled back to his birthplace.

I'd seen the police car take my father away. As soon as he returned to the house I went in to see him.

"Daddy what did the police want?"

"Nothing, pumpkin, they are investigating one of our properties in Yorkshire, but it is nothing to worry about. Just a minor misunderstanding, so do not concern yourself."

I knew from his reaction that it was serious, and he wasn't being strictly honest with me.

My men were still over at the site of the fire at the Cock & Bottle, clearing and sifting through the debris for clues, when after twelve days, they discovered more human remains in the cellar. I decided to head over there.

"Hi, Tony, what've we got."

"I'd say it's male, but apart from that, not a lot I can tell you, the body is so badly burned I'll need to X-ray the jaw and see if we can get an id through his dental records."

After Tony had removed the body back to the morgue and the pathologist had performed an autopsy on the remains, he came down to see me.

"Hello inspector, here are the X-rays from the victim in the pub fire, the cause of death appears to have been a blow to the back of the head with a sharp pointed instrument, like an ice axe with a serrated edge or something similar, you know the type that climbers would use. I'd say he was dead some time but it's difficult to estimate accurately because of the fire damage, but at least a month. The body was, late twenties early thirties about six feet tall, that's all I can tell you."

"Thanks, Tony, we'll start contacting local dental practices to see if they can identify who this poor unfortunate is."

It was late in the following day when Detective Masters informed me they'd been successful and the body had been positively identified as that of the missing property agent, Clive Harlow.

Another ex-lover of Megan Clemson meets an untimely and violent death when will it all end? We'd been searching for him since his wife had reported him missing, some weeks earlier, but we didn't expect to find him in circumstances like this.

I despatched two seasoned officers, one male one female to inform his wife we'd found her missing husband, this is always a dreadful part of our job.

As soon as the Chief Constable heard about this latest death, I got another rant about how inefficient we were and his patience was wearing thin. For God 's sake, leave us alone and let us get on with job, or do as you keep threatening to do, and take us off the enquiry.

We now had five murders to investigate, all were past lovers of Megan Clemson, and they all had met a violent end. I took a trip out to see Luke Clemson to see if he could throw any light onto the latest murder, as you can imagine, he was far from happy to see me.

I was at work, when our intrepid sleuth requested an interview with me.

"I'm making enquiries into the fire at the Cock and Bottle pub and the remains of the two victims we found inside. Jeff Landers, and Clive Harlow. Do you know anything about it?"

"Not guilty, Inspector, why don't you change the dammed record? I've been out of the country and only just returned. Your continual harassment is really beginning to piss me off, I'm getting the distinct feeling you're out to nail me."

"Just doing my job, Mr Clemson, there's no ulterior motive I promise you."

I glared at him, he'd no right to keep coming to my place of work, I know that Archie my MD was getting a bit fed up with it and felt it wasn't good for the image of the company.

"I'd appreciate it in future, if you've any further questions of me, you'd come to my home because the way you are pursuing me, I'm likely to lose my job. Now if you don't mind I've a gargoyle to finish carving, it's got a likeness not unlike yours."

Chapter 11

Mid morning I received a phone call from the Gardai in Ireland. Garda Superintendent, Tim Murphy, informed me they'd arrested two men, when they disembarked from the ferry from Fishguard to Rosslare, after they were recognised from the pictures that we'd circulated. One of them was identified as Thomas Clarke, his travelling companion, a Hugh O'Brien. They'd been removed to the station in Rosslare, and held pending further investigation.

"Rick, I want you and Detective Myers, to fly over to Ireland ASAP. The Gardai have arrested Thomas Clarke and one other individual called O'Brien, they're being held in the main Station in Rosslare. I'll apply for an extradition warrant immediately, but I know from experience that it'll take some time. There's a limit how long they can hold them, Superintendent Murphy has suggested we get someone over there and he'll allow us to interview them whilst they're in custody. You might just be able to get some information out of Clarke. Offer him a deal if he'll spill the beans on whomever he is working for, and who was behind the kidnap of Vera Maddox. If you can get some info out of him we might just start to make some progress in this fiasco."

Since my return from the US I'd not been able to adjust to a normal life, if you can call it that, with all the whispering and finger pointing. To add to that, I'd a run in with Megan's father that was a frightening affair.

I'd been sent over to do some restoration work on one of the cottages on the Wigglesworth estate when he spotted me.

He must've got out of the bed on the wrong side that day, because he came over and started to abuse me. He called me a spineless bastard for leaving Megan and not standing beside her in her time of need. As a result I'd made things worse for her. Not a mention of the nightmare scenario that had been mine for the past year or so.

I tried to ignore him, not wanting to get into any kind of confrontation with him. I was just placing my tool belt around my waist, when he pushed me up against my car with one hand around my throat. He reached into my tool belt and grabbed a large wood chisel from its holster then held it about an inch from my right eye. He was a big man and he was slowly squeezing the life out of me, I could feel myself going faint. Fearing for my life, I'd to do something quickly, I raised my right knee up as hard as I could and caught him right in the Crown Jewels. He cried out in pain then let go of me and fell to the ground. I gave him a couple of thumps, as I wanted to make sure he wasn't in a position to do any more harm to me. He still had my wood chisel held tightly in his hand.

He lay on the ground like a beached whale, when he finally came around, he started to make threats about my well-being for assaulting an MP.

At this point the occupant of the cottage came out, she'd seen him grab me by the throat and push a weapon into my face and force me up against my car, if I needed a witness she'd be happy to assist me. No love lost there I thought.

I returned to the factory and told Archie what had happened, so he decided under the circumstances to send my apprentice, Alistair, back out to do the repair.

He wasn't pleased about what had taken place, I felt it was another nail in my coffin. This single incident was the catalyst to prompt me to move on, enough was enough.

Stephanie and I'd exchanged a number of letters since my return from the US and she'd indicated her strong feelings towards me as I had to her. I phoned her later on that day to tell her that I'd decided to accept their offer of employment, and she was delighted at the news.

She said she'd prepare paperwork with an official job offer to assist me in my application for a green card, to gain permanent residency to live and work in the US. I knew this could take some time so, the following day I recruited the services of a local lawyer who specialised in emigration applications. I wouldn't be able to leave for the US with the pending murder trial coming up. I'd have to be available for that seeing as I was a major witness, or suspect, at times it was hard to differentiate. However, the ball was now rolling and my destiny would be firmly in my own hands, I'd be able to look forward to some normality in my life.

Detective Rick Masters returned from his visit to Ireland with a wealth of information.

"Have a good trip, Rick?"

"Brilliant sir, it couldn't have gone better, the Gardai were so helpful, and my only regret is that I didn't have more time to partake of the Guinness.

"Anyway, I offered Clarke a deal if he cooperated with us although he was a bit reluctant initially, but when I told him we'd found his prints at the scene of the kidnap, he started to realise he was in deep shit. He told me he did the odd job for Offington-Smythe, anything from removing difficult tenants off his property, to transporting livestock to and from his different farms.

"He was told to look after a woman at Lower Crag Farm for as long as was necessary, and at all times keep their identity secret. He told me Hugh O'Brien and a fellow called Morris kidnapped Vera Maddox then took her up to the Dales. Clarke and another chap called Clough, who is a gardener at Wigglesworth, kept her locked up. They also robbed the grave in Rochdale, then, planted the body in the copse just outside Kilmington.

"When they discovered she'd escaped and reported it to Offington-Smythe, he went ballistic. Clarke knew it was only a matter of time before he was rumbled because he'd a police record, so he decided to do a runner along with O'Brien, but a sharp-eyed Garda spotted him.

"He's willing to cooperate fully and I've a detailed statement duly notarised. O'Brien was less willing to talk but eventually he did, he said he abducted Vera Maddox but it was Chris Morris another gardener who had beaten her in the face, but it was his boss Offington-Smythe who'd made them do it.

"Both of them are still in custody, because of the gravity of the case, the Gardai got an extension to hold them until the end of the week, hopefully, the extradition warrant will be through by then."

"Bloody good show, Rick, let's get over to Wigglesworth and arrest these two gardener chaps, Clough and his colleague Morris, also our soon to be deselected MP."

There was intense activity all around the estate, I noticed many police cars parked over by the greenhouses, two of our gardeners were led away in handcuffs.

It wasn't long before they were knocking on the main door. I recognised Inspector Hyde.

"Can I help you?"

"May I see Mr Offington-Smythe please?"

"I'm sorry, Daddy's at Westminster, he won't be back until Friday evening, is there anything I can help you with?"

"Do you have a mobile phone number where I can contact him?"

"Sorry I don't, Daddy is not up to speed on such things."

"Really, I find that hard to believe."

"Believe what you like, I don't have a number, Ok."

The detective looked at me with disgust on his face, shaking his head he turned and walked down the path to get into his car.

As soon as they had left, I telephoned Daddy.

"What is wrong, pumpkin?"

"That inspector has being around asking for you, they've also arrested several of the gardeners and taken them away for questioning. What's going on Daddy?"

"Nothing to worry about, pumpkin. What did you tell them?"

"That you were at Westminster and wouldn't be back until Friday evening. He asked me for a mobile telephone number to contact you, but I said I didn't have one."

"Good, it is nothing to worry about, leave it with me I will take care of it. I will see you on Friday."

The main breaking news, on television that evening, was the arrest of newly elected Tory MP, Roderick Offington-Smythe.

He was arrested just after 7.00 p.m whilst he was having a meal in the Pugin Room at the Palace of Westminster.

He was later taken to Paddington Green police station, and detained for questioning.

News had been leaked, that he was being detained in relation to the recent kidnapping of Vera Maddox, who was the main police witness in a murder investigation involving his daughter, Megan Clemson. The police would be issuing a statement in due course.

As soon as I was aware my father-in-law had been arrested I felt that it was time I completed my break from Megan totally, so I instructed my solicitor to proceed with the petition for divorce.

He didn't think it would take long as I'd ample grounds for ending the marriage, with numerous cases of her adulterous behaviour.

I needed to distance myself from this family as far away as possible, as soon as the court case was over and I was in a position to move to the US permanently, I'd be off.

Of course, as soon as Megan got the paperwork, she was far from happy, saying I'd deserted her in her time of need and that she'd always been there for me. What a crock of shit.

She made several phone calls asking me to reconsider, but I was adamant my lawyer would carry on with the action.

Chapter 12

I was just out of the shower, when Jason Wimpole came hammering on the front door at Wigglesworth. He was standing there in an agitated state, shaking uncontrollably.

"What the hell's the matter, Jason? Come on in out of the rain." He rushed inside and turned to face me with fear in his eyes.

"God, you smell like a wet dog, Ok out with it, what's got you so wound up?"

"It's like this, I received a parcel in the post with what can only be described as a death threat inside, and to be perfectly honest, I'm bloody terrified. Every time I go out to my car I check underneath, I keep every door in the house locked it's like living in a siege zone. Only going out when it's absolutely necessary."

"Like now you mean, so why are you telling me, why don't you go to the police?"

"I've already done that, all they tried to do was pin the murder of Alan Walters on me. It seems like a lot of your friends are going down like nine pins, I figure I could be next."

He was getting more and more agitated, so I told him to get his wet clothes off whilst I made him some tea.

"Drink that, I've put a shot of whiskey in it. I don't know what to tell you, I've already been charged with two murders, of course I'm completely innocent, it's obvious whoever is responsible, is still out there trying to stitch me and all my friends up."

"You don't think your husband, Luke, has anything to do with this do you, after all, he'd have more reason than anyone else to start bumping off your lovers?"

"Absolutely not, Luke wouldn't be capable of violence and besides, he's a cast-iron alibi for his whereabouts when each of these murders was committed. He's been a regular feature down at the police station but they've let him go each time. It hasn't been pleasant for him being taken in for questioning every few weeks, with everyone pointing the finger in his direction. You can definitely rule him out."

Eventually he calmed down and asked for another shot of whiskey, which I duly supplied. I then produced a towel and dried his hair for him. I brushed it, and soon he was as good as new, the same old gorgeous Jason. After several more whiskeys his mood had changed dramatically and he was eyeing me with lust.

"What have you got under your dressing gown?"

"Nothing, would you like to take a look?"

I slowly disrobed and a couple of rubs in his nether region, he started to rise to the occasion.

"Same old Megan, when there's chaos all around, just think of sex and it'll make everything go away. Ah well, it might be the last shag I have before my stalker carries out his threat."

Jason and I had just finished several hours of Olympic style sex and were sweating profusely. We showered together before he left just after 11.00 pm. I must say he departed in a more relaxed state of mind than what he arrived in.

Not long after he'd left, Daddy's solicitor, Claude Thompson, called me to tell me they'd charged him with the kidnap of Vera Maddox and with perverting the course of justice.

"He's being held at Paddington Green police station and will appear in the Magistrates court first thing in the morning. He's cooperated fully with their investigation, to be honest, he didn't have much option because all of the estate workers had made statements that he'd given the instruction to kidnap her."

It took several seconds for it to register what he'd just told me, I knew he was up to something with all the police activity on the estate, and the arrest of several of our gardeners. Now it was becoming clear what he'd done.

"Oh the bloody fool, why'd he have to do that. I'm innocent, all this does is make me look guilty? He probably thought he was helping me, but all he's done is end his political career, probably get himself a stiff jail sentence into the bargain, and bring shame to the family name. All for the love of his daughter."

"I have to tell you, Megan, when this hits the press, they'll be all over you like bees around a honey pot. I've represented your father for over twenty-five years I never would've thought he'd be capable of orchestrating something like this. It was a revelation for me to hear the police reel off all the charges against him, from kidnapping, grave robbing, and several other associated charges."

"Grave robbing, you can't be serious?"

"Yes, they robbed a grave in the north of England, dressed the body up in women's clothes then dumped it outside Kilmington. They tried to give the impression it was Vera Maddox, whilst they actually held her captive in one of your farms in the Yorkshire Dales."

"I can't take all this in, Claude, it's just too bizarre, so unreal, every day the nightmare continues. Oh why oh why did he have to get involved like this?"

After I'd finished the phone call with Claude, I didn't know what to do, I've never felt so alone since mummy passed away. I thought about ringing Luke for some advice, then on second thoughts I decided not to do. He'd made it quite plain the last time we spoke that everything was over and his petition for divorce confirmed this. What a mess, every day a new revelation to test my ability to cope.

We had Offington-Smythe, more or less banged to rights. Although he was still at liberty until he was sentenced. He'd cooperated with us fully during his interview and we'd two of his staff in custody. We also had our extradition warrant granted. Two officers had been despatched to the Irish Republic to bring back James Clarke and Hugh O'Brien involved in the kidnapping.

That side of our investigation was pretty much under control, as a result, I was getting less flack from the Chief Constable. However, we still had five unsolved murders with a few suspects, but all who had plausible alibis.

I called a meeting of my senior investigating officers to run through everything that we'd uncovered in our investigation to see if there was anything that had been overlooked.

Megan Clemson had been charged with two murders, although I wasn't one hundred per cent happy that she was responsible. Her husband, Luke, would have more reason than anyone to exercise some retribution, but he could account for his whereabouts at the time of the murders.

Jason Wimpole had a plausible explanation as to how his fingerprints were found on a murder weapon. Could it be someone else who was deliberately trying to frame our suspects with fingerprints on the murder weapons? If so they were smart and calculating it would be difficult to catch them because we'd no idea who could be responsible.

As soon as the story broke about Megan's father, the press were camped outside my home and at my place of work. Even though it had nothing to do with me, they still kept up their harassment, looking for every crumb of information.

After a couple of days of this constant intrusion, they'd followed me to my place of work. Archie, my MD told them that unless they moved off the property and gave me some space, he'd take the matter into his own hands. They just looked at him with scorn and laughed in his face. Not long after, he came out with a bucket full of linseed oil and sawdust walked up to the group and threw it all over them. It was everywhere, all over their heads, clothes, and cameras.

"Don't come back, give this man a break, it has nothing to do with him. The next time it'll be something stronger."

They couldn't believe what had just happened, standing there like chips just out of the fryer, dripping from head to foot. Charlie Hargreaves, a photographer, distraught that his beloved Nikon had been baptised in linseed oil, "I'll sue the bastard, that's over three grand he's ruined."

I thought it best I should talk to them and give them what they wanted so Archie wouldn't need to get involved.

"Look, if you leave me alone I'll give you one interview and that's it, but it's on two conditions, that you do not pursue my MD for assault or for any damages, plus you leave me alone. Take it or leave it."

They mumbled between themselves for a couple of minutes. "Ok, we'll go along with that. What can you tell us about Offington-Smythe? Can you expand on what has been released on TV so far about his involvement in the kidnapping?"

"I've nothing further to add to what you already know, it came as a complete shock to me as I'm sure it did to Megan, to hear that her father had been involved with the abduction of Vera Maddox."

"Your wife has been charged with two murders, what've you got to say to that?" said Harold Lewis, a seasoned reporter with the Gazette.

"She isn't guilty of these two murders, she'll be proved innocent in due course, but she hasn't gone to trial yet, so anything further may be construed as sub judice."

"You've been a suspect in these murders, do you have any comment?"

"Jesus, is that the best you can come up with, do you expect me to stand here and say it was me? I'd no involvement in any of the murders, the police have been satisfied with my explanation as to my whereabouts at the times these poor unfortunates met their deaths."

"We understand that you've filed for divorce?"

"That's a separate private matter and doesn't concern you, so there'll be no comment on that."

"I understand there was an altercation between yourself and Offington-Smythe at one of the cottages at the Wigglesworth estate, I'm told he held a weapon to your face, any comment?"

"It was nothing serious, just a minor misunderstanding."

"Not according to Tara Bradley who witnessed it."

These guys were a bit more intrepid than I gave them credit for, as they seemed to have ferreted out snippets of information from a number of sources.

"Like I said, a minor misunderstanding."

"Do you have any idea who may be responsible for these murders?"

"None whatsoever, if I did the police would've been informed. I don't enjoy trips down to the local station each time there's an unexplained death. There's nothing more I can tell you, I've no direct link to the family anymore. That's all, gentlemen, I'd appreciate it if you'd leave me alone in future."

"One last question, what advice would you, have for any of your wife's former lovers?"

"Not sure what to say to that. They know who they are and have probably figured out themselves whether or not they'd be in the firing line. Just watch your back, whoever is responsible they're on a mission! That's all, I've nothing further to add."

With that they all headed off, squelching with each step, leaving an oil slick behind them.

"Sorry about that, Archie, I thought if I gave them an interview they'd leave me alone and not come down to my place of work. They also agreed not to report you to the police for assault."

"They call that assault, they haven't seen anything yet. I've got a pile of festering pig shit down on my farm, the next time they'll get that."

"Hopefully, they'll leave me alone now. I realise it's not good for the image of the company, having these little pricks and the police down here every few days. It's been a real strain these last few months with everything that's happened, I can only apologise, you've been very understanding."

"You've been with the company for a long time, Luke, we are all aware of the acute pressure you've been under since this started. We fully understand your position, if there's anything we can do to help, just let us know."

"Thanks a lot, Archie, that's very kind of you."

The headlines in the Gazette the following day didn't do anything, to calm the nerves of the Megan glee club.

'Husband of Megan Clemson says lovers will all die.'

It went on to say, 'he advises former lovers to watch their backs and to look at emigrating.'

The stupid bastards. I never said that, I gave them an interview but they still had to distort the truth for sensationalism. As a result, several other daily newspapers contacted me but I told them the Gazette had distorted the truth and I would not be issuing any further statements.

That morning just as I was about to leave for work, Jason Wimpole appeared at my cottage. He was tall and slim with a shock of black hair. His piercing blue eyes looked terrified as he confronted me.

"My name is Jason Wimpole, Megan and I are old friends. I have read what you said in the Gazette I want to know if I'm on your hit list."

"I know who you are. Remember, I found you in bed with my wife. It was only because of her I didn't beat the living crap out of you at the time. Now you've the nerve to come here and accuse me of murder. Because if that is what you're suggesting, you'd better walk away now, whilst you still can.

"Never believe what you read in the Gazette, they couldn't print the truth if their existence depended on it.

"They've grossly distorted what I said. In fact, I'll be issuing legal proceedings against them.

"Now piss off back into whichever rat hole you crawled out of, never let me see your ugly face around here again, otherwise, you might not need to emigrate."

By this point he looked as if he was about to burst into tears, his lip was trembling and he was as white as a sheet.

"I'm going straight to the police to report you for what you've just said."

"Report away, I've wasted enough time talking to you. So long shithead."

It was just before 9.00 a.m and I was only out of bed, when Jason appeared at the manor in an agitated state.

"What's the matter, Jason, you look terrified?"

"Just had a run in with your husband after what was written in the Gazette."

"Oh my god what have you done, I told you before, never believe anything they publish in that rag? What did you say to him?"

"He told the Gazette all your former lovers were targets because whoever was responsible for all these deaths was on a mission and they should consider emigrating."

"I'm sure he didn't tell them that, and even if he did, you'd no right to go around to his home, you're more or less accusing him of murder.

"Look, Jason, I enjoy your company, only yesterday you asked if you could move in with me and I said I would consider it, however, this has more or less convinced me that it would be a bad idea, so I've decided the answer's no."

"Megan, please reconsider, I realise I might've been a bit hasty going around to his home, but I felt it was time to confront him."

"Confront him about what? There's no evidence to link Luke to any of these crimes. Do you think he'd be walking the streets, if he were responsible? You're being such a prick, Jason, it's time you left."

I escorted him out. As we headed towards the door he begged and pleaded for me to change my mind, but I refused, I pushed him outside and closed the door behind him then headed into the kitchen for some coffee.

"Morning, pumpkin, what did that weasel want?"

"He's angry about what has been printed in the Gazette and thought he should tackle Luke about it, face to face."

"Really, he has more balls than I gave him credit for."

"That maybe so, but you can't go around accusing people of crimes they didn't commit."

"Are you sure about that, pumpkin, Luke had more reason than anyone to carry out these murders?"

"Daddy, I've told you before, it's not Luke and I think he's suffered more than anyone, probably even more than me. The last thing he needs is the likes of Jason going around to his home, complaining about what he did or didn't say to the Gazette. He wanted to move in with me but that's the last thing I need, I'll have to have a clear head to prepare for my trial."

"Do not worry about that, pumpkin, we have Oliver C Catchpole as our senior barrister, he has a ninety-five percent success rate as a defence lawyer. He is very confident, you will be acquitted of the charges."

"Inspector, Jason Wimpole is in reception, he wants to speak with you as soon as possible."

"Ok, Frank, send him up."

"Morning, Mr Wimpole, please take a seat. What can I do for you?"

He was nervously wringing his hands and seemed pretty

wound up.

"It's like this, when I read the Gazette this morning I didn't like what I saw, so I thought I should tackle Luke Clemson about it face to face. Being the number one suspect in the murders and him having the nerve to tell people they should emigrate. He made threats to my life and told me to get off his property."

"Well you can hardly blame him. You just can't go around making accusations against people based on what is printed in the Gazette. I've seen more fact printed in the Dandy and Beano than that rag, it's only fit for wrapping chips in."

"What's the Dandy and Beano?"

"Publications for children that would be far more credible than the local Gazette."

"What do you intend to do about it? He did make threats against my life."

"Well you probably asked for it, anyway, leave it with me I'll see what I can do."

As he left my office I felt a sigh of relief, having read the Gazette I'd no intention of pursuing this further, I'd more pressing things to deal with. Besides, he was a still a suspect in the murder of Alan Walters, maybe this was his way of throwing us off the scent.

I received a letter from Stephanie that said she'd like to visit me in England. This presented me with a major problem, as I'd never told her about my situation with Megan or the scandal about her past lovers being murdered. How do you tell someone something like that, it's a real conversation stopper? I'd fully intended to tell her in due course but didn't feel the need to do so when I was in the US. I'd told her I was married but that we were separated, that was all. I felt that anything further might jeopardise our friendship. There would be no way she could arrive in the midst of this nightmare and not be made aware of the problems. I didn't know her well enough, I'd no idea how she'd react and I was afraid of losing her, what was I to do?

I phoned her and told her just to hold off her visit, as we'd a number of restorations to do for the National Trust that had a strict time scale for completion. But as soon as they were completed I'd let her know, so that I'd be able to take leave from work and spend time with her when she eventually came over.

She was disappointed but said she understood. I felt terrible having to lie to her, but felt it was probably for the best.

After having dinner I'd just sat down to watch some soccer on TV, when there was a knock on the door.

"Evening, Mr Clemson, may I come in?"

It was master sleuth Inspector Hyde.

"If you must."

"I gather you know Jason Wimpole?"

"He said he was going to report me to you, so I'm sure you know he was around here first thing on Tuesday, more or less accusing me of murder. He was complaining about what I'd told the Kilmington Gazette. I told him to leave."

"Would you get your coat and accompany me down to the station?"

This was getting monotonous, but I grabbed my jacket and was driven down to the station and placed into the interview room.

"Can you tell me where you were between six p.m on the seventh and eight a.m on the eighth?"

"I was working on a project over at Romsey I think my apprentice and I got back to the factory around seven p.m. After I had dropped Alistair off, it would have been around seven thirty when I got home. I'd dinner and then went for a drink at the Pack Horse pub over near Bishop's Bluff. It would've been just before nine thirty. I left about eleven then came straight home."

"Can anyone verify this?"

"Of course, check with Cyril the landlord."

"Don't worry I will. Did you leave the house again that night?"

"No, I went to bed about midnight and got up just after six the next morning. I'm sure you're not interested in my social life, I assume it's about that arsehole, Wimpole?"

"He was found dead this morning by a dog walker on the tow-path alongside the Avon canal."

"Oh what a shame, he'll be sorely missed—I don't think."

"You might not feel so smug when you hear what I have to tell you. He was found with a large wood chisel embedded in his back, it had been stabbed in fourteen times."

"That's a good round number, twenty would have been better."

"The chisel had the name 'Bob Barron' inscribed into the handle."

"I don't believe it."

"Also, we found your prints on this weapon, not so smug now are we?"

I sat down taking in what he had just told me. He then produced the wood chisel in a clear plastic evidence bag.

"Recognise that?"

It was one of Bob's tools that had been gifted to me.

"The last time I saw that chisel it was in the hand of Offington-Smythe after he threatened me over by one of his cottages on the Wigglesworth estate."

"Your prints were on the handle. What do you have to say to that?"

"What would you expect? It was one of my tools that I used on a daily basis, taken from my tool belt by Smythe when he assaulted me and held it against my face."

"All very convenient, don't you think?"

"Convenient it may be, but it's the truth. If you talk to Tara Bradley she saw the assault and stated at the time she'd be a witness if need be. I'd also suggest you check the weapon for the prints of Smythe, that probably never occurred to you in your rush to pin it on me."

Smartarse. We should have cross-matched for prints but the computer system was down and we'd just checked the prints against our number one suspect manually.

"We'll be detaining you this evening until we check out your story, I'm sure you'll enjoy the comforts of this fine hostelry."

I took a trip out to see Tara Bradley, who confirmed that she'd seen Offington-Smythe assault Clemson. He'd held a knife of some description up to his face and he was choking him. She saw him struggling to get away from Smythe, he pushed him and he fell down onto the ground behind Clemson's car. It was at this point she came out to talk to him and offered to be a witness if needed.

I thanked her for her assistance and then took a drive over to the Pack Horse near Bishop's Bluff.

"Can I speak with Cyril please?"

"That's me, what can I do for you?"

"I'm Detective Chief Inspector Tyler Hyde, do you know a chap called Luke Clemson?"

"Indeed I do, nice guy, comes in here a couple of times a week, why do you ask?"

"Was he here last night?"

"Yes he was, came in just before nine thirty and left with a couple of other regulars about eleven."

"How can you be so precise about the times?"

"As soon as he came in he paid me for the pub raffle, it's a draw that we run every week for the local children's football team, it takes place around nine thirty. I remember he left at eleven p.m because I asked if he wanted another drink before last orders, but he declined, saying he'd an early start the next day."

"Ok, Cyril, thanks very much."

With that I left the pub disappointed that his story checked out so I headed back to the station.

"Tony, can you check to see if any of the prints found on the murder weapon used on Wimpole match up with those taken from Offington-Smythe?"

"Sure, but the system is still down so I'll have to do it manually, it may take some time but I'll let you know if there is a match."

Not long after Tony called me, "Sir I've a match for them, a thumb and four fingers belong to Offington-Smythe."

"Thanks, Tony, the plot thickens, seems like another nail in our MP's coffin."

I decided reluctantly we'd have to release Clemson as his story checked out.

"You are free to go, I've spoken with the different people and they confirm what you told me."

Clemson was far from happy that he'd been detained in this manner.

"Just when I was settling in, that is a bitter disappointment, however, the cell could do with some upgrades. It needs a few more home comforts, like a flat screen TV, snooker table, and the walls could do with some up-to-date wallpaper on them. Still, the rates are reasonable, but the downside is, the manager is a real prick. If I was in charge I'd send him for retraining, because his people skills are seriously lacking."

"I suggest you go, Mr Clemson, before I change my mind and lock this door and throw the bloody key away, you cocky little bugger."

"The one thing I'm not, is cocky. Pissed off definitely, but not cocky."

Chapter 13

Several of my men and I headed out to Wigglesworth Manor to arrest Offington-Smythe for the murder of Jason Wimpole. We passed the usual thugs at the entrance and drove up the long winding drive to the manor house.

"I'd like to speak with Colonel Offington-Smythe please."

We were shown into a small waiting room and asked to take a seat whilst they summoned him from the depths of this vast house.

Eventually he appeared. "Good day gentlemen, what can I do for you?"

"I'm here to arrest you for the murder of Jason Wimpole."

He stood there with his mouth wide open.

Megan Smythe went hysterical as soon as she heard this saying there was no way Daddy could be responsible, and poor Jason, who would do such a thing?

"Inspector, I co-operated fully with you over the kidnapping of Vera Maddox because I was guilty. I am due to be sentenced shortly, but you are not going to pin the murder of Jason on me."

"I'd like you to come down to the station with us and we can discuss this further."

"Megan, please ring Claude straight away, tell him what has happened."

"Will do, Daddy. Inspector, there must be some mistake. Jason was a good friend of both us, Daddy would never do anything like that, it's not in his nature."

"Our evidence says otherwise, anyway we'd better make our way down to the station."

Smythe protested his innocence all the way there and was threatening lawsuits and removal of me from office and the remainder of my staff being despatched to Siberia.

We led him into the interview room, not long after his lawyer arrived.

"Jason Wimpole was found murdered on a towpath alongside the Avon canal. Can you confirm your whereabouts yesterday, from nine p.m until eight a.m this morning?"

"I was at a meeting with the Conservative Party in London to discuss my position as an MP. I drove up to the City leaving home at seven thirty a.m the meeting took most of the day. Last night I had dinner with my political agent and I stayed over in my apartment in Kensington.

"I had another meeting this morning with the Conservative Party chairman and left London about lunchtime today and came straight back home."

"Can anyone confirm this?"

"Of course, numerous people can, I can give you a list of names with precise times of where I was during the course of the last forty eight hours."

If this was true, it threw my case into doubt.

"Can you account for how your fingerprints came to be on the murder weapon used on Mr Wimpole, namely a chisel?"

"No I can not, I do not possess such a tool."

"Let me refresh your memory. You assaulted Mr Clemson when he was doing repairs over at Ivy Cottage on your estate. You removed a wood chisel from his tool belt, then you held it against his face in a threatening manner, he'd to take action to avoid being injured. When Mr Clemson decided that retreat was the better option than valour, you still had the chisel clutched in your hand."

"Utter bullshit, wherever did you hear that?"

"We've an independent witness who saw the whole incident, also Mr Clemson stated that you removed the wood chisel from his tool belt then held it against his face."

"Not true, they are lying. It did not happen."

"How else can you explain your prints got onto the murder weapon then?"

He nervously looked at his lawyer and they whispered between themselves.

He had two choices, either, admit to the fact he had attacked Clemson with the wood chisel, this would explain how his prints came to be on this murder weapon. Or, deny the incident took place, but be unable to account for how his prints came to be there, leaving himself wide open to be charged with this murder. They continued whispering for several minutes.

"Very well, I admit there was an altercation, I did take something from his tool belt and threaten him. He is a spineless bastard for deserting my daughter the way he did, I am afraid I just lost my cool with him, but I did not take this tool I just left it on the ground, that is the truth."

"Right, I want details of your meetings yesterday, exact times and who you met with. I'll check everyone of these details, if one of them doesn't stack up, then you'll be back here in a flash. You can go for now but remember what I said."

I was just out of the shower, when I heard someone trying to break down the front door of the cottage.

"Oh it's you, Megan, what's wrong?"

She rushed past me in an agitated state.

"Luke you've got to help me. Jason Wimpole has been murdered and they've arrested Daddy for it."

I looked at her. Streaks from her eye makeup ran down her cheeks, for once her stunning good looks had deserted her.

"Jason was found murdered alongside the Avon canal, I just can't believe it, I was only talking to him the day before yesterday, they are trying to say Daddy was responsible. Can you help us, Luke?"

"Not sure what you expect me to do about it, I myself spent the night in custody over the demise of that little shit, I was only released a couple of hours ago.

"Your father took a chisel to my throat over at Ivy Cottage, he threatened to kill me. It was a tense moment I can tell you.

"As for Wimpole, I hated that smarmy prick with a passion, so I won't be shedding any tears over him."

She looked at me her lips trembled, and tears filled her eyes.

"Luke, I'm begging you, I've no one else I can turn to. I didn't know that Daddy had done that, I'm sure he didn't mean it."

"You'd better believe it. If I hadn't taken action he'd have jammed it into my eye, that's after he had strangled me. You don't know him like you think you do. If you don't believe me, ask Tara, she witnessed the whole event."

"Please, Luke, I'm on my own I need your help."

For once she realised Daddy was no longer there to solve her problems.

"I'm sorry, Megan, I don't see what I can do. I think your lawyer is the only person who can really help the both of you. You're up on murder charges shortly. As for your father, he already has the kidnapping of Vera Maddox to contend with, but now also a murder charge. It's all beyond my help. You'll definitely need expert legal assistance in getting out of this mess without a massive sentence."

The word sentence seemed to hit her like a bolt of lightning.

"You don't think they'll find me guilty do you, Luke?" she asked, with an appealing look in her eyes.

"You can't be sure of anything these days, Megan."

"You don't think I did commit the murders do you, Luke?"

"No, I don't, but I'm not the one you have to convince."

She sat down on the sofa buried her head in her hands and started to cry uncontrollably.

Chapter 14

The date for Megan's trial, was set for November 23rd 2006 and it was expected to take four weeks. As soon as this was announced, activity in the local press and on the local radio station was manic. They hounded Megan at every opportunity, also they didn't honour our previous agreement and constantly appeared at my home.

Because she'd pleaded not guilty at her earlier appearance in the Magistrates Court, she'd been sent for trial to the Crown Court in Winchester.

I was to be called as a witness for the defence, they'd retained the services of Oliver C Catchpole, an aggressive barrister who wasn't used to losing.

On the opening day of the trial, I arrived bright and early.

The jury had been selected and sworn in, it consisted of six women and six men of varying ages.

The senior prosecutor, Ms Olwyn Appleton, outlined the Crown's case to the jury, painting Megan the defendant, as a promiscuous women with low moral standards. She said she was akin to a praying mantis, killing some of her many partners after mating. The prosecution would show clear and detailed forensic evidence that linked the defendant directly to the brutal murders of Basil Thornwood and Neil Derek and, they'd be calling a reliable witness to one of the crimes.

The defence do not normally make an opening statement, but Megan's lawyer, Oliver Catchpole, was so incensed he went straight into the attack. He accused the prosecuting council of courtroom dramatics by calling his client a praying mantis, she must've been reading too many Agatha Christie novels. For this remark he received a strong rebuke from the judge.

Detective Chief Inspector Tyler Hyde took the stand and outlined the detailed investigation that led them to charge

Megan. After he'd finished answering questions from the prosecuting council, Catchpole got to his feet.

"Detective Chief Inspector Hyde, was there any doubt in your mind that Mrs Clemson was responsible for these brutal murders?"

Hyde looked hesitant for a moment.

"I can only go on the facts that our extensive investigation uncovered, her fingerprints were found on two of the murder weapons. She was also seen at the victim's house. To me that seems pretty conclusive."

"Not pretty conclusive to me. There's any number of reasons that her prints could have found their way onto these tools, as this case continues we'll explain how this is possible. Both of these murders were committed with a severe amount of brute force, not what you'd expect that a woman with the slight stature of Mrs Clemson would be able to muster."

"I've seen women perform physical feats that would astound you."

At this point there were howls of laughter from the court.

"Silence," shouted the Judge, "any more outbursts and I'll clear the public gallery. I'll not have this kind of hilarity in my courtroom."

"The only thing you have Inspector, are my client's prints on the two tools used as murder weapons without any hard evidence that she used these two tools to murder two of her close friends. No further questions."

The first independent witness for the prosecution was Vera Maddox. She took to the witness box, and swore the oath. She was dressed smartly in a black suit, as if she was going to a funeral.

Olwyn Appleton rose to her feet. She was small and fat in her mid thirties, she had a severe expression on her face like a bulldog chewing a wasp, ideal for a prosecuting council.

"Ms Maddox, can you tell me about the events you heard and witnessed on the evening of July seventh 2006?"

"Certainly, I was standing outside my mews cottage smoking a cigarette, when I heard a violent argument taking place at Glebe House."

"What time was this?"

"It started just after eight p.m, the shouting continued for about half an hour then it went quiet."

"Then what did you see?"

"I saw Megan Clemson come out of the house."

"Are you sure you saw the defendant leave the house?"

"Absolutely, no doubt whatsoever, I saw her walk out, climb into her Mercedes sports car and drive off at about nine p.m."

"Thank you, no further questions."

At this point Catchpole got to his feet.

"Ms Maddox, do you take a drink?"

"Why, are you asking me out for a drink?"

At this point there was laughter from the court.

"Silence, otherwise I'll clear the public gallery, this is your last warning," said the Judge.

"I'll ask you again, do you take a drink?"

"I used to drink quite a bit but now I only have the odd glass of wine."

"The odd glass of wine, that's all?"

"Correct, nothing more."

"So there's no way you could've been intoxicated and mistaken in thinking you'd seen Mrs Clemson?"

"I wasn't drunk, it was definitely her."

"Do you take drugs, Ms Maddox?"

Appleton rose to her feet. "Objection, Ms Maddox's personal habits are not on trial here."

"Your honour, I'm just trying to establish if the witness was in full control of all her senses when she says she saw the defendant."

"Overruled."

"I'll ask you again, Ms Maddox, do you take drugs?"

"In the past I've smoked the odd joint, but that was years ago when I was younger."

"The odd joint years ago. Is that what caused you to be admitted into the James Osborne Clinic for drug addiction, on two separate occasions within the last three years?"

"Objection, my client's previous drug addiction has no relevance."

"Overruled."

Vera Maddox stood there rooted to the core, she wondered how the hell did they find that out?

"Can you give me an answer, Ms Maddox?"

"What do you want me to say? I'd a bit of a habit for which I was treated for and it's now gone and is in the past."

"In the past you say, that remains to be seen. No further questions."

Forensics officer Tony Morehouse was called for the prosecution, he confirmed that prints found on the two murder weapons matched those taken from Megan. I felt so sorry for Megan, she had a look of sheer horror and desperation on her face as she listened to the evidence unfold. Her father sat there shaking his head at each revelation.

After the prosecution had presented their witnesses, I was called to the witness box.

"Please state you full name."

"Luke David Clemson."

"Do you know the defendant?" asked Catchpole.

"Yes, she's my wife."

"Can you tell me where you were from six p.m on the seventh of July?"

"I was at home with my wife. I arrived at our cottage at five thirty I'd finished work early that day. We'd dinner about six thirty then sat down to watch TV until about eleven forty five, at which time we retired to bed."

"Then what?"

"Not sure what you want me to say"

"What did you do then?"

"Are you serious?"

"Yes Mr Clemson, I am, what happened next?"

"We had sex a few times then fell asleep exhausted, is that what you wanted to hear?"

"So Mrs Clemson didn't leave the house at any stage?"

"She didn't have the energy."

At this point there were loud guffaws from the public gallery.

"I'll not tell you again, keep quiet," said Judge McCarthy.

"You're absolutely certain that your wife didn't leave your house at all that night?"

"Like I said, she didn't leave the house at any stage."

"No further questions."

Olwyn Appleton got to her feet.

"So you say your wife was with you the whole evening on the seventh of July. We don't believe your story, Mr Clemson, I suggest to you that you are lying just to give your wife an alibi."

"You can suggest what you like, the truth is she didn't leave the house at any stage, no matter what you think."

I could see she was angry, frustration was written all over her face, because she realised there was no way I was going to crack, however much she wanted me to do.

"I must point out that you have sworn an oath today, to tell the truth, the whole truth, and nothing but the truth. Perjury is a very serious offence punishable by imprisonment. Do you want to change your story, Mr Clemson?"

"I've no reason to change anything."

She stood there glaring at me and looked like she was ready to explode, she had her fists clenched.

"Very well, I'll prove you are lying and you'll suffer the consequences. No further questions."

I felt a huge sigh of relief when the judge said I could step down.

Megan was called next, she looked terrified.

"Please state your name."

"Megan Clemson."

"Did you murder Basil Thornwood and Neil Derek?" asked Catchpole.

"No I didn't, they were very good friends of mine."

"Did you see Basil Thornwood on July seventh?"

"Yes I did. I called over to see him around lunchtime, he'd been helping Daddy with his election campaign and we just talked about that. I stayed at Glebe house for about an hour then left for Wigglesworth Manor to see Daddy."

"Can you tell us how your prints came to be on two murder weapons?"

"When I was leaving his house I knocked over a number of garden tools that had been stood up against the rear wall of the property, I bent down picked them up and stood them back against the wall. I suppose my prints would be on several of the tools."

"No further questions," said Catchpole.

Olwyn Appleton rose to her feet.

"All very convenient don't you think? Can you tell the court, why you didn't tell this to Detective Chief Inspector Hyde, when he asked you how your prints came to be on two of the murder weapons?"

"I was too stressed out to think properly, being arrested for something I didn't do. How would you feel?"

"I'm not the one on trial here, and I don't believe you. You couldn't remember at the time when you were cautioned and questioned, but then your memory came back you had time to make up a cock and bull story."

"It's the truth, that's exactly what happened, no amount of pressure from you will make me change my evidence."

Well done, Megan, sock it to the bitch!

"No further questions."

Not long after this testy exchange, a messenger delivered an envelope to the defence team.

Catchpole rose to his feet.

"I would like to recall Detective, Tony Morehouse."

Applegate didn't like this, she obviously knew it wasn't good for their case.

"Mr Morehouse, when you tested the murder weapon at Glebe house, did you test any of the other garden tools for prints?"

"I'd no reason to do, the murder weapon was still in the victim so there was no need to look further."

"It may interest you to know that her prints were found on three other tools. A hay rake, a hoe and a spade. If you'd done your job thoroughly, you would've found this. These tools were in the evidence room at your own station until yesterday."

"Objection your honour, this is inadmissible, pure theatre for the court."

"Your honour, these fingerprint tests were carried out by Core Forensic Reports from Southampton, they're a respected organisation that have given evidence in numerous criminal trials. I've certified papers here that confirm Megan's prints were indeed found on these tools, to me that would indicate she was telling the truth."

"Why wasn't this evidence in the documents of discovery?" asked Appleton.

"These tests were only carried out yesterday and have only come to be in my possession in the past few minutes, delivered to me by courier."

The judge looked concerned.

"We will adjourn for thirty minutes. Mr Catchpole, Ms Appleton, I want to see you in my chambers immediately."

When the court resumed the judge advised the jury that the evidence from Core Forensic Reports was admissible, much to the disgust of Ms Appleton.

The next defence witness was handcuffed to a prison officer.

"Please state your name for the record?"

"Robert Wilson, they call me Wilson the candy man."

Again, there was loud laughter from the gallery. At this point, the judge had reached the end of his patience.

"I think this is a good time to take a break for lunch, we will reconvene at two p.m, this time without the public gallery."

As the court emptied, Megan looked at me and mouthed 'thank you' as she was led below.

I went to Chadwick's pie shop, to partake of one of their delicacies and a cup of coffee. Alistair, my apprentice was with me for moral support.

"Jesus Luke, that Olwyn is a right bitch, she looked ready to climb into the witness box and batter you into submission."

"Yes, she was pissed off all right because she didn't get the answer she wanted to hear, but that's her problem. Anyway, we'd better not discuss it just in case there's anyone listening."

We headed back to court at about 1.50 p.m, but they wouldn't let Alistair in because they'd decided to close the public gallery for the day, however, as a material witness, I was allowed in.

The proceedings got under way and Wilson the candy man took the stand accompanied by his prison officer.

Catchpole got to his feet.

"Mr Wilson, I'm sorry to drag you away from your hospitality suite. Can you tell the court your current address?"

"Sure, care off H.M Prison the Isle of White, at least for the next five years."

"Will you tell the court, what you're serving your sentence for?"

"Certainly, drug dealing, caught selling 'Charlie' that's cocaine, unfortunately it was to an undercover cop. This was my eighth conviction, so this time I've been sent away to repent on the error of my ways."

"Have you ever heard of a lady called Vera Maddox?"

"Bet your life I have, used to supply her, had a standing order for two hundred and fifty grams of 'White Widow' each week, that's marijuana."

"Can you tell the court how this arrangement worked?"

"Sure, I just drove around the back of her mews cottage every Wednesday morning, then went in for a cup of tea. I handed her the weed and she paid me, every week for over five years, that is until two months ago when unfortunately my enterprise was closed down."

"Can you identify the lady in this court?"

"Yes, she's the lady in the black outfit with the white collar at the end of the front row."

"Thank you, Mr Wilson, I've no further questions."

Vera Maddox looked decidedly uncomfortable, as the eyes of the court were fixed on her.

I could see what Catchpole was doing, he was trying to undermine the credibility of the only witness the prosecution had, so far he was doing a good job, even my uneducated legal brain could see that.

Olwyn Appleton tried to discredit his evidence but he gave as much as he got and my money was on Catchpole.

The next witness was called and sworn in. Catchpole got to his feet.

"Could you please state you name for the record, and what you do for a living?"

"I'm Howard Shuttleworth, the manager of the 'Economy Booze Store' in Kilmington."

"Have you ever heard of a lady called Vera Maddox?"

"Yes sir, we deliver alcohol to her mews cottage each week. We've a delivery service, it's all very discreet for the secret drinkers. You'd be surprised how many there are. She's a standing order for seven bottles of single malt Glenmorangie Scotch Whisky and seven bottles of Australian Merlot."

"Good God! That's every week?"

"Without fail, every week."

"Do you see Ms Maddox in this courtroom?"

"Yes, it's the lady in the black suit on the front row."

All eyes focused on Vera Maddox, who by this time was in floods of tears.

"Thank you, Mr Shuttleworth, no further questions."

The prosecution declined to interview this latest witness, it was at this point Catchpole rose to his feet and appealed to the judge.

"Your honour, I think we've more than illustrated that the prosecutions only eye witness cannot be relied on due to the testimony of the last two witnesses. They've testified that she needed an ample supply of drink and drugs on a continued basis. The quantities of drink supplied indicate to me, they're well above what one could call normal, it also appears she's a serious drug problem."

"I am inclined to agree, Mr Catchpole, unless the prosecution can offer further witnesses, I am reluctant to let this case proceed any further."

The prosecution team were frantically trying to find a way out of this dilemma, but their options were limited. Eventually they'd to concede defeat, Appleton got to her feet.

"I'm sorry your honour, we've no further evidence to produce."

"Very well, I am dismissing this case. The Crown Prosecution Service has wasted the court's time, not to mention putting Mrs Clemson through months of anxiety. Mrs Clemson you are free to go."

Megan was in tears and fell into the arms of her father, then thanked Catchpole for his wonderful work. She turned and smiled, and thanked me as they left the courtroom to be greeted by a plethora of photographers.

No doubt they were heading off for a major celebration.

Chapter 15

I was summoned to the Chief Constable's office.

"That was some damned pantomime you put on at the Crown Court, Tyler, what did you intend to do for an encore, pull a rabbit out of your arse?"

"I did express my concern to the Crown Prosecution Service, that I wasn't one hundred percent sure that Megan Clemson was responsible for these two murders. However, they wouldn't take my concerns on board, they felt there was sufficient evidence against her with her fingerprints being found on two of the murder weapons. It was their decision she should be charged and put on trial. I wasn't aware of Vera Maddox's drug and drink problem, there was nothing to indicate she'd any of these habits. Obviously the defence were able to find out, what we in hindsight, should've found out."

"So, a year later, Tyler, we're back to square one, with six unsolved murders still on our books.

"Do you have any idea the kind of pressure I'm under from the commissioner and various political groups?"

"What can I say, investigating these cases has been like trying to plait sawdust in a force nine gale?"

"What about this Clemson guy, do you think he's the culprit?"

"He's an alibi for each of these murders. In fact he was out of the country for one of them. I'd suggest caution before we head down that route, we don't want another fiasco like we've just had."

"Jesus, Tyler, I'd every confidence in your ability to solve these crimes, it seems like I was mistaken."

"It wasn't for the want of trying, so if you feel I should be replaced, that's fine by me."

"I want you to call your team together, go through every scrap of evidence you've gathered to date, see if there's anything you've overlooked."

I left his office and headed over to see my squad.

"Just had a meeting with the Chief Constable, he's not a happy camper, he wants us to review everything on file to see if we've overlooked anything."

I was glad for Megan that her nightmare was over, but she'd another one on the horizon as her father was due to be sentenced over the kidnapping of Vera Maddox. I'd never particularly liked him, even though he was my father in-law, I was amazed he could be so devious to do what he did to protect Megan. Apparently, he'd decided to come clean and avoid a trial in the hope that he'd get a reduced sentence. He also admitted threatening me with a wood chisel he took from my belt, because of this, his prints had been found on the murder weapon. It was either admit to assaulting and threatening me or, be implicated in Wimpole's murder.

Daddy knew he'd receive a stiff sentence for his stupid involvement in the kidnapping of Maddox, and was trying to prepare everything for when he would be away. He wanted me to take on the responsibility of running everything during his incarceration. I wasn't sure I could do it, after all, I'd never really had a proper job, apart from my brief employment in one of his advertising companies.

He'd been forced to resign as an MP, I think that hurt him the most. I'd several meetings with his estate manager for the past 30 years, Philip Knowles. He filled me in on everything about the running of the estate, from collecting rents, to looking after the maintenance of the gardens and the all the properties. Also making sure that all the produce from the farms got to market on time, he'd be my right hand man.

David Stoddart was Daddy's financial adviser, he brought me up to date on his investments and what we would need to do financially. Harold Winters was his general manager, a real hands-on kind of person, he said he'd help me find my feet.

After a couple of weeks I was quite enjoying the responsibility, if only it'd been under different circumstances.

A number of meetings were held with the different managers and supervisors in his various activities, as each day went by I felt more confident I could do it.

December 15th was the day for sentencing for all those involved in the kidnapping, I was with Daddy when he appeared in court.

Because they'd all pleaded guilty there'd be no trial and they'd all be sentenced individually.

Daddy as the instigator was sentenced first, the judge lectured him on the serious crime he'd orchestrated, the courts would not tolerate this kind of offence.

He received six years, there were gasps from people in the courtroom when this was announced, and the look on Daddy's face was absolute utter shock. Our lawyer, Catchpole, immediately announced that he'd appeal. The others received sentences from three years to probation. We were all shattered with the severity of the convictions, because we'd been led to believe that if they cooperated fully and pleaded guilty, they'd be treated leniently.

Daddy was expecting no more than three years, with part of it suspended. Tyler Hyde's, word meant nothing, he couldn't be trusted. Daddy had been truthful and honest with the investigation, making the inspector's job straightforward. He filled in all the blanks about his part in the crime, who else was responsible, everything from who kidnapped her from the mews, to who held her captive in Yorkshire. The intension had not been to cause any harm to Vera Maddox, only to stop her giving evidence. She'd been well looked after during her ordeal and she'd have been released unharmed after the trial was over. As it turned out, he needn't have got involved because I wasn't guilty.

Catchpole asked if the sentences could be deferred until after Christmas, but the judge refused. They were led away to start their sentences immediately.

I felt so alone as Daddy disappeared down the steps of the court to the waiting prison van below. Catchpole held my arm and told me to keep my spirits up. He would get Daddy out somehow.

My team and I spent hours going over all the evidence we'd gathered over the previous year. Tony decided to review some of the fire evidence from 'Walters Autos' and the 'Cock and Bottle' pub.

"Super, remember when we arrested the gardeners over at the Wigglesworth estate?"

"Yes, what have you found?"

"I've just had a thought. When we searched the tack room next to the stables, in addition to all the saddles and harnesses, there was a load of mountaineering equipment hung on one of the walls. Lots of ropes, shackles and crampons plus a couple of ice axes."

"Carry on."

"Remember the body we found belonging to Clive Harlow, I said the wound in his scull appeared to have been caused by a sharp implement like an axe. I don't know why I didn't think of it before, but they could be connected. I think I should take a quick trip out to Wigglesworth, if the axes are still there, see if we can get any forensics off them."

"Good idea, Tony, get onto it straight away, but get the necessary paperwork, we need to do this strictly by the book."

The following day, Tony was back with the two ice axes from Wigglesworth, he immediately started to process them for forensics. They were checked for fingerprints and DNA.

It was late in the day when he came racing into my office.

"Just found something that is very exciting.

"I've managed to match the serrated edge of the axe with the wounds in the skull of Clive Harlow, proving this was the murder weapon used. However, more interestingly, I've found a partial print on this ice axe that matched the one on the weapon used on Basil Thornwood. Further testing showed it matched the print on the pickaxe used on Neil Derek, the racket inserted into Alan Walters, it was also on the handle of the chisel used to murder Jason Wimpole.

"It wasn't so evident the first time around because it's not a full print, but I'm confident it belonged to the same person on each of the five murder weapons.

"I've put these partial prints up on the screen and merged them in layers using Photoshop software to create one full print. It has two deltas and quite a distinctive core. You could say it's a manufactured print and it might not stand up in court, because different sections of the print appear on each of these murder weapons. The puzzling thing is there is only one finger but there appears to be a partial print of the lower section of another finger, but I wouldn't be confident with this."

"They all matched, any idea who they belong to?"

"No, they're not a match for any of our current suspects and there's nothing in the national database that matches. However, there could be something in the files that go back a number of years, before the database was created."

"It's very interesting, but if it's pre-computer it will be big job to check it out. There are thousands of files in the basement, it will be like looking for a needle in a haystack, especially if it's not a local person."

"That's not all, I've been examining samples of ash taken from both of the fire sites and found something of interest. I didn't spot it when I was at the two sites originally, because there was so much debris. But when I re-examined samples taken from what we thought were the ignition points using an electron microscope, I've found minute traces of candlewick in the ash. As you know, this is a classical way of starting a fire. You place a candle in sawdust making sure there is something inflammable mixed in it, when the candle burns down to the sawdust, whoosh away you go.

"This method of arson can make it very difficult to spot, because everything usually gets destroyed in the fire. Depending on the size of the candle you use, you could be at the other end of the country when the fire starts and have a perfect alibi.

"I think this method was used in both fires because they each had minute samples of wick in them, indicating to me, this was how the fires were started. Also, I found residue of beeswax in both samples, so that narrows down the type of candle used."

"That's all very compelling, puts a different reflection on things, maybe we should have another look at Luke Clemson's alibi?"

Stephanie sent me another letter, saying she'd like to visit me late January if that was Ok. I felt it wouldn't be a problem now. My wife had been acquitted of murder and all the scandal that had been at the fore had now died down, plus all the rats from the Gazette had crawled back into their holes. I told her to go ahead and book her trip, then I arranged with Archie my boss to take some time off. Although we'd been in regular contact on the phone, I was looking forward to seeing her again in the flesh.

I was getting used to be being the lady of the manor, my serfs were all performing admirably, everything was running smoothly, the only downside was, it was very lonely.

I'd asked Luke to reconsider his position, but he'd refused as divorce proceedings had already been started. He said he'd moved on and I should do the same. This hurt me, as I felt long term he'd forgive me for my past indiscretions and come home. Sadly that was not the case, I was not used to being turned down, when he said he'd found someone else, it was like a knife through my heart.

We started to examine the timeline on each of the murders and Clemson's alibis.

The first murder of Basil Thornwood, took place between 6.00 and 10.00 p.m on the 7th of July 2006. Clemson stated he was at home with his wife during this time, was this true? We'd felt all along he was protecting her, maybe it was the other way around, it might pay dividends to talk to her.

The second murder of Neil Derek took place between 6.00 and 8.00 a.m on August the 16th the same year. Clemson claimed that he was staying at the Flagship Hotel near Salisbury and his apprentice could confirm this. It's only 45 miles away, he could easily have committed the crime and got back to the hotel, but he'd got his apprentice and the receptionist as an alibi. Here we'd two more people to re-interview.

Murder scene number three, the fire at 'Walters Autos' started sometime around 3.00 a.m on September 5th. Clemson was in Scotland, but like Tony said, the fire was started using a candle in sawdust. He could easily have committed the murder using a squash racket that belonged to Jason Wimpole inserted into Walters rear end, implicating Wimpole in the murder, then setting the candle alight before heading north of the border.

Murder scene number four at the 'Cock and Bottle' here we'd two bodies, the owner of the pub, Jeff Landers, and Clive Harlow. The fire started again with the use of a candle in sawdust. Where was our number one suspect? Flying over the Atlantic, what an alibi!

Murder scene number five, the towpath alongside the Avon canal, victim Jason Wimpole. Stabbed to death with a chisel belonging to Luke Clemson. He'd a confirmed alibi for most of the evening until midnight. Could he have committed the murder between midnight and say 7.00 a.m the following morning. He stated he was in bed from midnight until he got up at six the next morning, but we only had his word for that.

So what had we got, six people dead, what was the common denominator? We know they'd all been lovers of Megan Clemson at one time or another.

Luke Clemson had more reason than anyone to want them dead, yet it was all too obvious, however, I was under pressure to come up with something, he was the obvious choice.

I took a drive out to the Wigglesworth estate, noticeably there were no thugs at the gate. I parked outside the manor and asked to see Mrs Clemson, I was shown into the waiting room.

“Morning inspector, what can I do for you?”

"Just a couple of questions, Mrs Clemson, if you don't mind. You stated that on the evening of July seventh, that's the day Basil Thornwood was murdered, you and your husband were together all evening, is that correct?”

She thought about it for a while.

“To be honest, I took a bath between nine and ten on my own, so I can't confirm if he was in the house or not during this time, he could've slipped out.”

Oh what joy, bang goes this alibi.

“Are you absolutely certain about this?”

"Like I said, I took a bath during this time and he could've gone out or still been in the house watching TV I'm not certain that's all."

"Thanks very much, Mrs Clemson, I appreciate your time."

So alibi number one isn't so concrete.

I thought I'd take a trip out to the Flagship Hotel. I asked to see Veronica Rigby the receptionist who was on duty when we carried out our initial investigation.

"Morning inspector, how can I help?"

I turned to see her as she walked out of her office, she was a striking looking lady, tall, blonde with a slim figure and looked like a model out of the pages of Vogue magazine.

"Morning Veronica, you stated in your previous interview with Detective Masters that Luke Clemson was here at the hotel on August sixteenth and you assumed he was in his room all night and present at breakfast, is that correct?"

She thought about it for a minute, she had a worried look on her face.

"It's like this, inspector, we're not supposed to mix socially with the customers. However, there was a disco on the previous night and I was there helping the bar staff. In the course of the evening I got talking to Mr Clemson. We found we'd a lot in common, I'd one or two drinks, one thing led to another, then at the end of the evening I took him up to my room. It's not something I'm in the habit of doing. I put it down to the fact I'd taken too much alcohol. Please don't mention this to management, because I could lose my job."

"Did he leave the room at all?"

"No, he was with me all night until I'd to get up for work just before six a.m. I didn't see him again until nine a.m when he came to reception to check out, along with his roommate Mr Williams I believe his name was."

"Thanks very much Veronica, you've been very helpful, but it would've been better if you'd told us this at your original interview."

"I realise now that was a mistake, it's just I was frightened of losing my job, please don't say anything?"

"Not to worry, Veronica, your secret's safe with me."

I left the hotel with a spring in my step, two people had now offered a different version to their original statements. I wondered, could I make it three in a row as I headed off to see Clemson's apprentice, at his place of work?

I pulled into the car park at Heritage Craft Fine Furniture, and parked in the visitors' slot. I went into reception, asked to see Alistair Williams, and was shown into the waiting room.

"Morning, Mr Williams, I'm Detective Chief Inspector Tyler Hyde, I wonder if you wouldn't mind answering a few questions for me?"

"No problem, what do you want to know?"

"Do you remember the evening you stayed at the Flagship Hotel near Salisbury, along with Mr Clemson on the sixteenth of August? You stated at the time, that you shared a twin room with Mr Clemson and that he was with you all night. That isn't true is it? I've been talking to the receptionist, Veronica Rigby. She confirms that Mr Clemson spent the night with her, so he can hardly be in two places at once can he, so who's telling the truth?"

"It was just a slight distortion to give cover to the receptionist if she needed it, that's all."

"But in doing so, you also gave an alibi to Mr Clemson. From the previous evening in the disco when you last saw Mr Clemson to the following morning, what time did you see him again?"

"Just before nine, when he came back to the room to shower and to pick up his overnight things. We then went straight down to reception and checked out."

"You absolutely sure about the time you saw him again?"

"Yes."

"Ok, thanks very much, Mr Williams, you've been very helpful, but it would've been better if you'd told us this at your previous interview, goodbye."

On my way back to the station, I felt I'd achieved more in that one morning than we had in the previous twelve months, there seemed to be a pattern emerging that showed Mr Clemson had some anomalies in his story, could he be responsible for these murders?

He could've killed Neil Derek then got back to the hotel in time. However, we'd a long way to go to break down his sequence of rock-solid alibis and we could charge him.

I was in the workshop when Alistair came racing in to see me.

"Luke, I'm sorry, I think I might've dropped you in it. That inspector has been to see me about the night we stayed at the Flagship Hotel. Originally, I told them you were in my room the whole night as we agreed, just to provide cover for that receptionist. Well it turns out she told him the truth that you spent the night with her, so there didn't seem to be much point in me keeping up the pretence. I told him you got back to our room just before nine and we checked out shortly after, sorry."

"Not to worry, Alistair, we only did it to protect her, that's bloody women for you. My one time enjoying a bit of female company, and when they ask you to cover for them and you agree, they then play silly buggers and make it look like you've something to hide. Don't concern yourself about it, Alistair, it's not a hanging offence."

"I'm not so sure. He said I'd provided you with an alibi, whatever he meant by that."

"What's he up to now, still trying to pin something on me? Anyway, I have nothing to fear, I'll not lose any sleep over it. I think we'd better get on with the furniture restoration for Mr Paulton, he's due in this afternoon to pick it up."

That old bugger, was he still trying to pin the murders on me since Megan was acquitted in such a dramatic fashion? I'd better watch my back.

Chapter 16

When I got back to the station, Tony confirmed that DNA tests showed, the ice axe found over at the Wigglesworth estate, was the murder weapon used on Clive Harlow. Just another piece of the jigsaw.

"I think we should run a few tests on candles to try and be specific about the burning times based on the size of candle. We know Clemson was in Scotland, working at Hislop Castle when Walters garage went up in flames, so I'm just trying to put a timeframe into the equation to see if it's possible that he was responsible for this murder."

"Very well, Sir, I'll get onto it right away but it's not going to be an exact science, because whoever manufactured the candles, they could have different burning times, depending on the makeup of the candle and the type of wick used."

"I know what you're saying, Tony, so here's what you do. Go out and purchase a selection of candles from different shops, say in a ten or twenty mile radius, then do tests on all of them to try and establish an average burning rate. It may well be, there's just one manufacturer supplying all the local shops. We could be doing tests on candles that originated from the same source of manufacture. If that's the case it's not a problem, we just need to try and approximate how long it takes for a candle to burn down and create an ignition, then we may have a definitive timeframe to work with."

"Ok, Sir, I'll get a couple of my people as well and see if we can cover a bigger area to see if there is any noticeable difference in what we manage to find."

After Tony had left my office, I kept thinking it might be an idea to interview Clemson again, just to try and put some leverage on him. His wife had indicated she couldn't be sure he was in the house all night. This struck me as kind of strange, almost like she wasn't prepared to give him an alibi any more.

Had something happened in the interim, apart from, if the rumours were correct, him filing for divorce, that could have made her change her mind? It would be interesting to see what was behind it.

Tony and his team, managed to source candles from over 50 shops in a 30-mile radius.

When they were all compared, there appeared to be 12 different manufacturers. Some producing scented candles, some just normal and a variety of thicknesses and lengths.

They then proceeded to do a series of meticulous tests, placing each candle in a paper tray containing sawdust that had methylated spirits added. A stopwatch was used as each of the candles was lit then a close eye kept on it until it reached the sawdust and ignited it. It took quite a bit of time to complete all the tests, but at the end of the day, we'd all the data that we needed.

Tony brought all the detailed information through to my office.

"Quite interesting results, Sir, some of the larger scented candles would have lasted for days so I think we can rule them out for a number of reasons. Because of their size, if they'd been used in the two fires I think there is a strong possibility a lot more of the residue would've been found at the scene. It's also possible that some of the scent will also have been evident.

"With this in mind, we concentrated on the narrower and smaller candles. There was quite a bit of difference in burn times due to the different manufactures and the makeup of the candle. Some had used tallow and beeswax, some soy and palm wax, some paraffin wax and some had added synthetic materials. Different types of weave had been used in the wicks, all these different factors affected the burn times.

"A twelve-inch taper candle would burn for approximately ten to thirteen hours. An eight-inch taper candle would last approximately six to nine hours. The little tea lights between four and six hours. These are all approximate times, but it does show that you could light a candle and be at the other side of the world before they ignited, if you'd reason to do so."

"That's great, Tony, at least it gives us a sound base to work from to see if we can prove Clemson did set the fires. It shows he could've done it and be in East Lothian in plenty of time, as well as flying to America. All we've got to do is find that vital piece of evidence. I think it would be a good idea if you all went back to wherever you bought them with a photograph of Clemson, just to see if they recall him buying candles from their stores. It might just pay dividends."

I kept thinking about what Alistair had told me, that Inspector Hyde had said he'd given me an alibi. I thought I should go and see Megan to see if she'd heard from Hyde.

I took a drive over to Wigglesworth Manor to see her.

"Hello, may I help you, I'm Sybil, Megan's private secretary, she's in a meeting at the moment and can't be disturbed? Can I give her a message?"

This caught me by surprise, since when did Megan acquire or in fact, need a private secretary? Unless she needed someone to manage the many men she had in her life.

"Yes if you would, just tell her Luke would like to speak with her as soon as possible."

"Very well, I'll pass the message on."

Private Secretary, is this the same Megan we were talking about, never did a day's work in her life, now giving the impression she's one of the captains of industry? What next?

Chief Constable Atkinson requested my presence in his office to give him a progress update.

"What's the latest, Tyler, I notice you've been very quiet since our last meeting, what's going on?"

This guy was really starting to piss me off, let me get on with the job, as soon as we have made any headway you'll be the first to know.

"Nothing really concrete. I've re-interviewed a couple of witnesses, there are minor differences in what they're saying now. We've also found a partial print that is on a number of the murder weapons, but as of now we haven't been able to identify them. We're also running tests on candles to try and establish burn times, that's it."

"That's it? Do you have any idea the kind of pressure I'm under? I want to see some progress within the next forty-eight hours or there'll be changes."

"It's unlikely that what we've been unable to achieve in the last twelve months, we can achieve in the next forty-eight hours. I might as well book my retirement trip to Spain now."

"That's not good enough, Tyler, copping out when we're in the midst of the worst crisis this county has ever experienced, this just won't do. Is there anything further you want to add?"

"For Christ's sake, let me get on with the job! Stop badgering me! Every time you call me away you're stopping the flow of our enquiries. If you can't accept that then you can have my resignation now."

"Do you have any idea who you are talking to?"

"Yes, my Chief Constable. I suggest you start acting like one, because I've had more than enough of your damned pressure. Let me handle this investigation my way, when I've something positive to report I'll let you know. It's up to you, take it or leave it. I won't take anymore of your constant badgering and damned interference."

He got up from his seat, stood there glaring at me, he looked fit to burst, the veins in his neck were standing out like roots on a tree and he'd gone quite a nice shade of cerise.

"Very well, get on with it."

At this point he turned and stormed out of his office. That was easy. I bet no one ever talked to him like that before, but it was long overdue. No amount of browbeating will make the investigation go any quicker, the sooner he realises that, the better. Of course, that's how he's got to his present position, by constantly being an utter pain in the arse. Guess he'll be crossing me off his Christmas card list.

As I walked out of his office, several other officers who'd obviously heard the shouting gave me the thumbs up. I guess I just did what they would've all loved to do.

"Hello Luke, you wanted to talk to me? Sorry I was tied up when you called earlier today, just doing the monthly budgets with the estate manager, what did you want to talk about?"

"Hi, Megan, thanks for getting back to me, I don't like discussing things like this over the phone, are you free tomorrow?"

"Sorry, no can do, have to go up to London to see my investment manager, can you not tell me now what it is?"

"Very well, have you had a visit from Inspector Hyde, in the last day or so?"

"Yes, he stopped by the manor yesterday morning, just to check your alibi that you were with me all night."

"What did you tell him?"

"What else? That we were together all night, never left the house."

"Thanks, I'm not sure what he's up to, but he seems to be directing his investigation in my direction again. I suppose he's under pressure, they've to try and pin these murders on someone. Anyway, Megan, thanks for doing that I'll see you around, in between your business meetings."

"Yes Ok Luke, I'm really enjoying my new career, nice to talk to you again, bye."

She certainly seemed to have got the bit between her teeth, running her father's business interests, at least it'll keep her out of bed.

Late in the day, Tony and Rick Masters, returned from their tour around the candle stores.

"Inspector, I have some good news. I visited this place, it's a traditional old-fashioned hardware store. They recall Clemson came in to buy blocks of beeswax, methylated spirits and paraffin oil. It sticks in his mind because they didn't have any pure beeswax in stock at the time, they'd to get it in specially for him. They don't get much call for this product, all they normally carry is rosin for violin players, this wasn't suitable for what he wanted."

"Good work, Rick, but he'd hardly go to the trouble of making his own candles, would he? Not when they're so cheap. That doesn't make a great deal of sense does it?"

"Not really, unless he was making up his own kind of incendiary devices that would've less chance of being detected."

"I suppose that's a possibility, what do you think, Tony?"

"Rick could be right, we bought some of the beeswax that he supplied to Clemson, I'll run some tests to see if it matches with samples in the ash that I've got from the two sites. I might just be able to find something however, it won't be easy, but I can but try."

"Ok let me know the minute you find anything? I've got old 'bollock brain' breathing down my neck, I'm anxious to get back onto his Christmas card list."

I was counting down the days to when I'd see Stephanie again, I'd planned where we'd go and what we'd do. It would be a nice change to have a beautiful woman around again. I was tidying up all the jobs that we had on hand, making sure that Alistair would be able to carry on by himself during the time I was away. I felt confident he was capable of working on his own, but if he'd a problem, I was only a phone call away.

January 25th finally arrived, I headed down to terminal 5 at Heathrow to collect her.

When she spotted me, she raced over, flung her arms around me and kissed me full on the mouth. We both held one another tightly, oblivious to the crowds of people standing close by.

"Stephanie, lovely to see you again, have you had a good flight?"

"Great thanks, I slept part of the way but it was a very enjoyable journey. I must say, business class on BA is excellent, it's the first time I've experienced it but it's better than most first class services on the American carriers."

"That's good, glad you enjoyed it, I'll take you straight to my cottage and you can shower and freshen up. If you've the energy and you feel sufficiently rested, I've a full programme of things for you to see and do."

"That's very kind of you, I've been so looking forward to this trip and of course seeing you again. By the way, Chuck, sends his regards, he's looking forward to you joining us in the States."

"I've already applied for my green card, hopefully with your job offer and my immigration lawyer working on it nonstop, I should be hearing something quite soon."

Tony did further tests on the ash taken from both fire sites. He found that they matched the same beeswax sample purchased. Whilst it was not conclusive this particular beeswax was used in these two fires because beeswax was a standard material used in the manufacture of candles, it was a good indicator.

I felt that Mr Clemson should be brought in for further questioning. I visited his home but the place was deserted, so I went to his place of employment. They told me he was on leave. They'd no idea where he was, but he had his girlfriend over from the States. As soon as I heard this, the alarm bells started to ring, the last thing we wanted was him doing a runner, maybe he'd already skipped the country.

We notified a number of stations in the south of England, as well as all the main airports and seaports to be on the lookout for Clemson.

Chapter 17

Stephanie and I, had visited a number of tourist sites locally, then we drove down to Polperro in South East Cornwall, one of my favourite places. Not being the height of the tourist season it was very quiet. Some of the hotels were closed for the winter but we stayed in the Crumplehorn Inn and Mill, a lovely B&B full of history and this really appealed to Stephanie.

We spent several days there. She went out and took photographs of Polperro from every angle. We dined on the finest seafood in a number of different restaurants, and visited several traditional pubs. These all appealed to Stephanie, as they don't have anything like that in the US, with the exception of the odd Irish theme pub.

We'd just checked out of the hotel and were getting ready to leave, when a police car pulled in front of us blocking our exit. Two officers got out and walked over to us.

"Are you Luke Clemson?"

"Yes I am, is there a problem?"

"I've been asked to detain you and take you to see Inspector Hyde."

"Oh Christ, what does he want now, I'm on holiday?"

"Sorry about that, but I've been asked to detain you for further questioning."

I looked at Stephanie who wore a look of shock on her face. Why did that bastard have to do this, my newfound relationship would probably be over before it had begun?

"Constable, I can't leave my friend here, she's from America. I can't just abandon her here, can I drive her back with me, one of you can sit in the car?"

They discussed it between themselves and they eventually agreed.

As we drove off with Constable Beswick in the passenger's seat, there was an awkward silence. As I looked in the rear view mirror, Stephanie had a distressed look on her face, I felt that I should try to explain.

"I'm sorry about this, Stephanie, it's been a regular occurrence for me these past few months. My wife was in court recently on a charge of double murder, but the judge threw the case out of court. It would appear that they're now trying to pin it on me."

I could see by the look on her face she just wanted out of the car, she'd be on the first plane back home. I should've told her but I didn't know how to do it. Now I was paying the price, this bloody nightmare would never end. How could I possibly tell her that several of my wife's lovers had been murdered and I was the number one suspect? It's hardly the kind of thing you can talk about, not without people running for cover.

"Stephanie, take my keys and stay at the cottage until they've finished talking with me, I shouldn't be too long."

"I wouldn't be so sure about that," said Constable Beswick.

Once inside the station, I was taken in to see Tyler Hyde. Constable Beswick agreed to drive Stephanie to my cottage, at least I was grateful to him for that.

"Mr Clemson, you had us worried, we thought you'd done a runner to the US."

"And why would I do that?"

"Maybe because you know we've enough evidence to charge you with the murders of six people. It's been a long investigation, but we now have what we need."

"I've told you consistently, I'm not responsible for these murders, why don't you change the bloody record?"

"You won't be so cocky when I tell you we've found anomalies in your story.

"Your wife said you weren't at the house all night. Veronica from the Flagship hotel confirms that you were missing from six a.m until nine a.m. Your workmate Alistair confirmed you didn't stay in the same room as him. We have also established that the two fires were started with the use of beeswax devices, the same beeswax you purchased from the hardware store in Bishop's Bluff. Of course we've your prints on the chisel found in Jason Wimpole."

I couldn't get my head around this, what the hell had Megan said? The rest of it was all bullshit and I felt he was just fishing.

But why'd he chosen to do it now with Stephanie in the country, he couldn't have picked a worse time? I was more concerned with what she would think about me, than these trumped up charges that our intrepid sleuth had concocted.

"I'm not responsible for any of these deaths, the sooner you get that into your thick head, the better it will be for all concerned."

"Luke Clemson, I'm charging you with the murders of Basil Thornwood, Neil Derek, Alan Walters, Jeff Landers, Clive Harlow, and Jason Wimpole. You do not have to say anything. But it may harm your defence, if you do not mention when questioned, something that you later rely on in court. Anything you do say may be given in evidence."

I realised he wasn't joking, he was on a mission to pin it on me, this had been evident for a long time.

"It's not me, I'm not responsible for any of these murders, you have absolutely no evidence that connects me to these crimes."

"You'll be held at this station overnight and tomorrow, appear in the Magistrates court in Winchester. Take him to the cells."

As soon as he had been taken away, Tony Morehouse came into my office.

"Skipper are you sure about this, do we have enough evidence to charge him?"

"The Crown Prosecution Service think so, I'm just following what they have decided."

"What about the other print I found on the murder weapons, that is a critical piece of evidence?"

"Bury it, I don't think it would stand up in court seeing as you had to manufacture it. I retire at the end of this year, I want to go out on a high with this bloody case put to bed. It's been hanging over my head for a long time, I'm sick of the weekly rantings from the chief constable."

"I can't do that, I couldn't stand by and see someone getting jailed for something if they were innocent."

"Like I said, bury it, that print didn't exist until you made it, so it probably wouldn't be admissible, I don't want to hear another word about it."

There was frenzy in the local community as soon as the news broke. The headlines in the local Gazette read:

'Wiltshire Whacker Finally Caught.'

The media descended on the area in droves, along with TV crews from around the world. Serial killers always have that effect.

I appeared at the Magistrates' Court the following morning, after a brief hearing at which I pleaded not guilty to all of the charges, I was remanded in custody to appear at the Crown Court later in the year. My lawyer asked for bail, but due to the severe nature of the charges, this was refused. The police felt there was a high risk that I would flee the country. I was led away, to be held at Winchester prison.

What a nightmare. It was so unreal I'd a constant pain in my stomach, the tension I felt was so intense. I was held in captivity with real murderers, drug lords, wife beaters, you name it they'd committed it, every crime in the book. I'd always been a law-abiding person, never had such a thing as a speeding or parking ticket, yet I was mixed in with this lot!

Alistair and my boss Archie McGoldrick visited me in the Ritz several times. Alistair informed me that when he checked the house, Stephanie had left the day after I was arrested, she'd put a note on the kitchen table thanking me for looking after her. She wished me good luck with my life but she couldn't cope with this bizarre scenario and had returned home. I couldn't blame her, I would've done the same.

Chapter 18

I'd recruited the services of a good lawyer, Myles Heddigan QC, who made several visits to see me in prison. He felt that the prosecutions core evidence was all circumstantial and highly speculative. They'd no hard evidence, forensics or otherwise that linked me to any of the murders. I knew this, but it still didn't make me feel any better. Why did I have this feeling of impending doom? Hyde had been out to nail me from day one. Who knows what evidence he'd cook up? For me, this whole episode in my life had been a black period, one that I felt would never leave me.

This feeling was further compounded when Heddigan visited me.

"In my pre-trial preparation, your ex wife indicated to me she's reluctant to give evidence. I pointed out that we could issue a subpoena. It has now got complicated because the prosecution inform me she will be a witness for them.

"What the reason is for her changing her mind I'm not sure. It could be that the prosecution have offered her a deal if she testifies as a witness for them, by not pressing charges for any inconsistencies in her own trial.

"Who knows what Tyler Hyde has offered her. He has hounded you for years and is obviously a devious son of a bitch, not bothered about bending the rules to get you put away.

"It's probably better in some respects, because if we had her on the stand and she started to change her version of events from her original story, then she could be classed as a hostile witness. This would complicate how we could cross-examine her. At least as a witness for the prosecution, I can adopt a different approach."

I couldn't take in what Heddigan had just told me after all I had done for her.

What was her reason for doing this, talk about stabbing me in the back? I'd given her an alibi yet she'd chosen to repay me by screwing me in spectacular fashion. Maybe Heddigan was correct that they had done a deal.

The day for my trial was set for November 5th, with a bit of luck, someone would blow up the Crown Court!

I was taken from Winchester jail, handcuffed to a prison officer. As soon as I was in court I realised the prosecution council was Olwyn Appleton, I knew I was in for it. She'd an old score to settle with me.

She outlined the prosecution case, saying they'd prove beyond any reasonable doubt, that I was responsible for all six of these vicious murders. I remember her saying the same thing when Megan was in the dock. My lawyer addressed the court saying he'd prove that I was not responsible for these crimes.

The first witness the Crown called, was Megan.

She was sworn in and took the stand.

"Please state your name for the record."

"Megan Clemson."

"Mrs Clemson, do you recognise the defendant?"

"Yes, he was my husband up until we divorced nine months ago."

"Basil Thornwood was a good friend of yours, would it be fair to say?"

"Yes, we were very close."

"The seventh of July 2006 the day he was murdered, you're ex-husband states that he was at home with you between the hours of five-thirty p.m. until the following morning, the eighth, and never left the house. Is that correct?"

"No, he was out of the house between nine and ten fifteen."

"How can you be so precise about the time?"

"Daddy rings me every night around nine p.m. when Luke didn't pick up the phone I came downstairs to answer it. He wasn't there and the door of the cottage was open."

Oh Megan! What are you saying that's an absolute lie. You weren't even in the house, you didn't come home until two-thirty a.m.

"Did Mr Thornwood live nearby?"

"Yes, it's only about fifteen minutes walking distance from our cottage."

The questioning continued for another half an hour as the prosecution attempted to build their case. Eventually, Appleton reached the end of her interrogation.

"No further questions."

Myles Heddigan QC got to his feet.

"Mrs Clemson, you stated at your own trial for double murder, that Mr Clemson was with you the whole time, from five thirty in the evening and never left you at any time."

"Objection, your honour, Mrs Clemson was acquitted of this crime and it has no relevance in this case."

"It's absolutely of relevance, this was the critical piece of evidence that contributed to her acquittal in this previous trial."

"Objection overruled."

"You stated at your trial, that your then husband didn't leave the house that night, in fact that neither of you left the house and were together the whole time until the following morning. Yet now, you describe with such clarity, that when you came downstairs at nine p.m, the door to your cottage was open and Mr Clemson was missing. Which of these two versions is correct Mrs Clemson, because they both can't be right?"

Megan squirmed in the witness box, she didn't answer immediately.

"I'm waiting, Mrs Clemson."

"I was taking a bath between nine and ten and wasn't sure if he was in the house or not."

"Would it be normal to take a bath when you knew your father called you each night around this time?"

"Not sure what you're getting at, I took a bath Ok?"

"Mrs Clemson, may I remind you, that you are still under oath and perjury is a very serious offence, you're giving two conflicting versions of what happened that night. A man is on trial for a number of serious crimes, you'd better start telling the truth."

"I am telling the truth, it's just that I wasn't totally certain that Luke was in the house when I was in the bath."

"I wonder if the fact that my client sued you for divorce because of your adultery, has a bearing on why you're now changing your story. I'm sure the jury are taking note of your reluctance to answer truthfully.

"I'll ask you another way, was your husband in the house the whole time and never went out?"

"I'm not sure, I was taking a bath."

"So we've gone from, he was out of the house between nine and ten fifteen p.m to, you're not sure, you were taking a bath. Hardly convincing testimony, I'm sure the jury are taking note of your inconsistencies.

"In view of this new version of events that night, your previous testimony may well come in for more scrutiny. I don't need to remind you that perjury is a serious offence. Do you want to change your story again?"

"No, I don't want to change anything."

Heddigan looked intently at her, then at the jury.

"Very well, don't say you weren't warned, no further questions."

Good for you, Heddigan, but I think he let her off a bit lightly. I would've carried on until I got a truthful answer. However, I'm sure he knows what he is doing.

The next person the prosecution called, was the receptionist from the Flagship Hotel, Veronica Rigby. Appleton rose to her feet.

"Ms Rigby, you are the receptionist at the Flagship Hotel, is that correct?"

"Yes, one of them."

"On the evening of August sixteenth 2006, tell me what happened."

"I was working in the disco helping out the bar staff, because they'd a member off sick. It got very busy and they'd asked me to assist. During the course of the evening I met Mr Clemson and we got talking, we found we'd a lot in common, and got on famously, so much so that I agreed to meet him when I'd finished my shift. One thing lead to another, eventually we ended up in my room, where he stayed all night."

"So when he says he stayed in his twin room along with his workmate, Alistair Williams, that isn't correct?"

"No, he was with me the whole night until I left him just before six a.m"

Jesus it's hardly a hanging offence, she asked me to back her up but now I could see what Appleton was doing, I was being made to look a liar.

"No further questions."

Heddigan got to his feet.

"Ms Rigby, why do you think Mr Clemson said he was in his own room all evening?"

"Because I asked him to do so, I was afraid if the senior management found out that I'd entertained a guest, which is against company policy, I could lose my job. We're not supposed to associate with the clients on a personal level."

"Thanks for clarifying that Ms Rigby, no further questions."

It was obvious Appleton was nit picking, trying to make every little incident a hanging offence.

The next witness was Alistair. He looked terrified, when I looked around the courtroom I saw my boss, Archie McGoldrick who gave me a sly wink.

Appleton rose to her feet.

"Mr Williams, can you tell me where you were on the evening of the sixteenth of August 2006?"

"At the Flagship Hotel near Salisbury."

"You shared a twin room with your work colleague, Luke Clemson, did he spend the whole night in your room?"

"No he didn't, he spent the night with the receptionist at the hotel."

"Then can you tell me why you lied to the police in your original interview?"

"Because I was asked to do so."

"By Mr Clemson?"

Alistair was uneasy, he looked at me before he answered.

"Yes, it was in case the receptionist got into trouble."

"Thank you Mr Williams, no further questions."

She looked at me with a sly look on her face, but she was grasping at straws. This wasn't hard evidence, she was just trying to give the impression that I couldn't be trusted to tell the truth.

Heddigan stood up.

"Mr Williams, when Mr Clemson asked you to do this, did you consider you were committing a major crime?"

"No I didn't, it was just to protect her, she'd asked him to do it so we were only helping her out because she was afraid of losing her job."

"You've known Mr Clemson for a number of years, is that correct?"

"Yes, he's been my mentor for the past six years during my apprenticeship."

"In all this time, have you ever known him to be anything other than an upright citizen?"

"Objection your honour, leading the witness."

"Sustained."

"Let me put it another way, how would you describe Mr Clemson?"

"From my experience a man of the upmost integrity, I've enjoyed working with him every minute of my apprenticeship. He's extremely patient, kind, helpful, I wouldn't think he has a violent bone in his body. In all the years I've worked with him I've never seen him have any hint of aggression."

"Objection your honour, the witness isn't qualified to make such an assumption."

"Overruled."

"Thank you, Mr Williams, no further questions."

I nodded at Alistair as he sat down, the relief on his face was evident. The next witness to be called for the prosecution, was Inspector Tyler Hyde. Appleton stood up.

"Detective Chief Inspector Hyde, I understand you've been the main investigating officer into the murders of the six people, is that correct?"

"Yes it is."

"Has this been a very difficult investigation for you and your team?"

"Very much so."

"Can you tell the court why?"

"All the victims were murdered different ways, the perpetrator went to great lengths to cover his tracks. He used ingenious ways to set fires that destroyed evidence, but at the same time, creating an alibi for himself."

"Do you think the defendant in the dock is guilty of these murders?"

"Of course I do, otherwise he wouldn't be here. We've interviewed him on a number of occasions, my assessment of the defendant is, he couldn't tell the truth if his life depended on it."

"Objection your honour, that's an unfair assessment the inspector isn't qualified to make."

"Sustained."

"Can you tell the court what you found when you visited the home of Mr Basil Thornwood on July eighth 2006?"

"Certainly, the body of Mr Thornwood was lying face down on his kitchen floor. Forensics estimated he'd died between six p.m and ten p.m the previous evening.

"He'd a pitchfork embedded into his back, this had been stabbed in a number of times. The last one, had been driven in with such force, the pitchfork went through the body and was stuck into the wooden floor."

There were gasps from the public gallery at this revelation.

"What did you do then?"

"I made further investigations that lead me to the home of Luke and Megan Clemson."

"When you interviewed the defendant regarding the murder of Basil Thornwood, can you tell the court what happened, and outline subsequent events regarding the other murders?"

"Certainly, when I visited the family home the day the body of Mr Thornwood was found, Mr Clemson claimed that he and his wife had been at home all the previous evening and they never left the house. We now know from the testimony just given by Mrs Clemson, this indicates that this wasn't the case."

"Turning to the murder of Mr Neil Derek, can you tell the court what you found?"

"Certainly, the body of Mr Derek was discovered by his site foreman on August seventeenth 2006 at eight thirty a.m. when he started work. Forensics estimates he was murdered between six and eight a.m that day. He was found with a pick axe embedded in his skull." Again, there were gaps from the public gallery.

"When the body of Mr Derek was found on that day, I interviewed Mr Clemson at the station but he pointed out he had a cast iron alibi for the time of the murder and that he was at the Flagship Hotel near Salisbury. We've heard that there's an element of doubt about his whereabouts at this hotel, and there is a gap between six a.m and nine a.m when he'd ample time to travel the distance from the hotel to Kilmington, then carry out this murder, before returning and checking out of the hotel."

What utter bullshit, pure speculation, I've heard more convincing testimony coming from a children's crèche.

"The murder of Alan Walters was a particular vicious crime, can you tell the court what you found, Inspector?"

"This murder was a different story. He'd been killed in the most horrendous manner, left to burn to death in the trunk of a car. He was found with the remains of a squash racket that had been inserted into his anus. The state pathologist felt that he was probably still alive when he was placed in the car. Mr Clemson's alibi for this period was, that he was working on a project in Scotland and couldn't be responsible.

"We've established that the incident at Walter's Autos was a classic way of starting a fire. You set a candle in sawdust that has something inflammable mixed in it, when the candle burns down it ignites the sawdust and starts the fire. Depending on the size of candle used, you could be many miles away when the fire starts."

Surely to God the jury can't believe this crap, this isn't evidence it's pure fabrication.

"Can you tell us about the murders of Jeff Landers and Clive Harlow?"

"Certainly. The fire that took place on October seventeenth 2006 at the 'Cock and Bottle', a pub in Freckleston, was an attempt to mislead and confuse our investigation into who took the lives of Jeff Landers and Clive Harlow. Mr Landers had been killed by a blow to the back of his head with a blunt object. He was found in the remains of his apartment that had been over the pub before it collapsed to the ground. We haven't been able to find a murder weapon as of yet.

"Mr Harlow was killed with a blow to the head from an ice axe. This weapon was recovered from Wigglesworth Manor. He could've been murdered up to a month previously. Whether it was at this location or somewhere else, we just don't know. The fire started at approximately three a.m when the defendant was some way over the Atlantic on his way to America, all very convenient."

All very convenient it maybe, but it's the truth you pillock.

"Lastly, the murder of Jason Wimpole, can you tell us about this inspector?"

"Certainly, his body was found by an early morning dog walker by the Avon canal. He was murdered with a chisel that had the fingerprints of Luke Clemson all over it. A large number of stab wounds were found in his back, the pathologist estimated he'd been killed between midnight and eight a.m on the day he was found. Mr Clemson denied any involvement but he couldn't account for his whereabouts between the hours of midnight and the time the body was discovered."

Come on then, tell them the rest, why were my prints on the murder weapon?

"Thank you, Inspector, no further questions."

Right come on Heddigan, please get stuck in, I'm feeling a bit vulnerable at the moment.

"Detective Chief Inspector Hyde, when the first murder of Basil Thornwood occurred, you interviewed the defendant and his wife at their home. They both confirmed they were at home from five thirty p.m on the day of the murder until the following morning. We now have Mrs Clemson testimony that he was out of the house from nine p.m until ten fifteen p.m. Bearing in mind her originally testimony, that they were in the house together all night, and that this was a keystone in her acquittal at her own trial, we can't accept her version of events now, can we?"

"I can't be responsible for what witnesses say."

"I didn't ask you that, the point I'm making, which you conveniently seem to be side stepping is, that her change of testimony can't be taken seriously. You have to ask why has she now changed her story? Could it have something to do with the fact that Mr Clemson had divorced his wife because of her adultery, something that she would've found hard to accept, and there is an element of revenge in it?"

"What can I say? Women are unpredictable at the best of times, as I'm sure you know."

"Not from my experience. I'd say this women is being highly predictable, by changing her story, it undermines her husband's alibi, I'm sure the jury have taken note of her testimony, that may come back to haunt her in due course.

"You made great play of the time my client was at the Flagship Hotel, and the fact that when he was asked to do so, he gave the receptionist a cover story. Hardly the crime of the century, in fact, to me, it shows the caring side to Me Clemson, going out of his way to help someone when asked to do so. Yet you have set out to give the impression, he was devious, a liar and not to be trusted and could have travelled the distance from Salisbury to Kilmington, committed the murder and made his way back to the hotel in time for check out at nine a.m.

"The distance from the Flagship hotel to the murder site at Kilmington, is roughly forty-five miles. He would've had to drive from the hotel, find Mr Derek, and there would be no guarantee he would be at that particular building site, because apparently, he had three sites under construction at that time, and he could have been at any one of them. Then commit this dastardly act, drive the forty-five miles back to the hotel to appear normal to Mr Williams and Ms Rigby in reception. I suggest to you it's highly unlikely that this happened."

"I beg to differ, he would've had ample time, three hours is the window of opportunity he'd easily have enough time to do it."

"Yes, so you say, but did he? You've no evidence forensics or otherwise, that my client committed this violent act? It's all smoke and mirrors, Inspector, you're going to have to do better than that.

"I turn to the murder of Alan Walters. My client was in Scotland when this murder was carried out and the fire at his premises started. Yet you are convinced my client was responsible, what hard evidence have you that he carried out this murder?"

"We've established that samples of ash taken from two of the murder sites, contained traces of beeswax that matched the beeswax that Mr Clemson purchased from a hardware store in Bishop's Bluff."

"Tell me inspector, are you familiar with what is the makeup of candles?"

"I understand they can be made from a number of ingredients, from beeswax to palm wax to paraffin wax plus several synthetic materials."

"Very knowledgeable, but did you know that the majority are made from beeswax because it has a longer burn time and that figure is over seventy five percent? The samples you have, could've come from any number of candles purchased from anywhere. To suggest that my client was responsible, is stretching the bounds of possibility a bit too far.

"This also goes for the fire at the Cock and Bottle. When this occurred, my client was halfway across the Atlantic, but because this fits in with your theory, and that is all it is, he was also responsible for these two murders as well as setting fire to the pub. Again, you cannot produce one shred of evidence that my client was responsible.

"Inspector, throughout this trial, your so called evidence needs to be taken with a large spoonful of sugar.

"I now come to the murder of Jason Wimpole, found with a chisel embedded in his back. You made great play of explaining to the jury, that Mr Clemson's fingerprints were found on the handle of this murder weapon. What you failed to mention to them, was this was one of Mr Clemson's own work tools, so one would naturally assume his prints were bound to be found on this implement. Incidentally, the prints belonging to Mr Offington-Smythe, who is currently serving a prison sentence for kidnapping, were also found on this weapon. He has already admitted to you he took this chisel from Mr Clemson's tool belt and assaulted him. He's not sure what he did with it afterwards, the next he heard, it was used as a murder weapon. Something you failed to mention to the jury.

"None of your evidence is remotely convincing, it's pure speculation at best. The defendant's prints were not found on any of the other murder weapons, nor at any of the crime scenes. Neither have you produced any evidence that connects him to these murders.

"It beggars belief, that you can be so convinced my client is responsible for these crimes without any hard conclusive proof. It would tend to lead one to think you're on a mission to convict him of these murders without the standard procedural protocol, just because you don't like him and you think he is guilty."

"Objection your honour, this is an attack on the witnesses' good character."

"Sustained."

"No further questions."

Not sure how I felt about that testy exchange, but more importantly, how would the jury view it.

The next witness for the prosecution was Harold Nuttall, the shopkeeper. Appleton got to her feet.

"Mr Nuttall, I understand you're the manager of Stigfords Hardware store in Bishop's Bluff. Did you ever see the defendant before?"

"Yes, when he came into the shop to buy pure beeswax."

"Did this strike you as odd?"

"Not really, it's just we don't often get asked for it these days so we had to order it in specially. We only carry rosin that's what violinists use for waxing their bows. He said that wasn't really suitable so we placed a special order for the pure beeswax and he picked it up about a week later."

"Did he buy anything else?"

"Yes, paraffin wax and methylated spirits."

"Thank you Mr Nuttall, no further questions."

Heddigan sprang to his feet.

"When Mr Clemson ordered the pure beeswax, did he say what he wanted to use it for?"

"No he didn't."

"Then I'll tell you what he wanted it for. He intended to use it in his line of work as a master craftsman and repairer of period furniture. They use this to apply a finish along with a range of techniques to create a certain patina in wood. They also use paraffin wax and methylated spirits plus a number of other materials. These are methods that he and others have developed over many years in the trade as a professional furniture manufacturer and restorer, to age and to distress pieces. No further questions."

The next witness was Tony Morehouse, senior forensics officer. Appleton got to her feet.

"Good morning Mr Morehouse, I understand that as the senior forensics officer, you ran tests on the ash taken from the two murder sites? Can you tell us what you found?"

"I found minute traces of beeswax that matched the sample purchased from the same hardware store by Mr Clemson."

"Did the samples you retrieved from both murder sites match the samples from this store?"

Yes they did."

"Thank you, Mr Morehouse, no further questions."

Heddigan sat there for a few seconds before he got to his feet.

"Mr Morehouse, when you ran your tests and found traces of beeswax that matched the sample you purchased, how did you feel?"

"Just doing my job, I found a match from the two sites, I felt comfortable that the samples all originated from the same source."

"Would it interest you to know that when we ran our own tests on a number of samples of beeswax and candles, we got a match on eight out of the ten samples that we had tested? These tests were carried out by Core Forensics Reports from Southampton, the test results are here in these files. What this indicates to me, is that this is not an exact science. The samples that matched were sourced from a range of suppliers in the south of England, from Cornwall to as far north as Northamptonshire, a distance of two hundred and fifty miles."

"All I can say is that the samples that we tested indicated they all originated from the same source."

"Like I said, our test results would disprove your theory, because that is all it is, a theory.

"Did you find the defendant's fingerprints or DNA on any of the murder weapons?"

"No I did not, apart from the weapon used on Jason Wimpole."

"Did you find the defendant's fingerprints or DNA at any of the Crime scenes?"

"No I did not."

Bloody good show Myles, this emphasised further the lack of forensics they had.

"No further questions."

That concluded the evidence for the prosecution.

Heddigan decided that I shouldn't take the stand, even though I wanted to do. The prosecution hadn't produced any viable evidence that would convict me. Even so, I should've been allowed to give evidence, however, he was my lawyer and he wouldn't allow me. I had to respect that he knew best.

The judge decided to adjourn for the day so I was taken back to Winchester prison. Overall, the prosecution hadn't done a great job, but it was how the jury saw it, and that was unknown.

The following day the trial resumed. Most of the witnesses for my defence were there to provide character references. My boss, Archie McGoldrick, gave me a glowing report, as a diligent employee, always willing to put in extra effort to ensure the customer was happy. He stated that I was honest, trustworthy and a pleasure to work with.

The manager of the Scottish National Trust confirmed that Alistair and I'd arrived on site at Hislop Castle, one of their properties just after 10.30 a.m on September 5th and didn't leave until the work was completed four days later.

Archie's son, Donald, confirmed that I'd travelled with four other's from Heritage Craft Fine Furniture to Raleigh Durham in the US on 17th October, the night before the 'Cock and bottle' went on fire.

The trial had taken just over six weeks. It'd attracted press and TV correspondents from around the world. There was intense media activity outside the court, to hear the trial of the so-called 'Wiltshire Whacker.'

Both Olwyn Appleton, the Crown prosecutor, and my lawyer Myles Heddigan QC, had completed their summing up. The judge gave the jury specific advice when reaching their decision before they retired to the jury room to consider their verdict.

I started to get nervous, when after a full day, they hadn't returned to find me not guilty. They were sequestered to a nearby hotel overnight, with instructions not to watch any TV or read any newspapers. When they came back into court the next day, they asked the judge for further instruction and to review some elements of the evidence.

At this point I was starting to get a bad feeling about this, what was the problem, surely they hadn't been convinced by the pantomime that the prosecution had put on?

At the end of their second day of deliberation, they eventually came back into court. The clerk of the court asked the foreman of the jury, if they'd reached a verdict.

"Yes we have."

"How do you find the defendant, Luke Clemson, on count one, the murder of Basil Thornwood, guilty or not guilty?"

"Guilty!"

Oh, fuck, no.

"How do you find the defendant on count two, the murder of Neil Derek, guilty or not guilty?"

"Guilty!"

This can't be real.

"How do you find the defendant on count three, the murder of Alan Walters, guilty or not guilty?"

"Guilty!"

Utter madness.

"How do you find the defendant on count four, the murder of Jeff Landers, guilty or not guilty?"

"Guilty!"

No. This can't be happening.

"How do you find the defendant on count five, the murder of Clive Harlow, guilty or not guilty?"

"Guilty!"

At this stage I realised I was doomed.

"How do you find the defendant on count six, the murder of Jason Wimpole, guilty or not guilty?"

"Guilty!"

Six out of six.

"Is that the verdict of you all?"

"It is."

What just happened? This can't be right, that's totally unbelievable, how could they possibly come up with those verdicts? I can't stop shaking, I think any minute I'm going to have a bowel movement.

You call this British justice, they can't possibly think that the evidence provided proves beyond any reasonable doubt I was responsible?

Not a single piece of evidence, either forensics or otherwise linked me to these murders. All they had was beeswax that our tests showed could have come from anywhere.

I looked at my lawyer, he was shaking his head. I should've been allowed to take the stand, it was a mistake not to let me do so. The jury obviously thought I'd something to hide, but I was guided by what Heddigan advised. What a major cock-up.

The judge thanked the jury for their diligence and he excused them from any further duty for ten years. He adjourned the court for two hours, he would proceed with the sentencing then.

I was taken to the cells below in a state of absolute shock. The nightmare continues.

Just after 2.30 p.m. the court resumed, and I was brought up from below.

"Luke Clemson, the jury have found you guilty on six counts of murder. These particularly violent and heinous crimes have resulted in the loss of loved ones to a large number of families. Wives have lost their husbands, children have lost their fathers. Parents have lost their sons, sisters their brothers. Family members have sat through six weeks of harrowing testimony, listening to the catalogue of injuries you inflicted on their loved ones.

"You were very calculating in your mission of murder, and have shown no sign of remorse for these terrible crimes. With this in mind, it is the sentence of this court that you serve thirty-five years on each count of murder, the sentences to run concurrently, with a recommendation that you serve a minimum, of at least twenty-five years. Take him down."

Oh what fucking joy! 35 fucking years, how can they do this to me?

I was driven straight to Winchester prison. Two weeks later, I was transferred to Wormwood Scrubs with all the hardened criminals. Heddigan immediately appealed the sentences but this would take time to go through the process. By now, I was cursing the day I first set my eyes on Megan Offington-Smythe. If I'd never met her, none of this would have happened.

My lawyer visited me several times to discuss my appeal, but by now, I'd given up any hope of being released.

Megan had played a major part in my conviction. All I'd ever done was love her, now she'd knifed me in the back in the most spectacular fashion. I stupidly gave her an alibi, then she went and lied under oath to convince the jury of my guilt. Was she that upset that I'd decided to divorce her, and that this was her retribution? How could I've got involved with this woman who was hell bent in seeing me suffer?

I was looking forward to my retirement, my workmates had arranged a celebration for me in the 'Rose and Crown' pub. 'Commandant Eric Lassard' had stopped his weekly rants since the conviction of Clemson. I'd be going out on a high.

One day I found Tony Morehouse searching the old records store in the basement.

"Hi Tony, what're you up to?"

"Just seeing if I could put a name to the print that I found."

"I told you before, to forget it, the culprit has been tried and found guilty. I retire in under a few months, I don't want anything to blot my copybook." What was his problem? The case was closed we didn't need any complications at this stage.

He dumped the files on the floor, but I suspected the minute I left the room he'd continue to search. However, the files were so old, not in any kind of order, he'd draw a blank.

The Wigglesworth estate was performing nicely, I was enjoying my new role as director of operations. I'd visit Daddy every month to give him an update on his different businesses. He was thrilled that I'd taken to the job, I was a changed woman, well almost.

I'd met Father Cleary, the local Catholic priest attached to St Joseph's church. We met at a children's charity fund raising function, and got on famously, afterwards he started to call around to the manor. One thing lead to another, eventually we finished up in bed. But my God, he'd the biggest pecker I'd ever seen, it was like an arm. He should've been in 'Ripley's Believe It Or Not'. Instead of being a priest, he could've been their star attraction.

But bedding a priest, I ask you, had I reached the bottom of the morality pit? I thought I should finish it, but before I'd time to do so, the Bishop for the diocese was tipped off about our exploits. As soon as he heard about what we'd been up to, he'd Father Cleary removed to another parish.

Chapter 19

As I said at the start of this book, I'm sat in a confined space, about 8' by 6' and the light is not very good.

So, I'm just about to go above on deck to help my wife, Stephanie, drop the main sail because we are about to enter the Cat's Paw Marina, at St Augustine, Florida.

You thought I was in jail, I was, but the truth eventually came out and I was released. Thanks to the work of the intrepid forensics officer, Tony Morehouse.

I'd spent months going through old files, despite being threatened with flogging and incarceration in the salt mines by Chief Inspector Tyler Hyde.

There were thousands of files that were not in any kind of order, either by date or name. It was a daunting task, they were just dumped on the floor. On many occasions I felt it was a pointless exercise. The details belonged to many people who were long dead, so I eliminated them purely on that basis. I figured it was unlikely we'd a 95-year-old nutcase hell-bent on reducing the population of the UK. The others I scanned into the system if there was a possibility they were still alive. After much searching over many months, I found one file that stopped me dead in my tracks.

The name on the file was:

Tyrone Offington-Smythe

Megan's brother! Could this be our murderer? I would have to compare his prints with what we had on file so I immediately started to process them.

Fingerprints off this individual, showed he had suffered an injury to both hands as he only had full joints on the thumb, forefinger and little finger on his right hand. His left hand only his thumb, and middle finger were intact. Prints had been taken of the lower sections of his fingers but were unclear.

He'd been despatched to Tasmania, some twenty-five years previously. The attached details showed he'd been supplying drugs on a large scale until he was caught in an undercover sting operation. A bit of a rebel is how you'd probably describe him, he certainly didn't need the money. Judging by what was on the file he's a real hothead. He'd been shipped out to the family's tea plantation to avoid prosecution.

It took me several hours to process the prints. As soon as I compared them on screen and eventually, after much effort found a match, I couldn't hold back this information and took it to Tyler Hyde immediately.

"Tony, what the blazes have you done? I retire in two days time, this is the last thing I needed."

"That may be, but this shows that an innocent man has spent the last nine months in jail, that the person who had handled every murder weapon, was Tyrone Offington-Smythe, and his prints that we have on file confirm this. He was supposed to be in Hobart, but apparently it seems he was over here."

"Why the hell couldn't you have left well enough alone, this is going to have massive ramifications, I told you months ago to leave it but you wouldn't listen? Now I've to figure out what to do. Put the file on my desk and I'll go and see Commandant Eric Lassard, police academy's spokesman for the insane. I know he'll be thrilled at the news, of course the Crown Prosecution Service will be ecstatic."

This was the last bloody thing I needed, retirement imminent, flight booked to Spain in fourteen days time, what a cock-up.

I phoned the Chief Constable to advise him what Tony had found, then made my way up to his office.

When I opened the door, he looked up from his desk with a look of pain on his face, that gave the impression, he'd either a severe case of piles, or he was about to give birth.

"Tyler, we've a monumental problem, do you realise what the press are going to do to us when they find out about this, what have you got to say?"

"Not a lot, the Crown Prosecution Service studied the evidence, it was their decision to go ahead with the trial not mine. To be honest after this Friday, it's not my problem."

"You can't leave then, retirement is not an option until this bloody mess is sorted out. It's your baby, so don't even think of leaving this to someone else."

"My flight to Spain is already booked and paid for, my only commitment to you is I'll stay on until then, roughly two weeks, not a day longer. I've had more than enough of this particular investigation and trial. Anyway, can't stay here chewing the fat, better find out where this brother is. Also, I don't want any daily requests for information, just let me get on with it."

As I left his office, he sat there opened mouthed, he wasn't used to be spoken to like that.

I gathered the team together.

"Rick, I want you to contact the tea plantation in Tasmania, find out if Smythe left the country at any stage in the last few years. If he did, find out exactly where he went. Tony, set out in detail that we can understand, with photographs of the partial prints relating to each of the weapons used on the victims. We have less than two weeks before I head off to Spain to sort this out, so get on with it."

Rick Masters, contacted the tea plantation and spoke with the office manager Olive Chan. She told him that Mr Offington-Smythe was overseas at conference in Germany, she wasn't sure when he'd be back. She'd no idea where he was staying and had no way of contacting him, she wasn't particularly helpful.

"Skipper, didn't get very far with the tea plantation and it's going to be very difficult trying to do it long range to establish his movements."

"How do you fancy a trip out there?"

"Are you serious? Bloody love to go."

"We've only fourteen days to establish if he's our culprit. I have a few friends in the Australian police and they're responsible for policing the island, so let me make a few phone calls. Get a bag packed just in case."

"Hello Howard, how's the weather down under?"

"G'day Tyler, you old Pommy bastard, thought you'd retired to your home in Spain, what happened, did they class you as an undesirable alien and refuse you entry?"

"No, not yet and not so much of the old. Just wondered if you could help one of my men if I send him over? It's regarding a murder enquiry involving six people who have met a violent and untimely end. We've a suspect who was supposed to be in Hobart, a chap called Tyrone Offington-Smythe who owns a tea plantation there."

"Struth, six murders, can't say I've ever heard of him, but I'll run a check and see if it throws anything up. But if you want to send your man over we'll look after him."

"Thanks, Howard, I'll let you know what we decide. His name is Rick Masters he's one of my senior detectives."

Later that day Howard sent me an email confirming they'd run a crime check but nothing showed up, not even a parking ticket. They'd established the location of the plantation and the residence of Smythe. Apparently, they were one of the biggest tea and lamb producers in the country, in the top fifty exporters. He'd send officers out to the plantation to try and establish the whereabouts of our suspect and if he'd made any trips overseas.

I advised Rick and told him we'd hold off with his visit for forty-eight hours until we got more information through from Australia.

"Hello Tyler, Howard here, my men have just got back from Hobart and have some interesting news. The Sheila on the desk wasn't very helpful initially, slightly suspect immigration papers, so we told her she could be looking at deportation. Amazing how helpful people will be in such circumstances. Anyway, my friend, it appears this chap has made several trips to the UK in the past few years. He was there from April until November in two thousand six and has made two more trips since. We have a Quantas Airlines first class counter foil showing he departed for the UK on April thirtieth and returned on November tenth that same year. However, the interesting thing is, he's probably over there now!

"We weren't able to establish fully his whereabouts for the entire time he was in the UK, but we do have several hotel invoices. We've a hotel receipt for fourteen nights in Romsey. He stayed at the White Swan Hotel from the first of July until the fifteenth, we've found another receipt for a stay at the Wilton Arms Hotel in Winchester from the twenty eighth of July until the nineteenth of August. No idea where he stayed in between.

"He stayed in Totton at the Mill House Hotel, from August tenth until the twenty fifth. After this he moved to Kingsworthy, stayed at the Wayfairer Inn from August twenty ninth until September sixth.

"He then stayed in a place called Ringwood at the Mount Wilson Hotel from September seventh until the twenty second. We've another receipt for the Holiday Inn in Winchester from October third until the nineteenth.

"After this there's nothing, so we don't know where he stayed in between each of these hotels, or where he was until he got the flight back to Australia on November tenth. He left for Germany sixteen days ago, but he could be in the UK by now, we've no way of knowing. He could've travelled across to your country on the Eurostar or a flight or any number of ferries.

"I've left one detective at their offices and have banned the secretary from communicating with Offington-Smythe just in case she tips him off and he decides to leave the UK, that's assuming he's there."

"Thanks for that Howard, do you think she'll keep quiet?"

"We've told her in no uncertain terms, if she tips him off she'll be on the first bloody flight back to Singapore. So I think she'll keep her pie hole shut."

"What can I say Howard, you've been very helpful, can you send me copies of whatever documentation you have?"

"Will do, I'll also email you a current photograph of your suspect. There were several in his office, mostly posing with models, politicians and film stars, but some with awards they've won. He's a handsome bugger, shouldn't think he's a problem with the opposite sex. Anyway, I'll send all his hotel invoices through, if my men find anything we feel is relevant, we'll pass it on straight away. Good luck with finding him!"

I called Rick into my office, "The trip is on hold, may even be cancelled, my contacts out there have managed to find out a great deal of info on our suspect, plus they think he's already over here somewhere."

"That's a disappointment, I was looking forward to the trip, just got my surfboard down from the attic, ah well, maybe when I win the Lotto."

"We understand Tyrone Offington-Smythe, was here in the UK at the time each of the six murders were committed, staying at different hotels. Howard Donnegan from the Australian police is sending a current photograph through, plus details of where he stayed. As soon as we get this information, I want you and your team to head out and check to see if he is staying at any of these hotels. Be careful, he could be very dangerous, try not to alarm the hotel staff if they ask, maybe say a family member is ill or something like that, for Christ's sake don't tell them he's the Wiltshire Whacker."

I'd received a letter from Luke, imploring me to come clean and tell the truth to help with his appeal, but how could I? Not without revealing I'd perjured myself at his trial, knowing what a dim view the courts take of that, I wasn't prepared to go down that route. I filed it in the round tray.

After Daddy had been violently attacked in prison, his lawyer, Catchpole, requested that he be moved to another location, the authorities were giving it every consideration. I didn't realise it was so severe until I made my monthly visit to Winchester prison. I got a shock when I saw him, he'd a scar down the left side of his face about four inches long. He'd also been stabbed in the chest.

"Oh, Daddy, what've they done to you? Who did this?"

"They have got the guy, he was from E wing his name is Bull, a real hard case, doing twenty five years for double murder. They think he did it under instruction."

"What do you mean, instruction?"

"Someone presumably on the outside told him to do it. He certainly meant to kill me, the chest wound was serious, just missed my heart by half an inch. They have got him in solitary and he will remain there until he says who gave the instruction."

"I'll contact Catchpole the minute I leave here, this is just too scary, if they can't guarantee your safety here, then they should transfer you to another prison until your appeal is heard. What about the scar on your face, will they not allow plastic surgery?"

"Already had some, and I will be having more later this week, the surgeon said I will still have a scar but not that noticeable."

"I hope not, you'd frighten the crap out of Boris Karloff looking like that."

"That is my girl, always the one to give out compliments. But do not worry, pumpkin, I will be fine, Catchpole is already on it, he reckons I will be moved by the weekend. He is confident my appeal will be heard by the end of the month, hopefully I should get a reduced sentence. But the way you are running things I might just retire and leave you to it."

My team had been checking all the hotels we know that Offington-Smythe had stayed at in 2006, but to date had drawn a blank. Just before lunch, I received a phone call from her father's lawyer, Oliver C Catchpole.

"Inspector Hyde, I've been informed by the governor of Winchester prison, that an inmate called Bull attacked my client with a knife injuring him seriously. This was a determined attempt on his life that almost succeeded. After a period in solitary confinement for violent behaviour, he's come clean that he carried out the attack on my client Offington-Smythe on an instruction from outside.

"When pressed, coupled with a miserable time on bread and water, and being locked up twenty-four-seven, he eventually cracked. He divulged that the instruction came from one of his visitors, a farmer called Dobson who farms over at Kilmington. We paid him a visit but initially he wouldn't speak to us, however, he did talk when I told him he could be facing a charge of conspiracy to murder. He said he was threatened and did it under duress by wait for it, by Tyrone Offington-Smythe!

"That's the son, he was told to offer him a guaranteed payment of five thousand cigarettes a month, the main trading currency in prison. Not sure how they intended to get the contraband into the jail but Dobson conveyed that information onto Bull, who made the attempt on my client's life. I expect that you will be interviewing this farmer for his involvement in this conspiracy to murder.

"My client is being moved this week to Woodhill prison in Buckinghamshire, and is also having ongoing treatment for his wounds. However, another reason for my call, is that we're concerned that there may be an attempt on his daughter's life. We've just informed Megan, that she's possibly a target for her deranged brother, Tyrone.

"As you may be aware, since the incarceration of her father, Megan has been running his different businesses. It's possible her brother became aware of this arrangement and is none too happy because there was a lot of bad blood in the family. Seeing that Megan was critical in you securing a conviction for the so called 'Wiltshire Whacker,' can you provide any kind of cover for her?"

"Perhaps he should recruit the services of Baseball Bat Security, like he did before?"

"We've already done that and they'll be covering the main entrance into the estate, but if we could please have a police presence at the manor house itself, it would be greatly appreciated?"

"Very well, Mr Catchpole, I'll see if I can spare someone, but only until we apprehend the son."

This was a going to create a minor staffing problem, because it meant three men in rotation doing eight-hour shifts.

I then despatched Rick Masters and two other detectives over to 'Reece Farm' in Kilmington to apprehend this chap Dobson and bring him in for questioning. Hopefully, he could give us information that would enable us to track down the son in the next twelve days.

Chapter 20

When I became aware that my brother, Tyrone, had ordered an attempt on Daddy's life, I felt extremely vulnerable, I'd no one I could fall back on for support. None of my past friends would help, they were barely speaking to me, in fact, they were running for cover, probably wearing flak jackets for added protection.

The police presence would be welcome. If he became aware they were there, he was less likely to come to the house, although that couldn't be ruled out. I searched Daddy's gun cabinet and eventually selected a small pistol I felt comfortably holding. It was a Beretta Cheetah, a lightweight .22 caliber that Daddy used to use for target shooting over in one of our quarries. It wouldn't stop an elephant, but it'd give me a bit of comfort just to know I'd got it in my purse.

I was aware he should've handed the guns in after the law was changed in 1997 and handguns were banned. But Daddy vehemently refused to hand them in, saying it was introduced by an over zealous, crass Labour Government and he wouldn't comply, in view of my current situation, I'm glad he didn't.

I made sure that all doors and windows were securely locked at all times, and told all the gardeners to keep a sharp eye out for Tyrone, or any strangers on the estate.

As soon as we'd all the information from Tony, that showed that Clemson could be innocent, I'd to figure a way to release it without it looking obvious that we knew about the other prints. The press would have a field day because our relationship had been strained, they would relish this. I called him into my office.

"Tony, this is what I'm going to say to minimise the amount of criticism that we might be in for. I'm going to say that after extensive investigations, a print we couldn't previously identify was eventually matched to one taken over twenty-five years ago. I know you warned me about this and in hindsight, maybe I should've listened to you. However, this whole department will get serious flak if this should come out. I'm appealing to you to go along with what I'm suggesting for the sake of all your colleagues."

"Not sure if I'm prepared to take that risk, you're retiring in a few days, the after effects of this could've major consequences for me. It's a lot to ask."

"I know that, Tony, you were right and I was wrong, but if you knew the kind of pressure I was under with daily ranting from old bollock brain, you would've done the same.

"At that time you'd to take partial prints to create on computer, a full print to match up with one taken twenty-five years ago. It was not conclusive evidence I know I'm right, when I say it wouldn't have stood up in court. The defence could've argued that we'd used computer software to generate the print. Now you're on your high horse, inferring I withheld vital evidence that resulted in Clemson going to jail."

"We put an innocent man inside, that's wrong by any standards, now you expect me to lie for you?"

"Look, it wasn't conclusive proof, you only had one fingerprint and you manufactured that. It was only after reading his file all those years later, you realised he'd lost a number of fingers as a result of catching meningitis as a child. We couldn't have used this as hard evidence at the time, if we'd said this print belonged to any suspect, the fact that the print was generated the way it was, the defence would have walked all over us.

"I did what was right at the time, hindsight is a great thing, but believe me my action was the correct one to take. Anyway, I don't intend to spend any more time trying to justify what I did, the ball is in your court, do what the fuck you want, I've had enough. But, understand one thing, it'll destroy me and I'll probably lose my pension, not to mention I could end up in jail for withholding so-called evidence. But, like I say, it's up to you. However, you won't come out of this squeaky clean, as well as tarnishing your workmates."

He stood there looking at me, I knew he was thinking he should spill the beans, then he walked towards the door and turned to face me.

"I'll leave it up to you as to how you word it to the press, but if it implicates me or throws any blame in my direction, then I'll tell what really happened." With that he left the room.

I talked to the Chief Constable and gave him a written statement that I felt should be released to the press. The print that we found was only partial on each of the weapons, it was only by months of painstaking technical analysis, that we were able to piece a full print together and match it with one taken twenty-five years previously. It'd been stored in our old records office, it took months to find and was only discovered by a stroke of luck.

He read over it and felt it was probably the way to go.

As soon as the statement was released, there was frenzied media activity. TV and the press from a number of countries were camped out outside the station, we constantly got harassed each time we passed in and out.

Clemson was released from Wormwood Scrubs, in glaring publicity. His lawyer immediately announced he'd be suing the police for his incarceration. We knew he'd a strong case and would be in line for a huge payout, it'd be best to settle as quickly as possible. Ultimately, a long, drawn-out situation would be a lot more damaging to the police than a quick financial settlement, however much it cost the state.

The defence lawyer, Myles Heddigan, asked very awkward questions, he informed us that he'd press for a public enquiry, as to why his client had been jailed, when this evidence was available during his trial.

In an effort to prevent this happening we explained at the time we didn't consider it evidence as we didn't have a full print, it was only after many months of painstaking forensic application using computer software, we came to the current situation.

Clemson had been signed up by a major Sunday paper, this would be the first of many financial paydays.

We'd endeavoured to keep the identity of the person responsible for the murders under wraps, but after a few days, it became public knowledge who the prints belonged to. Fearing that Tyrone Offington-Smythe might flee the country, we'd all the air and seaports on high alert.

I was quite surprised when my ex-husband was released from prison, I was half expecting a visit from him because of my testimony, however, I'd more pressing things on my mind. Tyrone it would appear wanted Daddy and I dead. I didn't sleep easy at night, every little sound made me nervous, living in a house like Wigglesworth, the noise is constant. Several times, I drew my pistol and walked the corridors at night, but I couldn't carry on like this, I was becoming a nervous wreck. Even though I'd police protection, I felt very vulnerable, especially at night, as a result I moved my bedroom to another part of the house, just in case Tyrone decided to pay me a visit.

We tied *Excalibur* up in the 'Cat's Paw' marina and went into St Augustine for dinner. We were on the eighth day of our honeymoon, having sailed from South Carolina across to the Bahamas, before heading for Florida.

Stephanie and I had been married in Myrtle Beach at her local church, where she was christened, and had attended all her life. Alistair was my best man, my old bosses Archie McGoldrick and Tom Wilson came over for the wedding, by all accounts, had an absolute blast.

My financial situation had improved dramatically since my release from prison. I'd been paid £350,000 from a Sunday paper for my story, I received an advance part payment of £200,000 from a top publisher for my autobiography, there was also talk of a film deal. The settlement from the UK Government over my imprisonment had been agreed and was due any moment. Overall, it meant I was now a millionaire. However, no financial reward could compensate for the nightmare that had been mine over a number of years.

The first thing I did when I was released from prison, was to fly to the US to see Stephanie. She was a bit reluctant to meet me initially, but her brother, Chuck, said she should do so out of courtesy. The fact that I'd flown all that way, it was the least she could do.

I explained everything that had happened to me since I first met Megan, including her affairs, the murders that both of us had been accused of. I'd asked that Chuck be present, I didn't want to hold back anything, after I'd told them my story, they could judge me. If they didn't want any further involvement with me, I'd understand, and return to England.

They'd both sat there open-mouthed whilst the details unfolded, I told them everything, even highly personal things that my ex-wife had done and the hurt and shame that I'd felt.

When I'd finished my one-hour monologue, or maybe it was longer, Megan got up from her seat and embraced me tightly for what seemed an age. Chuck shook my hand and thanked me, saying, "Only an Englishman would be so honest."

I stayed on in the US for three more weeks, during which time Stephanie and I got to know one another better. We both felt that we belonged together, when I asked her to marry me, she said yes without any hesitation. She said she'd never met anyone before that she felt she could settle down with, that's until she met me. Her parents had been very religious and had given her and Chuck a very strict upbringing, she'd no intention of jumping into bed with anyone before the final commitment was made. This was a comforting change for me, to meet someone who's life didn't revolve around bedding as many men as possible.

As my departure time arrived, we decided to fix a date for the wedding, as soon as I'd tidied my life up in the UK, I'd be back.

I'd been worried that my application for a green card could be affected with everything that had occurred, but my lawyer said I'd been acquitted of all charges after wrongful arrest and conviction, in fact he expected that the necessary paperwork would be through within the next two weeks.

Rick Masters had a lead on Tyrone Offington-Smythe. He called into a hotel in Kingsworthy on the off chance he might be there. It wasn't on our list but as all the hotels had been checked and we'd drawn a blank, we'd decided to widen the search. The receptionist confirmed he was indeed staying there, she checked his room but apparently, he was out.

We decided to put an armed team in an unmarked car outside the hotel on a 24-hour watch.

The press had been relentless in their quest for the truth, awkward questions were being asked. Myles Heddigan was pressing for a public enquiry and there was a strong chance, that, there would be an enquiry of some kind.

I'd to defer my retirement and postponed my flight to Spain for a few more weeks. Old bollock brain had exerted so much pressure on me, with all kind of threats regarding my pension and my involvement in a cover up, that I'd no option. It was looking likely that I'd be pegged out to dry. If I stayed on to defend myself, I'd have a better chance of being exonerated, rather being in Spain getting buried under tons of shit and accusations.

We were concerned that our suspect would not return to the hotel, because the press had been tipped off and had now named him, despite our request for a news blackout. I contacted the editor of one of the papers, the 'Winchester Globe,' and vented my anger, calling him irresponsible for reneging on our agreement not to name the suspect. He'd probably have high-tailed it out of the country by now, just when we'd located him. This was a major setback for us. I told all the press they'd get no further cooperation from us in any future cases and if any more people met an untimely end, I'd hold those newspapers to account.

The farmer, Martin Dobson, was detained and interviewed, he told us he knew Megan's brother from his teens. He was originally one of his distributors for his drugs, but only in a small way, he'd received probation for his involvement with Tyrone.

He hadn't seen him for over 25 years, when he arrived at his farm unannounced. He threatened to disclose his ill-spent youth and destroy his life if he didn't help him. Dobson was a senior member of the parish council, he was also a respected associate of the farmers union, being a past president as well as being on a number of committees. He felt he'd no choice but to comply and pass the instruction on. He realised now that it'd been a stupid thing to do, and he should've gone straight to the police. Too late! We charged him as an accomplice with conspiracy to murder.

Daddy's appeal was heard and his original sentence was upheld, he was lucky not to have it increased. The judges on the panel were of the opinion that it was on the lenient side for such a serious crime.

However, taking into account his age, coupled with his remorse and expression of regret for such a stupid offence, they decided to leave the sentence as it was. His original, substantial financial remuneration for causing distress to the family of Jane Mills, and Ms Maddox, was also in his favour.

He was bitterly disappointed, because he was having a hard time in prison and had been subjected to more physical abuse on two occasions. However, this shouldn't be a problem anymore as he was being moved to Woodhill open prison where the inmates were of a less violent nature, with the possibility that eventually in a few years time, he may be allowed home for the odd weekend.

I was still living in somewhat of a siege zone. I'd upgraded the alarm system in the manor and had cameras installed at different locations covering every access point into the house. I'd persuaded my secretary, Sybil, to move in with me for company. Oh, how things change, only a short time ago I'd have had no problem having the opposite sex around, now they would run a mile if they even saw me and would continue to do so until Tyrone was apprehended.

I'd visited inspector Hyde and explained to him now it had been made public that my brother was wanted in connection with these murders, with his picture splashed all over the papers, I felt more than ever he would come after me. He agreed this was a strong possibility, and said their attempts had been hampered by the press revelations. He said they'd provide additional patrols around Wigglesworth, also when he could spare it, put an extra man on duty during the hours of darkness.

The highly visible police presence should help to deter my lunatic brother, although nothing could be taken for granted.

I'd monitors in my bedroom that covered every camera view, with a panic button linked directly to the security company, even so, I didn't sleep easy at nights.

Chapter 21

Stephanie and I arrived back in Myrtle Beach after a month-long honeymoon. We'd a wonderful time away, and we were deliriously happy. For me another life changing experience, I'd undergone several in the past few years.

I'd a lot of catching up to do, not to mention dealing with correspondence that'd accumulated during our absence.

The fact that Megan's brother, Tyrone, had been named as the 'Wiltshire Whacker' and was the subject of a massive worldwide police hunt, astounded me

Megan had told me when we were first married, what her father had done to get Tyrone out of the country to avoid a prison sentence. It was up to him to make a success of running the tea plantation and sheep farms, and that this would be his only inheritance.

Since his enforced departure, there'd never been any contact with him. Offington-Smythe had cut him off completely, so Tyrone was on his own.

Obviously, he'd made a go of it, because apparently he'd built up this tea producer from being a modest operation to be a major exporter. The sheep farm had more than trebled in the 25 years he'd been in control. His annual turnover on the two enterprises was estimated to be in access of Australian $ 140 million and he was treated as a celebrity in Hobart.

It seemed his resentment had continued to grow over the years, the fact that he'd be excluded from the vast wealth of the estate, roughly estimated at £1.95 billion was too much for him to accept.

All that dosh and I walked away from Megan without a penny, I know people that would've hung in for a settlement, but for me it was never about the money, I was just glad to get away.

Myles Heddigan my lawyer, had been pressing for a public enquiry, seeing as the whole justice system was under the spotlight, it was finally granted. It was decided that the enquiry was to be chaired by Sir Marcus Munstead, a retired crown court judge, a highly respected figure who'd been in public service all his life.

The committee would be made up of a mix of politicians and lawyers, some retired, some practising, plus several other high profile people.

Munstead was apparently a tough cookie. If anyone could get to the bottom of what exactly had gone on, it would be him. Myles was happy with the choice of chairman, he'd sent me a letter telling me the start date for the enquiry, he also confirmed that my expenses would be met in full so that I could travel back from the US for the event.

"Stephanie, we'll be going to the UK the month after next, that's when the enquiry starts. It should be an interesting experience. No doubt the police will be scurrying around trying to get their story straight."

"Do you really want me to go with you, because it could go on for weeks, I can't really afford to be away for too long? We're only just back from being away for a month. We've lots of orders on hand with more coming in, all as a result of our participation at High Point again."

"I don't intend to sit through weeks of testimony, just to hear inspector Tyler Hyde's version of events, then I thought we'd carry on from where we were so rudely interrupted, I'd lots more to show you. If I have a word with Chuck about covering for you and he said it will be Ok, will you come?"

"Of course I will."

Making sure that Wigglesworth was secured for the night, I retired to bed about 11.00 p.m. After a couple of hours, and being quite a light sleeper, I became aware of someone in the house. The sound of footsteps coming out over the speakers on the monitors woke me. The clock beside my bed, indicated it was 2.30 a.m. As I turned my head to look at the screen, I saw a male figure on the landing, he turned and started walking along the corridor towards where my old bedroom was. Reaching into my purse I took out Daddy's gun, I made sure the magazine was locked in position. Then just before he reached the room, the intruder unwittingly broke an invisible laser beam about ankle height, then the interior alarm went off. The sound of the klaxon horns being activated, coupled with a high-pitched whine that had a serious affect on your middle ear and balance was frightening.

The policeman on duty outside, called me on my radio to check if I was Ok. The monitor showed the person racing down the stairs, out through the great hall into the kitchen.

"Constable, we've an intruder, he's raced into the kitchen, be careful!"

Sybil raced into my room, hysterical with the noise of the alarm. I managed to calm her, but when she saw me holding a gun, she went frantic. I left her to deal with her fear whilst I went to investigate. The alarm-monitoring company had already dispatched someone to check it out. Just as I got to the foot of the stairs, a shot rang out.

As I entered the kitchen, I found the body of Constable Jacobs lying on the floor, he'd been shot in the stomach but he was still alive. I immediately called for an ambulance and the police, then placed a large swab of kitchen paper towel over his wound and pressed hard to help stem the flow of blood, whilst I tried to make him comfortable.

Within minutes, the emergency services had arrived and started to attend to the policeman, who by this stage, had fallen unconscious. Our own security people appeared in double quick time and surrounded the property. Inspector Hyde arrived as soon as they made him aware, that he'd a man down.

"Any idea who it was, Mrs Clemson?"

"I'll give you two guesses as to who it was, but my concern is how the hell did he get into the house? All the windows and doors were secured and the locks have been changed since Tyrone was here twenty-five years ago. Plus they're all alarmed, so even if he'd have used a key, the minute he opened a door or window, the alarm would've gone off."

"I assume you've cameras inside the premises as well as outside, and it's all on disk, can we take a look at the recording to see if we can make out for sure who it was?"

"Yes, not a problem Inspector, the disk-drive is in my bedroom."

We made our way upstairs, following a well-worn path, no doubt taken by half the male population of Wiltshire.

"My god, it's like a major control room here, you seem to have every part of the house covered."

"It still didn't stop him getting in, despite spending a bloody fortune on all this equipment. I'll scroll back through the recording to see if we can make out who it was.

"Here we go, he appears first coming out of the scullery, that's insane, why the hell would he go in there? Then he goes up the rear stairs to the servants' quarters, where I first heard him because the steps just here creak a lot. Then he walks along the corridor that leads into the main bedroom area, this is where he trips the beam. I'll freeze it here and zoom in. Can't see for sure if that's Tyrone. This guy has a full beard and is wearing a hoodie, but the height is right. I remember he walked with quite a limp because he lost several toes and part of his left foot as a result of contracting meningitis as a child, he also lost a number of fingers as well. According to Daddy he was lucky to have survived.

"Just going to play back that section. Right, coming up now, yes I think that's him all right, you can see his pronounced limp, it's more evident as he's running down the stairs. But how the hell did he get into the house? That's a very worrying aspect."

"I think we should go and investigate the scullery and see, I've a man seriously injured and not expected to live. So we could be looking for a murderer."

The scullery was about 14' square, each wall had numerous shelves stacked with tin goods, and an assortment of foods. Large maturing Cheddar cheeses were stacked on one shelf. Several Serrano hams plus a number of strings of Salami sausage hung from large metal hooks in the ceiling, there were also two large freezers at one end.

"There doesn't seem to be any doors or windows in here, it would appear he just came in here by mistake."

"Inspector, I don't think I can stay here anymore, not after what has just happened, the next time I might not be so lucky."

"Can't say I blame you, but it's your decision if you stay here or not, however we'll continue to station officers outside in case he returns."

After all the activity had died down and the inspector had left, I went back upstairs to find Sybil. She was crouched in a linen cupboard in my en suite, shaking uncontrollably. I led her out and tried to comfort her, but the whole experience had been traumatic for her. It was all too much, she informed me she couldn't stay with me anymore and as soon as it was daylight she was leaving, I couldn't blame her.

The police had a highly visible presence with an officer stationed inside the house along with a patrol car parked outside. Even so, I couldn't sleep and counted the hours until sunrise.

This day just happened to be visiting time to see Daddy in Woodhill prison, it would give me the opportunity to tell him about the events of the previous night.

"Hello, Daddy, how are you coping?"

"Not great pumpkin, been attacked twice in the last two months, it seems there is a concerted attempt to kill me. They have got the culprits responsible, one of whom is already doing time for grievous bodily harm, the other on a similar charge of wounding a nightclub bouncer. I have taken the bold step of getting my own minder, nice chap, over six feet tall and weighs over eighteen stone. He is an ex wrestler, built like a tank, it is costing me a thousand cigarettes a month. I did not have much option because the prison governor would not do anything."

"You'd think they could protect you, it's so ridiculous that they can't. But it seems you are not the only one at risk, we'd a serious incident at home last night. Tyrone got into the house somehow, but he tripped the new alarm system. Then as he raced out, he shot a policeman who was on protection duty, he is in a serious condition. He got away although nobody saw him outside. Do you have any idea how he could have got in?

"He was first spotted coming out of the scullery at around two thirty."

"Are you sure it was him?"

"Positive, even though he'd a full beard he'd got his unmistakable limp, it was definitely him."

"So it is confirmed then, he is back in the country? It would appear being in exile has not changed his demeanour, his campaign of murder was obviously an attempt to frame you for these crimes. Thankfully, that failed. But shooting a policeman he must be completely deranged and must be caught. Catchpole has investigated the people behind the attacks on me and he is pretty certain he is also responsible for instigating these. How could I have fathered such a demon, he should have 6,6,6, tattooed across his forehead?

"If I had any thoughts of re-including him in my will, that is certainly not going to happen now, not after what he has been doing.

"Be careful, pumpkin, it would appear he is on a mission to destroy our family, he will not stop until he achieves this."

"How could he have got in?"

"When I think about it, there are several ways he could have got into the house. Remember, Wigglesworth was built in fifteen sixty-five, there is a possibility that even at this stage, there are entrances into the house that we do not know of. There are at least three priest holes that were built into stairs and cupboards that we only discovered when I was a child."

"What the hell are priest holes?"

"In the sixteenth century, there was a lot of intolerance depending on what religion you were. The old ruins down by the lake near the boathouse, are testament to this, as it was once a church before it was burned to the ground. Catholics were constantly being hounded, they used to build in escape tunnels and small hiding places, known as priest holes.

"When Elizabeth I was in power, they would raid and purge people they thought were Catholics. If they were having a mass they would hide the priests in these places until the coast was clear, hence the name. If they were caught, it usually meant certain death.

"Our family have changed religion a number of times over the years, so it was no surprise that there were priest holes in Wigglesworth.

"There is one built into the stairs that lead up to the old servants' quarters, one inside the fireplace in the great hall that comes out in the kitchen. The other one is in the scullery, this leads into a tunnel that goes all the way across to the cottage rented by Mavis Lawry. It comes out in the floor of the barn just behind her property. I suppose it is possible Tyrone could have found out about this, to be honest I do not really know. The whole of one wall in the scullery moves out, if I remember correctly it is activated by lifting up a shelf on the opposite wall to release it, all very clever. There is a steel gate at both ends of the tunnel, so I doubt if anyone could get in that way, I know they were sealed shut, but I have not been down there since I was a child."

"How come I never knew about these priest holes?"

"You never asked, when did you ever concern yourself about the history of Wigglesworth?"

"Well I'm making up for it now, running the whole estate, and even if I say so myself, doing a dammed good job!"

After visiting was over, I said my goodbye and left the prison.

As soon as I arrived back at Wigglesworth, I called inspector Tyler Hyde and told him about the escape tunnel in the scullery. Within the hour he arrived with his forensic team and we set to work finding the entrance. This involved emptying shelves of their contents, then attempting to raise them to activate the door release. Eventually, after about an hour we'd success. One shelf slid to the side then lifted up and immediately released the opposite wall and it swung open.

"That's bloody ingenious," said the inspector.

Shining torches into the darkness, they ventured down the tunnel. It was just a short distance to the steel gate that'd been sealed shut years before. They confirmed that the whole lock mechanism had been cut through and removed so the door swung freely. They spent several hours collecting forensic evidence, before they moved along the tunnel to the steel gate at the far end. This had been treated in a similar manner.

It was late in the day when they'd gathered all their evidence and left. I contacted a local engineering company to come out to Wigglesworth. They took accurate measurements then gave me a quotation to manufacture and install two new toughened steel doors. They'd have substantial locks that could only be opened from the side facing the house. The downside was, it would take several days to manufacture and install these. I decided to move into a hotel until the gates were ready.

I kept thinking about what Daddy had said. There could be other entrances into the manor that we didn't know about. I instructed the garden staff to search the grounds for anything that looked remotely like a trapdoor or an entrance. They spent several days, checking all the grounds and outbuildings, but found nothing out of the ordinary.

Inspector Hyde, confirmed that they'd indeed found the fingerprints belonging to Tyrone on the gates and shelves in the scullery.

What was I to do? The place was like Fort Knox, yet he'd been able to get inside. I contacted the alarm company and had a series of modifications done to the system. The tunnel would have extra cover, night vision cameras and passive infrared sensors. They installed a series of extra beams on the ground floor so that any movement in any part of the house on that level, would trigger the alarm. At least with all this extra security, I should be able to sleep easier in my bed.

When all the modifications to the alarm system had been done and the new doors fitted, I moved back in. I removed all the guns from Daddy's gun cabinet and placed them in my new bedroom. I decided I needed more firepower, so I selected a .44 Magnum pistol, guaranteed to stop anything, providing I could hit it. A Remington pump action shotgun also caught my eye, although by the time it was fully loaded with cartridges I could hardly lift it, so I reduced the weight by just putting in two shells, if I hit my target that should be enough. Come on make my day!

My officer, John Jacobs, who'd been on protection duty at Wigglesworth when he was shot, was in a serious condition in hospital. He'd suffered very serious wounds to his liver, complications then set in. He contracted septicaemia, despite the valiant efforts of the medical team, he died five days later. We were all in shock, John was a much-loved member of the force, due for retirement the following year. We'd not relish having to break the news to his other half, Sandra. What a lousy job!

This was now another murder investigation, we'd to catch this son of a bitch before he could kill again.

I contacted our cousins in Australia and spoke with Howard Donnegan, I asked if he could enquire to see if he'd slipped the net at our end and arrived back in Hobart. He later confirmed that they'd checked with immigration, there was no record of him entering the country at any of the ports either air or sea. Since the shooting, they'd officers at his residence and office but there was no sign of him. They'd keep up their surveillance and we'd be the first to know if he should return.

We'd a police watch at all our air and seaports and a high-visible police presence at Wigglesworth Manor. Seeing as details of our suspect had been released in most of the press we decided to release a photograph of our suspect and this was broadcast on TV to see if we could flush him out. We didn't have a lot to go on, he could be anywhere and probably by now, had changed his appearance.

When you lose a member of your team it affects everyone, even in neighbouring forces, we are a family, so everyone was determined to get this killer.

Chapter 22

It was show time!

Stephanie and I arrived at Heathrow Airport, we hired a car then made our way towards Winchester for the start of the enquiry.

We were booked into the 'Fox and Hounds Hotel' in nearby Crawley, a traditional English pub full of character, Stephanie loved it. After settling in, we took the opportunity to look up several old friends, including Alistair and my old bosses Archie and Tom. Alistair by now had finished his apprenticeship. He'd now got his own pupil to pass on his skills to, so the cycle continues.

We read most of the local newspapers, they all had coverage of the intrusion at Wigglesworth and the shooting of a police officer who had since died. It appeared to follow the same pattern of killing. I looked at a picture of the suspect Tyrone, finally putting a recent face to all the stories I'd heard about him. He was a handsome sod, very much like Megan, with stunning good looks, he could've been in the movies, instead, he'd become a serial killer hunted worldwide.

The press speculated about the forthcoming enquiry, they were looking forward to the appearance of the principals in this debacle.

The following day we arrived for the enquiry, of course there was an abundance of press present, several I recognised from my earlier persecution.

The chairman, Sir Marcus Munstead, outlined the terms of reference for the enquiry, he said a number of witnesses would be called to establish the sequence of events that lead to this gross miscarriage of justice.

Detective Inspector Tyler Hyde was called to the table first. He was asked to outline the timeline and events that lead him to the conclusion that I was guilty of these murders.

He was arrogant and not the least bit apologetic, for the gross mishandling of the original enquiry that lead to my incarceration. Munstead got stuck in and eventually had him reduced to an unsure bumbling nervous wreck, so much so, I almost felt sorry for him. Several of the committee pressed the boot home. When it was disclosed that Detective Tony Morehouse had informed him he'd found evidence that proved that another party could be responsible, he got buried under an avalanche of vitriolic abuse.

Eric Dawson, a Labour MP, was like a dog with a bone, he kept hammering away at Hyde, calling him inept and less than truthful and convincing in his testimony. Chairman Munstead had to intervene a couple of times to reign in Dawson, because he was getting carried away. It got so bad he eventually refused to answer any more questions unless they changed their attitude to him. He wasn't on trial, he was there to help with the enquiry. The tone of the questioning didn't change, so he got up from the table, said he'd nothing further to contribute and left the room. Security tried to restrain him but Hyde wasn't having any of it, he pushed them aside and stormed out of the building.

This would be the end for him, even if he'd made an attempt to justify his action at the time, he might have stood some chance of coming out of the enquiry with a degree of credibility.

But to react the way he did, there was no way back. The committee would eventually publish their recommendation. This could well mean trying him for conspiracy to pervert the course of justice, or at the very least, withholding information.

I was soon called to give evidence and sat at the large horseshoe-shaped table. I gave the committee a detailed account of the whole series of events that led to my conviction. Irrespective of the withheld fingerprint evidence, it was felt the judge had swayed the jury in his summing up and it was an unsafe conviction.

The very fact that there was no physical evidence of mine, either fingerprint or otherwise, found on any of the victims or at any if the scenes, compounded the feeling that I should never have been convicted. Munstead asked me several pertinent questions as did a number of the committee, I answered truthfully and eventually I was excused.

Megan was called next, within minutes she was reduced to tears. Munstead put it to her that she'd been far from truthful with the court when she disclosed I'd left the house around the time Basil Thornwood was murdered. She stuck to her story. She couldn't do otherwise, anything else would prove she'd lied under oath, come to think of it, so had I.

A few woman committee members obviously knew of her reputation and didn't approve of the way she lived. They questioned her for several hours, in what, could only be described as truly brutal. As the enquiry heard her stomach-churning testimony, I felt they'd gone too far. Even though her evidence had condemned me to a life in prison, and if capital punishment had still been in force, by now I would've been put to death. I felt sorry for her, she was a forlorn figure with no support from anyone, other than the family lawyer, Catchpole, who was there more in a supportive than a legal role.

The police came in for an awful scathing, the Chief Constable Atkinson felt the full wrath of Munstead and the committee in general. He sat there with a red face looking like a scolded child, I quite enjoyed seeing him squirm, after all I gather it was his constant pressure that had forced Hyde to pursue me.

An independent fingerprint expert, Noel Dyson, was called, he explained that none of the prints was complete on any of the weapons. He displayed on a board an enlarged picture of each portion of the prints found on the various weapons and how it was understandable that this could have been overlooked. He then went on to show how these had been merged together to make a complete print, that was later identified as belonging to Megan's brother. He outlined that this would not have been standard procedure to obtain a set of prints, it may well not have been admissible as evidence. This one expert had thrown a lifeline to Hyde.

By the end of the second week, I'd heard and seen enough. Stephanie had sat through the whole proceedings absolutely gripped by the events as they unfolded. Initially she was a bit reluctant to come to Britain, but here she was, enjoying every minute of the enquiry. She'd studied Megan with great interest, saying she was a beautiful woman, she could see why men would be attracted to her.

I'd made myself available to the committee should they want to re question me, but when I spoke with chairman Munstead he felt they wouldn't be calling me again. The fact that I'd been wrongly accused and convicted wasn't in question, they just needed to know how it had happened. The reason for the enquiry was to try and establish in an impartial manner, how this miscarriage of justice had occurred.

"Right that's enough of that, Stephanie, let's head to Cornwall to carry on from where we left off."

That was the worst week of my life, after spending over 20 years in the police force serving the British people, to end my career in such a manner. They made me look like a common criminal, but I only acted on the information that I had at the time. A committee of jumped up has-beens, hell bent on inflicting the greatest amount of culpability on me. The only good thing about this enquiry was, I understand old bollock brain got humiliated just as much.

Perhaps I should've stayed rather than storming out, but the questioning was very biased. It was obvious from the start they held me personally responsible. The committee would make their recommendations and that could possibly see me tried for my actions. I'd barely had chance to settle down in Spain, before I was summoned to this witch-hunt. I could finish up in exile along with all the other criminals on the run, what a strange quirk of fate that would be.

Apparently, the one good thing that came out after I left, was the testimony from the fingerprint expert. He explained the difficulty that we had and how it would've been very easy to miss this print. Our beloved Chief Constable expressed his disappointment that I'd stormed out, but he felt this testimony took a lot of the pressure off us.

The enquiry had taken up so much of my time, I was glad to be excused and get back to running Daddy's empire. The whole experience had been far worse than my previous appearances in court, in many ways. This time every single person on the enquiry panel had the opportunity to question me. The women I found particularly distasteful, one of them Marjorie Knutsford a retired magistrate gave me a hard time. It was obvious she didn't approve of my lifestyle, and seemed to be on a mission to make everyone aware that I was the devil's disciple.

She'd apparently never been married, looking at her, I could understand why. Ugly, didn't described her, she'd a face like a slapped arse, and had probably never experienced the joy of real sex. She tore into me with venom in her questioning. After a while, I gave as good as I got, what had I to lose? They seemed to be overstepping their remit with no one to protect me other than the chairman keeping them in line. I held my nerve, consoling myself it'd soon be over, when they obviously felt they'd exhausted every avenue of character assassination, I was allowed to leave.

There'd been no further incidents at Wigglesworth, but I couldn't drop my guard. Tyrone was still on the loose, and until he was caught, I couldn't rest easy.

It was obvious he'd attempted to frame me for these murders, but why? I couldn't get my head around this. It wasn't my decision to exclude him from Daddy's estate, but it was obvious he'd a deep-rooted hatred of us.

I was only thirteen when he was caught drug dealing. We never really spoke as children and didn't have a normal brother-sister relationship. It's not as if we were constantly fighting, he was just so distant. After this he was sent to Tasmania, so I'd no contact with him whatsoever. Someone must have been in touch with him over the years, keeping him up to date as to what was going on at Wigglesworth, seeing as he was able to pick off my friends at will.

By now, Daddy had been moved to an open prison where the regime was less rigid, and the inmates were low-category offenders.

He became involved in a number of activities, talking to and encouraging some of the young offenders to forego a life of crime and to embrace the path of righteousness and hard work. This seemed to be his forte and helped him mentally just as much. Hopefully he'd be allowed home at weekends within a couple of months.

The weather was glorious as Stephanie and I continued our tour of Cornwall, taking in all the splendid scenery as we moved along the coast towards Devon. She was in her element, and particularly looked forward to the evenings, as we sought out places of character for our evening meal, usually a pub with a good restaurant, and somewhere that we could sample real ale.

Each night we'd view all the spectacular pictures she'd taken that day. She really was a very accomplished photographer, her work had been exhibited in a number of galleries in New York.

When we'd finished our holiday, we made our way back to be present at the enquiry as it was nearing its end.

The committee had heard the evidence from all of the police involved in the original investigation, from the humble detective to the chief constable. Megan had been humiliated in spectacular fashion. They also heard the testimony of experts who gave their measured assessment on different aspects of the case. From what was published in the press on a daily basis, the police came in for a huge amount of criticism for their sloppy and unprofessional approach.

The committee would ultimately publish its report and make recommendation on whether any further action should be taken.

Chapter 23

Catchpole called me to let me know that Daddy was being allowed home for the weekend as part of the prison's rehabilitation program. He'd be free on Friday afternoon after 3.00 p.m with the proviso that he returned to prison by 5.00 p.m on following Sunday evening. It would be a once monthly occurrence, eventually leading to a weekly event, if the rules were adhered to.

This was great news, at last he seemed to be getting somewhere. He'd been a model prisoner, even giving talks on being in business. Daddy was an entrepreneur having started many successful businesses. With the approval of the prison governor, he'd started a training program to encourage inmates to set up on their own in business after they were released. He felt that because of his involvement in this program the authorities decided to reward him by bringing his weekend release forward.

I'd finished my appearance in front of the committee in a premature fashion, as a result, I was looking forward to going back to my new home.

Relations between myself, and Tony in particular, had taken a downward path. For someone who I'd taken under my wing many years before, he didn't hold anything back in his testimony. It was evident he'd no intention of covering for me or shouldering any of the responsibility. The Chief Constable was concerned that this fiasco had damaged his chances of a knighthood, what a disappointment after years of brown nosing his way to the top.

I decided I'd head back to Spain and polish my sombrero, before I came in for another slating when the committee published its report and recommendations.

By the time I got to Ford open prison in West Sussex, it was 3.30 p.m. Daddy was pacing up and down outside, anxious to get back to Wigglesworth, but roadworks on route had held me up.

"Sorry I'm late, Daddy, got here as quickly as I could, how are you feeling now?"

"Great, pumpkin, it feels wonderful to be free and going home, although we have had several supervised trips outside. We went to an old folk's nursing home last week to do the gardens, it was hard work but a great day out. Most of the people in here are a lot younger than me, some are only in their early teens, but mostly a genuine bunch of lads. They call me Granddad.

"When they tell you the kind of background they have come from, with no money to buy the basics, with no job prospects, possibly facing a lifetime of being unemployed, it seems inevitable they would turn to crime just to exist. I tell you, now I have a much better understanding of the prison system, the inmates, and how it works.

"Anyway, I do not intend to spend the rest of the weekend reminiscing about Disney-World, I just want to get home to see the old place and see how you have been running things in my absence."

"We've got Channing Caterers coming in tomorrow, Daddy, I've invited a lot of your friends to come over for dinner, I thought it would be nice change after the experience you've been through."

"That is great, I look forward to it."

Stephanie and I left the enquiry then started to head back to Bishop's Bluff, it was the last few days of our trip. The intention was to show her where I'd grown up and all the places I'd frequented, before I emigrated to the US.

As we drove past Wigglesworth, she was awestruck at the size of the house and the grounds. We stayed in the 'Hare and Hounds' pub, one of my previous haunts and somewhere I'd spent many hours of my formative years, learning the art of a good pissup.

We called in to see Alistair, Archie and Tom, my old bosses who by now, only put in an appearance a few hours a week. The company was growing from strength to strength, they'd also been recommended for the Queens Award for exports. The young blood had done good!

Saturday morning I was up bright and early, after exercising Pegasus, my chestnut stallion, I made my way back to the stables.

"Morning, pumpkin, if you had called me I would have come with you for the ride."

"Sorry, Daddy, when I looked into your room you were out for the count so I decided to let you sleep on, we can do it tomorrow if you want.

"The caterers called to say they'll be here just after lunch to start preparing for tonight's dinner."

"Are we having anything nice?"

"You'll love it! First course will be a choice of stuffed quail, or spinach with bacon stuffed mushrooms. The soup course will be broccoli and blue stilton. The fish course will be fresh salmon or trout from our own river. Main courses will be a choice of lobster thermidor or, 'Civet de Lievre' jugged hare to you and me, or for those who prefer it, prime rib of Kobi beef from our own Wagyu herd. To finish, a selection of greenhouse grown exotic Wigglesworth fruits with ice cream.

"We'll dine in the great hall of course, then afterwards I've got Mario and Lola from the Sportsman's club to run the roulette and poker tables in the games room, should anyone feel inclined."

"Sounds lovely, Megan, it will be a welcome change after prison food but I hope you are not going to too much trouble?"

"It's only what you deserve, I feel I'm responsible for you ending up inside, so it's the least I can do. I've told your guests they can stay over if they wish to do so, no doubt a few of them will.

"I thought we could raid the cellars and bring up some of your 1973 Château Lafite Rothschild Bordeaux and Château Coutet Sémillon-Sauvignon Blanc."

"Why not it is only gathering dust, it has been a while since we popped a cork."

"The Marshmen Quartet will be the entertainment for the evening, we'll put them up in the minstrels gallery, it's always a great sound from up there. Seems like an age since there was any real life in the house, it'll be like old times."

"Yes, I am looking forward to seeing my old friends again. It will feel like my rehabilitation back into society is well under way."

The rest of the day was a madcap rush, making sure everything was going to plan. The housekeepers had been busy organising the guest rooms in the west wing, Channing caterers were in the kitchen putting their finishing touches to the food.

Just after 7.30 p.m the first guests started to arrive, several cars pulled into Wigglesworth and parked in front of the manor.

The first people we greeted, were retired Chief Constable Richard Porter and his wife Melanie. He was in his late seventies but still a fit man, tall and slim with silver hair and moustache, someone I'd always had the hots for in my earlier life, sadly, he was never one of my conquests.

A lot of senior Tory politicians started to arrive, this surprised me somewhat as I expected a number of them to bow out, but obviously, it was good to be seen with Daddy again, especially as he was a major contributor to the party.

It was getting exciting as the number of people arriving started to grow and the atmosphere began to build.

Stephanie and I'd just gone down to the reception in the 'Hare and Hounds' where we met Alistair and his girlfriend, Marion.

"Lovely to see you both again, let's go through to the restaurant, they've a table ready for us?"

"When do you return to the US Luke? I know you did tell me but I've so much going on in my head these days I'm constantly forgetting things, guess I'm showing my age."

"We leave the day after tomorrow, but I must say we've thoroughly enjoyed our visit and we'll be back again later in the year."

"Yes it's been fantastic, it's a lovely part of the world, we've some marvellous pictures to remind us," said Stephanie.

"I hear there's a big party on over at Wigglesworth tonight Luke, according to my boss, Archie. He knows a couple of people who are going. Apparently, Offington-Smythe has been let out of prison for the weekend, so there's a party being thrown in his honour."

"Out so quick after what he did, just doesn't make sense to me, what's the point of giving someone a long prison sentence, then being so lenient?"

"Obviously, Luke, his contacts have helped, apparently he's been a model prisoner having implemented a training program to encourage people to start their own businesses when they eventually get out."

"Even so, it seems wrong to me, but having seen firsthand how screwed up the justice system is, it's not a surprise."

After we'd finished dinner, we went through into the bar for a few drinks.

Just after 10.00 p.m I noticed a figure in a dark tracksuit wearing tinted glasses come into the bar. He'd long wavy black hair and a thick bushy beard. After ordering a beer he took a seat in the lounge and was later joined by a female. She was in her late thirties early forties, tall, good-looking with blond hair. They seemed affectionate to one another, oblivious to people around them. She looked familiar but I couldn't put a name to the face.

"I know her," said Alistair, "that's Connie Knowles, her father's the estate manager over at Wigglesworth."

"That's where I've seen her."

At one point he got up from his seat and left the bar, it was at this stage I noticed he'd a limp.

I don't normally stare at people, but there was something about him that caught my attention, so when he came back in I followed his every move until he returned to his friend and took his seat.

They stayed for about another fifteen minutes then got up to leave. As they passed our table he turned and looked directly at me. At this precise moment, his dark glasses slipped down his nose. I looked at his piercing blue eyes. I might as well have been looking at Megan!

This one brief moment was enough, I would know that look anywhere, it had to be Tyrone. As he slid the glasses back up his nose, I noticed he'd several fingers missing on his left hand, this was surely him.

"Bloody hell, I think that's Tyrone, Megan's brother. Alistair can you call the police let them know he's just left and is probably on his way to Wigglesworth? I'm going to follow him, Stephanie, can you go up to the room and wait for me, I shouldn't be long I just want to see where he's going?"

"Negative, I'm coming with you."

I thought about it for a moment, "Very well, but be careful this guy is lethal."

We raced outside just in time to see a white Ford Mondeo estate leaving the car park.

By the time we'd got into our car and were mobile, he was almost out of sight, speeding along the road that passed the Wigglesworth estate.

We made up some ground and saw him turn off the main road down Pickwick lane that ran adjacent to the grounds. Fortunately, there was a full moon and visibility was good.

He stopped by the west side of the grounds, climbed out of his car and was quickly over the wall that surrounded the estate. We parked up in a field opposite and decided to follow him. Was this really him? A worldwide hunt was on for him, yet as brazen as you like he'd sat drinking in a pub where he could've easily been recognised by any number of people.

Stephanie and I scaled the wall and dropped into the estate grounds. We came out just behind the boathouse on the edge of the lake and approached with caution. We waited for several minutes, but there was no sound or any sign of movement. Searching the walls I found a light switch, as I threw it I was anticipating finding Tyrone, but there was no sign of him.

There were two rowing boats tied up inside, several fishing rods and a couple of life jackets hung on the walls along with a few pairs of waders. I knocked on the walls for any false opening but they were all rock solid. We inspected the boathouse thoroughly but he'd simply disappeared

"Where the hell did he go, I distinctly saw him come in through this door?"

"I think we should go, Luke, let's leave it to the police, I'm getting a bit nervous."

"Ok, Stephanie, you're right, I shouldn't be putting you at risk."

We left the boathouse then climbed the wall back onto the road, only to discover the white Ford estate had disappeared.

"He either sneaked back to the car or his girlfriend drove it away, I didn't even think to get the registration number although, it's probably a hire care. Let's get back to 'Hare and Hounds', I'm sure there'll be some activity there."

As we drove into the car park there was a high police presence. After we entered the hotel I could see Alistair in conversation with an officer, just then I felt a tap on my shoulder.

"Mr Clemson, we meet again, I gather you think you saw Tyrone Offington-Smythe?"

I turned to see detective Tony Morehouse, an old adversary and one of Tyler Hyde's team.

"Not sure if I should be talking to you, in view of the anguish you put me through."

"If anyone had any doubts about your guilt, Luke, it was me, I expressed on a number of occasions to Tyler that I wasn't comfortable with the decision to charge you."

"Pity he didn't listen to you, it would've saved me a lot of grief, not to mention costing the state over a million pounds as well as a public enquiry."

"What can I say Luke, we've all been humiliated in public in spectacular fashion with our whole operating procedures laid bare. I can tell you this, when the committee produce their recommendations, we'll come in for a real slating. However, whatever we both feel personally about past events, we need to catch this madman. I gather you think you saw him?"

"I don't think, I know, it was definitely him all right, we tailed him down Pickwick lane to the west side of the estate, where he climbed over the wall then disappeared into the boathouse. We followed him and checked to see if we could find him but he just disappeared into thin air. I suggest you get your men over there just in case he's holed up somewhere."

"Thanks for your help, Luke, I'll get men over there right away, once again I'm sincerely sorry for the nightmare that we put you through."

With that Detective Morehouse left the hotel, along with a convoy of police cars.

We met up with Alistair, had a nightcap before we retired to bed for the night.

The party was in full swing at Wigglesworth, when, just after midnight, security at the front gate called me to say the police were on their way up to the manor.

"Good evening, Mrs Clemson, I'm Detective Masters, can I have a word with you?"

"Is it important, we've a major celebration taking place?"

"It's important, but it won't take long."

"Very well, please step inside, we'll go through into the library."

"We believe your brother, Tyrone, was spotted in the 'Hare and Hounds' hotel this evening, then after he left he was tracked to your boathouse."

"Are you sure it was him?"

"Your ex-husband Luke is staying there, he was sure it was him, when Tyrone left the hotel he followed him to Wigglesworth. He drove to the estate climbed the wall into the property and went into the boathouse, but then simply disappeared. I've men searching the building and grounds at the moment, plus we've tracker dogs to see if we can locate him. May I suggest you keep a sharp eye out for him and keep the doors locked."

"Thank you detective, all the doors are securely locked, we've a doorman on duty to monitor everyone that comes into the only open access point into the house."

"I'll check back with you later to give you an update, Mrs Clemson."

With that he left, I felt somewhat concerned at this news but we'd a vast number of people in the house as well as a strong police presence so this gave me some comfort, that he'd hardly try something.

Just after 2.30 a.m. Detective Masters returned to the house.

"Sorry to bother you again, Mrs Clemson, but we've drawn a blank. We've searched the grounds thoroughly and gone over the boathouse with a fine toothcomb, but there's no sign of your brother. We'll leave a patrol car here and some extra men around the property just in case he shows, but please be vigilant. We'll return at daylight with a lot more men and give the estate a more detailed search."

"Ok thanks, officer, goodnight," I went back to my guests who were oblivious to the drama that was taking place outside. I decided not to tell Daddy, as I didn't want to spoil his first weekend out of prison.

Only a few guests had elected to go home, the remainder had indicated they would prefer to stay the night, and why wouldn't they, five star treatment at no cost? My one problem was I would have to leave the alarm system off as we'd so many guests strolling around the corridors of the house, they'd be sure to activate it.

One by one they retired to their rooms, by 3.30 a.m they were all tucked up in bed. I was totally exhausted coupled with consuming a serious amount of alcohol, I was glad to call it a night.

Chapter 24

The police had a strong presence around the house and this gave me comfort. When the last of our guests had gone up to their rooms, I checked with staff to ensure that all the doors and windows were securely locked, then I made my way up the stairs.

I had put my school friend and clone, Monica Devlin, into my old bedroom along with her boyfriend. Retired Chief Constable Richard Porter and his wife I placed in the 'Green Room' next to Daddy. The rest of the guests were housed in the west wing.

I had a quick shower and got into bed. As I glanced at the monitors for one last look I checked the view from each of the cameras. It was then I noticed someone walking along the corridor towards my old bedroom. They quickly went inside, shortly afterwards I heard a couple of gunshots and saw someone come out and start racing down the corridor.

I picked up my pistol and ran out to investigate. As I opened the door, my old friend, Monica was draped lifeless across the bed, shot through the temple, her boyfriend was lying on the floor with a shoulder wound. I helped him to his feet, told him to make his way outside to the police and tell them what had happened.

Several more gunshots followed, I left him and went straight to Daddy's bedroom.

Smoke was filling the corridor. I could hear the sound of wood crackling and this increased as flames took hold.

When I opened the door to Daddy's room, he was sat on the floor resting his back against the bed. He'd been shot in the chest and was barely breathing. He was pale and his lips had turned blue, as I cradled his head he whispered.

"Tyrone shot me ...be careful... pleaded... evil look on his face... pointed gun... fired... Sorry... pumpkin...aaah."

With that, he closed his eyes and expired as I held him. That bastard brother, why'd he do this to Daddy, how could he possibly kill his own father, it was obvious he was deranged? He thought he'd shot me, when in fact, it was my old friend, Monica.

By now smoke was coming into the room, I couldn't do anything further for Daddy. I'd to get out, the heat was becoming too intense.

With a cloth over my mouth and nose, I ran out. I checked the 'The Green Room' and found retired chief constable Richard Porter lying face down, he'd been shot in the back of his head, his wife lying beside him in a crumpled heap with bullet through her face. Jesus my brother was on a mission of slaughter but how the hell had he got into the house?

By now, both stairs down were well ablaze, the only way was up to the next floor. I could hardly see as I raced upstairs, along the corridor past several bedrooms until I came upon one with an open door. Staggering inside, I switched on the light then opened a window. I was screaming and shouting to the crowds below, but they obviously couldn't hear me with all the noise, flames were shooting up obscuring me from view.

Time was not on my side, it was minutes at the most before this level caught fire. This floor was somewhere not often visited by me, it held items of old furniture that had been dumped there over the years, I think the last time I was in there was when I was a child.

As I searched the room, I noticed a bulge in a large faded tapestry that hung on a stone wall. When I pulled the fabric back, there was a section of the wall that appeared was on a hinge. It was about a metre in height and half a metre wide, enough for someone to squeeze through. As I pulled at the stone, it swung back and there was a narrow passage behind it. Was this one of the priest holes that Daddy told me about?

I couldn't stay in the room any longer, flames were already coming through the floorboards, igniting several pieces of furniture.

The heat was becoming intense, I could hardly breathe with all the acrid smoke. My options were limited so I climbed inside the priest hole. It was all stone hopefully it wouldn't burn, maybe I could hold out here until the flames died down. With that I pulled the wall shut and I was in total darkness.

Eventually, I could feel the heat coming through the stone, it was getting uncomfortable, I moved along the passage, feeling the walls as I went.

I stumbled down a step, then discovered another step below that, so I sat on the floor and slid down to the next level. There was another step below that, even though I couldn't see a thing. It was a circular stone staircase that went on and on.

After 10 or 15 minutes, of shuffling down from step to step on my backside, I figured I was below the basement in the house. At least I was away from the direct heat of the flames, although there was a serious amount of smoke getting into the tunnel. I sat there for several minutes asking the question, was this where Tyrone entered the house? It had to be, I wondered where in the grounds it would come out?

I groped my way along the tunnel for what seemed an eternity, water was up to my ankles, the walls were covered in slime, it was damp and smelly. Every so often I felt creatures run across my feet. Eventually I came to a dead end with a solid damp wall in front of me, there had to be a way out, but finding it in the dark was the problem.

It was 4.30 a.m when I awoke to the sound of the emergency services not too far away from the hotel.

I drew the curtains back to investigate. In the distance I could see the glow of a massive fire, with flames leaping forty or fifty metres into the air. When I was fully awake, I realised the location of the fire was Wigglesworth.

"Holy shit, Stephanie, it looks like there's a huge fire over at Wigglesworth Manor, I'd better get over there, it looks serious."

Stephanie raised her sleepy head from the pillow, when she was fully awake she said, "Please don't go Luke, I'm afraid you might get hurt."

"I feel I must go they might need help. Don't worry I'll be careful."

"You're acting like you are still married to her, I'm your wife now, please don't go."

"Stephanie, that's ridiculous, of course you're my wife, it's just this looks serious and they might need some assistance. I'd never live with myself if I could've helped and didn't. It has nothing to do with my former wife, it's just there could be dozens of people trapped in there seeing as there was a large party taking place this evening, I'm sorry, Stephanie, I need to offer my services."

"Very well, but I may not be here when you get back."

"Sorry you feel that way, Stephanie, don't do anything stupid."

That was our first altercation of any kind since we first met. She obviously felt that even at this stage, Megan was still part of my life. She'd never indicated to me at any point she was threatened by my previous wife's presence. Megan was history I'd no feelings for her, not after all she had done to me, but this was serious.

As I drove into the estate, a number of fire engines were in attendance, several more had just arrived. I counted nine appliances, with officers racing around laying hoses down into the lake to draw additional water. The fire had really taken hold, virtually every room seemed to be ablaze, several of the flying buttresses had collapsed and a large portion of the roof had already caved in. The great hall was no more along with the ornate wooden staircase.

It was such a tragedy to see this magnificent building being reduced to a pile of ash. It would be a huge loss to the nation to lose such an historic building dating back to 1565.

Vast amounts of water being poured onto the raging inferno had little effect, even with the addition of several more appliances.

The heat from the flames was so intense the police had moved the crowds a long way back. A large number of guests in their dressing gowns and night attire, visibly shaken by the whole experience were standing around, several of the women were hysterical.

Four ambulances were treating the walking wounded, a couple raced out of the grounds with the more seriously injured for hospital.

There was no sign of Megan, as I walked through the crowds I bumped into Detective Rick Masters.

"We meet again, Mr Clemson, I don't suppose you've any idea how this started?" he said with a smirk on his face.

"Fuck off, I resent the implication of that comment, I saw the fire from my hotel room and just came along to see if I could help. Don't think about trying to pin this on me you evil little prick."

"Sorry if it upsets you, I have to ask the question seeing as you'd have as much reason as anyone to torch the place."

"Well I didn't you nasty little shit, I don't suppose it occurred to you it started accidentally, your obviously programmed to think the worst of everyone and be suspicious of every scenario?"

"That's the way policemen think. It's part of the job."

"That may be, but just remember what I said, I'd nothing to do with this, so don't go down that route, unless you want a harassment order served on you. You and Hyde are in enough trouble so I suggest you back off. Now get out of my way whilst I see if I can locate any people I know."

Masters sloped off, no doubt to see if he could pin it on someone else.

As I walked amongst the traumatised guests, I eventually saw Thomas and Lucy Crown who I knew from my days at the manor. He was a headmaster at the local school and someone who I'd always been friendly with.

"Hello Thomas, Lucy, are you both Ok?"

"Oh hello Luke, yes we're Ok. You weren't inside, were you?"

"No, I was staying over at the 'Hare and Hounds.' I woke up with all the activity from the emergency services. When I looked out of the window I saw the place on fire, so I came over to see if I could help. How did the fire start any idea?"

"It seemed to be coming from the great hall or the base of the stairs, with all that timber it was soon ablaze. To be honest we didn't stand around to investigate we just got out as quickly as we could down the rear stairs. That's the scariest thing we have ever been through."

"Any sign of Megan?"

"Haven't seen her, we heard four or five gunshots, when we came out of the bedroom to investigate, we saw flames shooting up the main staircase. We just hammered on a few bedroom doors screaming, 'Fire', then we raced out through the servants' quarters.

"I think most people got out, but several of them had serious burns, they've already been taken to hospital. Haven't seen Roddy Smythe though, or Megan, so no idea what's happened to them."

"Gunshots, are you sure?"

"I'm not an expert, but that's what it sounded like, someone going from room to room shooting, but to be honest, if we hadn't have heard the shots we would have died."

"Did you tell the police about the gunshots?"

"Yes, Luke, we have told them everything, it seems unreal, an absolute nightmare."

Most of the guests had got out of the fire although several of them had serious burns. Even though I was divorced from Megan, I was still concerned for her safety.

By now there was huge activity around Wigglesworth. The emergency services were everywhere, TV companies had set up cameras filming the fire, the local press were in attendance. They spotted me but being reluctant to be interviewed, I made my way to my car.

The whole building was ablaze, attempts by the emergency services seemed futile. Several firemen had been injured when a flying buttress collapsed on top of them. The general feeling was it was too dangerous to enter and it should be left to burn itself out. I looked at this and thought about the work I'd done on the staircase and the beautiful interior of this magnificent building being reduced to a pile of ash and rubble.

I tried to call Stephanie but she didn't answer, I figured she was annoyed with me. Was Tyrone responsible for this fire? That gunshots had been heard made it seem likely.

I don't know why, but I thought I'd drive around to the boathouse as I'd a feeling after my first visit, this could be relevant.

I was trapped inside this tunnel and couldn't find my way out, I had visions of being lost in there forever starving to death. In desperation I started to call out in the hope that someone would hear me.

"Help me, help me."

I parked up beside the boathouse and went inside to investigate. I threw the light switch and walked around looking for anything that might indicate this was an entrance into Wigglesworth. Then, after several minutes, I thought I heard the muffled sound of a woman's cry.

"Help me, help me."

I raced to the other side of the boathouse and put my head to the floor.

Again, I heard, "Help me, help me."

The sound seemed to be coming from somewhere under the large flagstones that ran around the edge of the boathouse.

"Is that you, Megan?"

"Yes, who's that, is it you, Luke?"

"Yes it is, can you not get out?"

"No I've been trying but there's a brick wall in front of me I can't figure out how to get out of here it's pitch black. Please help me, Luke. I don't want to die."

Several of the flagstones had large metal rings cemented into them that the boats were tethered to. I pulled at them one by one, thinking they might release something, but they were reluctant to move.

"Try pushing on the roof if you can reach it."

"That's not a problem it's only just above my head."

After several minutes, a flagstone, just a few inches above the water line, started to rise up. A distraught but relieved Megan raised her head outside the tunnel. She had fear in her eyes, and looked like she had been down a coalmine, she was wet and bedraggled.

"Luke, am I glad to see you, please help me out."

I reached down pulled her up. She threw her arms around me and held me tight for several minutes.

"Are you Ok, Megan?"

"Much better for seeing you, I've just come out of what can only be described as a bloody nightmare, I nearly perished in that inferno. How come you're here, how did you know where to find me?"

"Pure luck. I followed Tyrone here earlier tonight after I spotted him in the 'Hare and Hounds'. I saw him come into the boathouse but lost him after that.

"I told the police, they sent someone over to check this out but obviously they failed to find him. He must've got in here then waited until the party was in full swing before he went on the rampage."

"Actually, we'd all retired to bed for the night when he set fire to the place, then went on his shooting spree. Daddy's dead, shot by my brother, he also shot dead three other people and wounded another guest.

"Most of them were asleep in the west wing, I was just checking the monitors one last time after getting into bed, it was then I spotted someone walking along the corridor. He walked into my old bedroom shot dead Monica Devlin an old school friend and wounded her boyfriend Robert. Poor Monica, Tyrone obviously thought he'd got me.

"As soon as I heard the shots, I went straight to the room but it was too late. Then I heard another shot so I raced to Daddy's room, again it was too late. He'd been shot in the chest and was barely alive, he said that Tyrone had done it then he died in my arms. I heard two more shots and checked the main guest room on that floor and found ex-Chief Constable Richard Porter and his wife dead, he was the person responsible for sending him to Tasmania all those years ago.

"He torched the place I was lucky to get out, he'd set fire to both sets of the stairs, my only chance of escape was up to the next level.

"I raced up and tried calling to the police but they couldn't hear me with all the noise, the flames were shooting up past the widow so they couldn't see me.

"I made my way into a disused bedroom that was stuffed full of old furniture. I was getting desperate, the flames were starting to come through the floorboards, the heat was unbearable and I could hardly breath with all the fumes.

"I found an entrance in the wall that led into a tunnel so I climbed inside figuring I would be safe from the flames. Daddy did say there were probably ways into the house that we didn't know about, obviously Tyrone was aware of this tunnel from when he lived here before, he probably got out the same way I've just come out of.

"This goes all the way into the house, a distance of I would think seven hundred metres, then at the far end there's a circular stone staircase that goes all the way up to the third floor.

"He thinks he's killed us all as well as destroying the house and he's probably on the run, however, if he finds out I'm still alive he'll be back.

"I think I'll stay at our old cottage until morning, then collect some clothes and leave town until this nutcase is caught. If the police ask, please don't tell them I'm alive, let them think I perished in the fire. The longer I can keep up the charade, the better chance I have of staying alive. Will you do that for me Luke?"

"Of course, I think it's probably for the best."

"Can you drop me off at the cottage so I can get out of these wet clothes?"

"Not a problem Megan I also need to get back to the hotel, Stephanie will be doing her nut, keep safe."

With that she gave me a hug and a kiss on the lips then I dropped her off at our old cottage.

Chapter 25

As I raced back to our hotel, it was now daylight but the smoke from the fire was everywhere, visibility in places was quite bad. Some of the fire appliances were leaving the estate, but others would no doubt still be there damping down for several days. As I drove into the car park at the hotel, there was a lot of police activity. When I got inside, Detective Masters caught my arm. I was sure he'd some other caustic comment and I was ready for him.

"Luke, can I have a word please, there's been an incident. A short time ago, a man burst in here and abducted you wife, when the owner tried to stop him, he shot him in the chest and he has since died. We're not sure, but we think it was Tyrone Offington-Smythe. The manager was able to get a few words out before he expired, he said 'Tyrone' not exactly a common name and he'd have known him seeing as he has owned this place for the past thirty five years."

"Oh my god, why did I leave her alone? If I had stayed with her, this wouldn't have happened.

"I don't think there is any doubt it was him in view of what he did last night, did anyone see where he went?"

"The staff who were preparing the tables ready for breakfast, say he just bundled your wife into his car after knocking her unconscious, then he drove at speed out of the car park up Rawton Road in a white Ford estate car they are not sure what model."

"Thank you, Detective. I've something to do." With that I raced back to my car, I had to go and see Megan before she left her cottage.

She was just loading a few bags into her Mercedes sports car when I screeched to a stop. "Glad I caught you, Megan, your brother has kidnapped Stephanie from the hotel, he shot Lewis Tate the owner when he tried to intervene, he died a short time ago."

"Oh dear God, I'm so sorry, Luke, my family have made your life an absolute nightmare, not to mention the horrible thing that I did to you at your trial. I keep asking myself, how could I have done such a thing? I'm still in love with you, when you said you'd found someone else, I just couldn't handle it, can you ever forgive me?"

"What's done is done, Megan, my immediate concern is where Tyrone has gone with Stephanie, but more importantly, what does he intend to do with her?"

She thought about it for a while, "He can hardly take her to a hotel can he? My guess is he would take her to one of our properties, assuming god forbid, he doesn't kill her in the meantime."

When Megan said this I went cold, the whole episode was like something out of a horror story.

"We have over sixty properties in our UK portfolio, a lot of them are farms. They are all rented out and occupied. Come to think of it with one exception, 'Lower Crag' in the Yorkshire Dales.

"It needs a lot of money spending on the family home to make it habitable, it has serious damp issues. In fact, we've just finalised plans with a local builder to carry out the necessary repairs starting next month.

"The place hasn't been lived in for over ten years, but we've a sheep farmer who wants to move in, so that's why we're doing the modifications.

"It's the farm where Vera Maddox was held in captivity after she was kidnapped from her mews home."

"Would he know it was vacant, Megan?"

"He knows everything that is going on. Someone has been keeping him up to date about our current situation."

"I think I know who that might be, Alistair pointed out his lady friend in the pub, was Connie Knowles, the daughter of your estate manager."

"That old bag, I caught her and Tyrone in the stables having sex years ago. She was completely naked and was only about thirteen at the time. She just turned and laughed at me and carried on humping him like a professional. Obviously, her father has been keeping her up to date with everything that has been going on at Wigglesworth. He'll have some explaining to do before I put my boot up his arse."

"This Crag Farm, is it far, would it take long to get there?"

"Can't remember is the honest answer to that, even though I was there, Philip Knowles took me up last month to see the builder about the repairs. Let's punch it into the sat nav and see what it says.

"Here we go, roughly three hundred miles, in current traffic will take five and a half hours."

"Do you know where this farm is, Megan?"

"I was there but I can't remember what route we took, but don't worry, the sat nav will direct us straight there."

"You said us, I was going to ask you if I could borrow your car it will be faster than mine, as well as the fact you didn't want to meet up with him."

"That was before I knew about Stephanie. Please let me drive you, maybe I can make up for some of the hurt that I've caused you? Come on jump in, the sooner we get going the better, it's worth a try to see if he's there, because I can't think of anything else we can do."

With that we raced out of the grounds and headed north for the Yorkshire Dales.

Megan's a good driver, she'd spent a number of years competing in and winning, a lot of rallies. I felt comfortable with her at the wheel, but no doubt she'd be getting several notifications in the mail after posing for a number of speed cameras on our mercy mission.

We made a brief pit stop on the motorway before heading north. We were running a little behind schedule because of roadworks, and a contra flow situation on part of our route, but Megan floored it whenever she could.

Just after 1.00 p.m., we were getting close. We turned off the narrow road onto a dirt track and after about 20 minutes we saw 'Lower Crag Farm' up ahead, we approached with caution.

As we drove into the yard, everything seemed normal with no sign of Tyrone.

We both got out of the car and started to walk across to the farm, when suddenly, a white Ford raced out from behind a farm building. We both dived out of the way, but he struck the front of the Mercedes as he sped away. This took us completely by surprise, he must have been expecting us the way he drove at us like a maniac. We soon realised we'd a problem with our car as something was pressing onto the wheel.

"That was the bastard. He'd Stephanie in the front seat, so at least she's still alive whatever his intensions are. I hope to god he doesn't kill her I'd never be able to live with myself if he did."

As I inspected the front of the Mercedes, part of the wheel arch was pressing onto the tyre. I found a piece steel pipe in one of the farm buildings and I was able to force the metal away from contact with wheel so at least we were mobile again.

This had cost us valuable time, but Megan was soon gaining on them, as we came off the dirt track onto the main road she floored it. Several times she made an attempt to overtake them, but each time she was forced back.

As we headed south, both of us took chances but then we found ourselves stuck behind a farm tractor and trailer and lost a lot of time, we could see them disappearing into the distance.

Eventually we got past the obstruction and made up time, we headed south of the village of Aysgarth. Up ahead we could see the white Ford travelling at speed when Tyrone lost control on the narrow road.

He skidded, as he tried to negotiate a sharp corner at speed. He hit a low wall then somersaulted several times, scattering glass and various bits of metal, before he rolled the car then slammed into a van travelling in the opposite direction, coming to an abrupt stop in a cloud of dust and steam. My heart sank, would Stephanie still be alive?

We screeched to a halt, I raced over to what remained of the Ford. My stomach churned as I approached the crashed car lying on its roof. Tyrone climbed out through the driver's window, he got to his feet then staggered towards me. He'd a pistol in his hand, he raised his arm and fired. The bullet went through the lower part of my left ear, the pain was intense. He dropped his arm as he was obviously injured. I'd no intention of taking a second shot, so before he could raise it again, I gave him a Choku Zuki Karate punch to throat with as much force as I could muster. I then jabbed two fingers into his eyes blinding him before I then gave him a Mae Tobi Geri front kick to the chest. At this point, he sank to the ground. He lay there motionless.

My next concern was Stephanie, she was still trapped upside down in the car, petrol was dripping from the fuel tank that'd become ruptured, I was afraid it would ignite any minute. I undid her seat belt, held her to prevent her from dropping down then I lowered her as gently as I could. She was unconscious and had serious facial injuries and God knows what other internal organs had been damaged.

With help from people in the other vehicles that had stopped to offer their services, we managed to get her out of the car as carefully as we could, then moved her well away from the crash site. Her hands and feet had been bound with duct tape so we carefully removed this, minutes later the Ford exploded in a ball of flames setting the van on fire.

Within a short time, all the emergency services arrived, the paramedics immediately attended to Stephanie. Her vital signs were recorded, it was not good. They put in a saline drip as she was losing a serious amount of blood. A neck brace was applied and she was secured onto a spinal board, at the same time I got a lecture from one of the doctors.

"Great care has to be exercised with injuries of this kind, the head must be made secure to prevent movement, before they are placed on a spinal board, otherwise permanent damage can be done."

"I'm aware of the normal procedures, but it was either do what I did, or she would have burned to death."

They didn't comment further.

Because of her serious injuries it was decided to call for the air ambulance, I held her hand whilst we waited for the arrival of the helicopter. Ten minutes later it put down in a nearby field, she was quickly loaded onto it, then flown to Leeds General Hospital.

I was in a state of shock and couldn't take in what had just happened. My wife barely hanging onto life, would she die before they could get her to hospital. Megan was by my side holding onto my arm.

The van driver approached me, "Bloody hell, I've never seen anyone deliver punches with so much speed and effect, it was awesome."

"That bastard has killed a total of twelve people, six in the past few days, it was the least he deserved, plus after he'd kidnapped my wife I was determined to rescue her, although it doesn't look like she'll make it."

As soon as I'd said this, it dawned on me of what may happen to Stephanie. Subjected to a horrifying experience in a foreign country by this maniac, as a result now barely alive.

The police had initially arrested me for killing Tyrone. Fortunately, the van driver was able to explain in graphic detail, how the accident had occurred and what had happened when Tyrone got out of the vehicle, and shot and injured me before he was stopped.

He confirmed that I acted in self-defence having been shot once, and had very little option.

After making several phone calls to the police in Wiltshire to establish I was telling the truth, they allowed me to go. We gave detailed statements to them, because this was no ordinary road traffic accident.

He was wanted for a number of murders in Wiltshire as well as the abduction of my wife from Bishop's Bluff.

The paramedics then applied a dressing to my left ear and recommended I go to hospital to get the injury attended to.

I expressed my gratitude to the van driver for his help and exchanged details with him.

We made our way to Leeds General Hospital and while we waited for news of Stephanie, I checked into A&E to get treatment on my ear. Megan sat with me the whole time until I was called. After a thorough examination, my ear was cleaned then stitched with a follow-up treatment recommended for cosmetic surgery.

Stephanie had X-rays, plus a CT scan to establish the extent of her injuries. One of the doctors came out to give me an update.

"Mr Clemson, my name is Charles Hanson I am the senior consultant neurologist. I am afraid your wife is very sick, she has a fractured skull and a serious bleed on her brain. We have got her in a state of induced coma to help prevent the brain from swelling further. I have performed surgery on her to relieve some of the pressure. She will be closely monitored over the next few days, if her condition improves she'll be slowly brought out of this coma.

"She also has a broken pelvis, her right leg is fractured in two places, she has lost her right eye.

"I have to warn you, she is in a serious condition, her chances of recovery are very slim, so please prepare yourself for the worst.

"We will let you know if there is any change, may I suggest you go and get some rest, I gather you were shot at the scene of this accident."

"Yes I was, but my injuries pale into insignificance compared to Stephanie's, but I'll stay here for the time being if you don't mind, thank you for everything you are doing."

I realised with everything that had taken place, I'd forgotten all about her twin brother, Chuck. I called him, and told him what had happened, also, gave him the extent of her injuries and the doctor's prognosis.

He was in total shock when he heard this. He'd be on the evening flight from Raleigh-Durham into Heathrow, then the first available connection up to Leeds-Bradford airport.

Megan was with me the whole time and kept apologising for everything that had taken place, saying that she was responsible for causing all my problems. To be honest, I was more concerned with Stephanie and if she would pull through or not.

We booked into a hotel close to the hospital, I also reserved a room for Chuck. The hospital confirmed that there was no change in Stephanie's condition, she was still clinging onto life in the intensive care unit. Chuck called me to say he was arriving at Leeds-Bradford airport at 9.30 the following morning so I arranged to collect him.

However, I needed to talk with Megan as I felt there could be a problem meeting her brother.

"Megan, I want to speak to you regarding Chuck, because I feel there could be an issue.

"When I was released from prison, I flew to America to see Stephanie and Chuck, I explained everything that had occurred and your part in it. I have to say they didn't think very much of you, and whilst I may be able to forgive you to a degree for what has taken place, he may find it difficult to be in your company. I don't want to sound cruel or ungrateful, I'm just trying to avoid any unpleasantness."

"I understand, Luke, I'll head back to the cottage, there's a lot I have to tidy up, of course let the police know I'm still alive. No doubt that will disappoint a number of people. Will I leave you the car? I can get a flight down."

"That's not necessary, you'll need the car plus we don't know how long we'll be here. Thanks for everything, Megan, I appreciate all you've done, I'm sorry for everything you've lost."

With that, she threw her arms around me and gave me a long affectionate hug.

"I hope she pulls through, Luke, if I can do anything for you, please let me know."

I felt terrible for everything that Luke had lost and the mayhem that had taken place at Wigglesworth. I had to get back to arrange the funeral for Daddy, if and when they recovered his body.

There were also the other unfortunates who had been shot by Tyrone, I know that poor Monica Devlin's parents lived in Ireland and they wouldn't be aware of her demise.

Retired Chief Constable Richard Porter and his wife Melanie had no children but he had a brother who was in politics, he would have to be contacted. Of course I didn't know how many other people had perished in the fire.

I suppose I would have to arrange for the funeral of my brother but he would be cremated and disposed of, he would definitely not be interred in the family plot on the estate.

Chapter 26

I was there to meet Chuck when the Heathrow flight touched down. He of course was distraught, and was finding it hard to remain composed. Knowing there is supposed to be a special bond between twins, made it more difficult.

When we arrived at the hospital, we were suitably gowned and allowed into intensive care, but as soon as Chuck saw his sister, he broke down. She was barely recognisable, most of her head was swathed in bandages, there were drips and pipes everywhere, monitoring her breathing and all her other bodily functions. He just stood there holding her hand, sobbing constantly. I didn't know what to do, no amount of consoling from me seemed to make any difference.

Eventually, they asked us to leave, so we headed to the hotel. Chuck looked exhausted, I told him to try and get some rest, if there was any change in her condition, I'd let him know immediately.

It was late in the day when I arrived back to my cottage at Wigglesworth. I phoned the police to give them an update and Detective Masters accompanied by several other officers paid me a visit. I explained what had happened, that my brother had got into the house through a secret tunnel that came out on the third floor. He set fire to the house before shooting Daddy dead, as well as four other guests before he escaped back out the way he had got in.

They knew about the kidnapping of Stephanie. I just filled them in on the car chase through the Yorkshire dales before the crash that seriously injured her and ultimately brought Tyrone's trail of destruction to an end.

When they heard this, the relief on their faces was evident. This madman had caused havoc over the past few years.

Just before 4.00 p.m Chuck and I were summoned to the hospital, I knew it wasn't good news. Charles Hanson the senior neurologist was waiting to meet us.

"Good afternoon, gentlemen, I am afraid Stephanie's condition has taken a turn for the worse. We haven't been able to stop the swelling on her brain, despite operating a second time to relieve the pressure. I am afraid we can't do anything further, I think you need to look at turning off her life support. Her brain has suffered irreversible trauma, she is in a vegetative state, I am very sorry."

Chuck just broke down completely at this news, I felt so helpless it was so surreal. 24 hours ago, we'd everything to live for, I'd never been so happy, now here we were in the depths of despair because of Megan's lunatic brother, now being asked to turn off her life support machine.

Hanson left us alone to contemplate what he'd just asked us to do. Life can be so unfair at times, being asked to extinguish the life of someone you deeply love. I wouldn't be able to do it, I knew Chuck would never do it.

We stayed in the room for the best part of an hour, when Hanson returned.

"My apologies but I think you should come and say your goodbyes. Stephanie is sinking fast, she is barely alive."

We followed him into intensive care and held her hands as we watched the monitors indicating her vital signs give their last flickering indication of life, before the heart monitor flat-lined and the buzzing sound told us she'd died.

It was a numbing feeling. We both hugged one another in our time of grief, not knowing what to do next. The hospital staff was very understanding, they led us into a special room reserved for the next of kin.

We didn't speak, we just sat there trying to take in what had just happened.

Not long after a woman came into the room.

"Hello, my name is Amanda Lamb, I'm very sorry for your loss, we'll do everything we can to help you through this difficult time.

"Please allow me to explain something. I'm one of the organ procurement officers for the National Health Service. I know this is very hard for you, please forgive me if you feel this is insensitive. It's my job to try and help with the organ transplant scheme by asking relatives of the deceased if they would be prepared to donate any usable organs. There's an acute shortage of organs for transplant purposes plus there is a limited time frame that allows for the successful removal of them, that's why I'm approaching you now to see if you would consider this. Forgive me for asking, if you feel I'm being heartless I understand and I apologise but, you could help a lot of people."

Chuck just broke down at the thought of his sister being put through this.

"I've just lost my wife, Chuck has lost his twin sister, being hit with this so soon after she has died, is something we didn't expect. However, I realise there is a time limit that you have to work with.

"Stephanie was such a wonderful person, if I thought part of her could live on and bring life to someone else, then I'll agree to the removal of her usable organs."

"Thank you very much, Mr Clemson, your decision will bring a better quality of life to a large number of people.

"I understand that you live in the US and you'll want to return your wife's body home as quickly as possible. I'll help you to organise this. We've a support team that will start work on this straight away and we'll be able to release her body to the undertaker by the end of today. They'll negotiate with the airlines about handling the casket."

Having thanked Ms Lamb, then signed various documents, we stayed on at the hospital for the rest of the day, exchanging all our details. Eventually we returned to the hotel, both of us in a state of shock, this was the worst day of our lives.

It was all my fault, if I hadn't insisted on Stephanie coming to England for the enquiry, she'd still be alive, how could I've been so selfish?

We were back in Myrtle Beach five days later. The funeral took place at her local church where she was christened and we'd been married just a short time before. She was laid to rest beside her parents, in a ceremony participated by the whole town.

Chuck was never the same again, even after several months he was still lifeless, like his soul had been ripped from him. I also found it very difficult to carry on with our line of work without Stephanie by my side. Our home was so empty, everywhere I looked, I was reminded of her, I knew I couldn't carry on.

"Chuck I need to talk to you. Since the passing of Stephanie, we've both been struggling with life. I don't feel I can carry on, it's not fair to you or the company if I can't give it one hundred percent.

"So, with this in mind, I've decided to return to England. It may be that with the passing of time, my enthusiasm may return, but the way I feel now, I think it's a big ask. Your sister was the best thing that ever happened to me, life without her is very difficult to handle."

"I know, Luke, it's also like part of me has been torn away. I do know that my sister loved you very much. She told me many times how she felt about you. I understand your need to return to the UK, but please feel free to come back anytime, you have a home here as well as a job."

"Thanks, Chuck, I have enjoyed knowing you and I'll keep in touch."

Ten days later, I was back in Bishop's Bluff looking for a new home. Eventually, after several weeks of searching, I found a grade A listed period property called 'Hazelhurst Manor' dating back to 1575 that was in need of some love and care.

The place hadn't been lived in for 30 years, but I could see the potential. It was a major restoration project that might take my mind off things and help get me from the depths of my depression.

The roof was in a serious condition, so the first thing I did in conjunction with English Heritage, was to bring in specialist people to make the building weatherproof.

By degrees I made inroads into the repairs, working with my hands I began to feel I was living again, and rose each day with a little more enthusiasm for life. It'd been over a year since

Stephanie's tragic death, there wasn't a day that I didn't think of her.

The hospital had initially given me brief details of the donor recipients, it was extensive. Her heart had been transplanted into a 20-year-old girl from London. Her liver into an 18-year-old boy from Edinburgh, her kidneys into 10-year-old twin girls from Coventry, I felt this was appropriate. The cornea from her left eye was transplanted into a 50-year-old lady from Newcastle. A 55-year-old man from Luton with a history of pulmonary fibrosis received her lungs. Her pancreas was transplanted into a 35-year-old chronic diabetic woman from Manchester.

They had all recovered from their initial procedures, there'd been no rejection with any of the recipients.

I telephoned Chuck, to give him an update on the people who had received her organs, but he was still in the depths of depression and didn't seem too interested. This surprised me, after all, it meant parts of his sister had helped a number of people to a better quality of life.

He told me he rarely visited the factory and was lucky to have staff that could carry on the business without him.

He'd sold their boat, *Excalibur*, because it brought back too many memories of him and Stephanie. The old cliché of 'time heals' didn't seem to be working in his case, even though I told him Stephanie lived on in a number of people.

My old protégée, Alistair, was a frequent visitor to Hazelhurst, he helped me with a lot of the repairs. As we finished each room, the two of us would search antique shops to search for suitable furniture. We found several gems from the period but I made other items and I would challenge any of the experts to tell if they were genuine or not.

My friend, Keith, a textile designer and printer, created a range of fabrics for curtains and upholstery and they blended in perfectly.

By the middle of the first year, I'd restored the kitchen, the great hall and 12 bedrooms, but it was going to be a long job. I'd another 20 rooms to renovate, however, I was in no rush. My only restricting factor, was how much physically I could do each day.

I didn't need to work for a living anymore, I'd many millions in the bank.

Stephanie had named me as beneficiary in her will, although it didn't feel right to take her money. I raised the point with Chuck, but he said she'd divided her estate between the two of us. She'd discussed it with him on a few occasions, it was her wish in her will, that I receive her house, as well as half the proceeds of her bank account and her other investments.

He didn't have a problem with this, it was what Stephanie wanted, however, I insisted that he take her house and when he reluctantly agreed, I had my lawyer deed the property into his name.

Not long after I'd got back from America, the Munstead Report was finally published.

They found the police investigation was severely flawed and they came in for serious criticism, however, they were excused for the fiasco regarding the fingerprint.

The detailed report from the independent expert, confirmed that only parts of prints appeared on each of the murder weapons, as a result, they could be excused for missing this evidence. He also felt that the fact that a print was created using computer software, this would not have been admissible in court.

They also found the fact that prints from Tyrone had originally been taken 25 years previously, so no blame could be attached to the police. It was pre-digitisation and was only found purely by chance, after many months of searching.

However, the report felt the actions of Detective Inspector Tyler Hyde, highly unprofessional with a cavalier attitude to the gathering of evidence, without due care for the correct process of the law.

He received a serious reprimand that would have gone on his record, but seeing as he had already retired, nothing further would be done.

I served over six months in prison as a result of the actions of this bastard, and all he got was a slap on the wrist. I'd expected more, but deep down I wasn't surprised, not after my experience with British justice.

He was now in residence on the Costa del Sol, Spain with a lot of the other dregs of society.

The Chief Constable came in for a serious amount of criticism, because it had happened on his watch. After this report it would be seriously damaging to his career he could kiss his chance of a knighthood goodbye.

This document would have far-reaching implications for the police service in general and for the gathering of evidence. An innocent man had been jailed for a crime he didn't commit, and this must never be allowed to happen again.

It was felt that Inspector Hyde had used his position to exert his influence unduly, disregarding concerns of fellow officers to bring this case to court.

The Crown Prosecution Service came in for a serious amount of stick for proceeding without any clear forensic evidence. They'd been careless and negligent in their rush to judgement.

The judge didn't escape a mention. He gave the jury incorrect and highly biased direction, and as a result, he'd been forced to retire.

Overall, none of the people involved with the prosecution and conviction escaped the wrath of Sir Marcus Munstead.

His report was scathing and far reaching, with a number of recommendations that related to the gathering of evidence and the chain of command.

My only regret was that Tyler Hyde had been allowed to escape without any disciplinary action for his vendetta against me.

Alistair told me that Megan had gone to Tasmania to sort out the estate of her brother, Tyrone. He'd died without making a will. He hadn't married, so Megan being the next of kin, inherited everything.

"How do you know so much about her, Alistair, I haven't seen hide nor hair of her since I arrived back into England?"

"My auntie was a housekeeper for her, just a few hours a week, but when she went to Tasmania she laid her off, that was eight months ago, apparently she hasn't been back since."

"Not at the main house surely?"

"No, Luke, that was destroyed totally, I don't think it will ever be rebuilt, it would cost millions to bring it back to life and years to do it. She had rented out your old family cottage and was staying in Copse Lodge at the far end of the estate, it's a sizeable property.

"I know it, did a lot of work on it several years ago."

"Apparently, it was the only house on the estate that wasn't occupied. If you ask me I think she'll probably remain in Tasmania. She's had time to sample the life out there and it's far enough away from here to make a fresh start."

"Yes, Alistair, but it would be in the shadow if her brother and a constant reminder of the carnage he caused here, a purely evil little shit who should have been drowned at birth."

"I gather your old karate skills came in handy when you caught up with him, I know my friends used to talk about how good you were, they learned a lot from you when you taught down at the club."

"I relive that moment every day, when he raised the pistol and fired. I swear I thought I could see the bullet coming at me. It went through the bottom part of my ear, the wound is not as visible now after my cosmetic treatment. But at the time the pain was so intense, I just reacted. Another half an inch to my right and I wouldn't be talking to you now. I just flew at him, I wanted to make sure he didn't take a second shot, I've never felt such rage.

"I punched him so hard in the throat I gather his windpipe was severed, he was also blinded when I jabbed my fingers into his eyes, but it was my kick to his chest, apparently breaking four ribs that punctured his heart finally stopping him.

"I've never done that to anyone before, but it was the culmination of him beating and kidnapping Stephanie, the frantic hunt from here up to the Yorkshire Dales, to being shot at. I think I would've torn his head off but for the van driver, who pointed out he was probably already dead.

"I was arrested of course, after all, I'd killed someone, but the van driver's testimony showed that I'd acted in self defence after receiving a bullet through my ear, so no further action was taken.

"I lost my wife as a result of that evil bastard, my life will never be the same again, but at least I can talk about it now without getting too emotional."

"Sorry about that, Luke, I didn't mean to bring it all up again, you've had a torrid time the last few years, I don't think I'd have coped like you have."

"Let's change the subject, Alistair, I think we've earned a pint down at the Hare and Hounds."

Since I'd arrived in Tasmania, I'd travelled extensively throughout the tea plantation and the sheep farms, both of which covered vast areas of land.

Our green tea apparently, was classed as very high grade and commanded a huge price.

It was November when I was there, and the tea was being harvested. The buds and tips were handpicked then blanched to stop them going black then it was mulched and allowed to dry on trays.

Part of the harvest was processed to produce regular tea. It was interesting to see the different processes involved. The staff was very helpful in explaining each stage.

The sheep farms had over 500,000 head of stock, most of which would be processed then frozen and sent to Europe, but mainly to the UK.

We covered most of the farms on horseback. It was enjoyable being back in the saddle again. Although, several of the more remote farms we visited by helicopter.

There was no doubt that Tyrone had built these two enterprises up to be highly successful, I know under different circumstances, Daddy would've been very proud of him.

He'd excellent managers in place who'd no idea of the carnage that he'd caused in England, all they knew was, he'd been killed in a car accident and that I was here to take over.

I looked over the accounts of both operations, they were highly profitable businesses. What was I to do, stay here or return to the UK?

Both enterprises had superb managers they could be trusted to run things in my absence.

The other option, was to sell them as going concerns, they'd bring in many millions should I decide to go down that route.

It was Christmas, I invited Alistair and his girlfriend and my old bosses and their spouses to dinner on St Stevens day.

It was the first time I'd felt like celebrating anything, but my main reason was to show off my restoration skills.

Archie was very impressed. "You've certainly done a good job so far, Luke. I used to drive past this place every day on my way into the office and saw it deteriorating year by year. I think you rescued it just in time.

"Your ability in restoring all the original features is truly spectacular, however, I put it down to the training you got at our company!"

"Of course, where else? But I can't take credit for all of it. My old apprentice, Alistair, has put in a lot of time here. It's been a labour of love for both of us.

"It hasn't been easy though, having to work with English Heritage and the listed building people is time consuming, needing to get approval before I did any kind of replacement or repair, at times it's been very frustrating.

"I know they're only doing their job, but they can be quite anal at times, if I hadn't taken this restoration project on, this place would've been a total ruin within a couple of years, then nobody would've touched it."

When dinner was over, we retired into the lounge and had several more bottles of wine. We talked about old times the projects that we had worked on over the years until late in the evening when, suitably anesthetised they eventually left.

Here I was, lord of Hazelhurst Manor, not as splendid as Wigglesworth once was, but impressive none the less. It needed more life in it, a few kids running around, that was something that Stephanie and I'd talked about, but sadly, that was not to be. Was I getting broody, maybe I was but I realised it probably wouldn't happen?

After Christmas, I decided to leave Tasmania and return to England to weigh up my options. Rory Palance was my general manager who'd overall control over both enterprises. I felt comfortable things would run smoothly in my absence.

He'd send me weekly reports on both companies, although reading all this information was time consuming as well as taking care of all the other business interests that Daddy had left to me.

I was a very wealthy woman, although that had never really concerned me. My life had always been comfortable, Daddy saw to that, but seeing on paper what I was worth was quite a sobering thought.

The insurance on Wigglesworth had not yet been paid out and was the subject of many letters between my lawyer and the assessor. The claim ran into many millions and they were disputing a number of items, as well as the main claim for arson.

They were nit-picking trying to pay out as little as possible, but Catchpole my lawyer known in the trade as the 'pit bull' wouldn't let them away with anything.

They initially suggested it should be rebuilt and payments would be made at each stage of repair, but when they received the estimates from three independent companies for the total rebuilding, they took a deep breath and decided a lump sum settlement was the best way out and the least expensive.

Of course, the loss of this historic building was causing a lot of concern for various heritage groups in the country. They'd been exerting pressure for the place to be rebuilt, but unless the insurance company could be compelled to do it, this was unlikely to happen.

One day whilst at Copse Lodge, I was confronted by a group of people to see what did I intend to do with Wigglesworth, or to be more precise, what did I intend to do with this a pile of rubble.

I didn't think it was any of their business, it was my property to do as I saw fit.

They more or less insisted it was my duty to restore the home to its former glory, irrespective of the cost involved, or where the money was to come from.

How dare they, come into my home and start dictating to me, what I should or shouldn't do with my own property?

One particular tree-hugger really started to get up my nose, when she said it was common knowledge that I was a seriously wealthy, and I could well afford to pay for the rebuilding of Wigglesworth.

Bloody nerve of her, fat little barrel of a woman, she pissed me off so much I thought I'd have some fun.

"Actually, only last week I was approached by a consortium to bulldoze the site and develop it as a theme park with all kinds of rides. I'm seriously considering their proposal.

"One suggestion was, we put a paddle steamer on the lake, then have a monorail going around the perimeter into the different theme sectors in the park.

"We'll have a safari section complete with robotic animals, a futuristic section with actual rockets that can be bought from NASA at a knock down price, apparently they're surplus to requirements.

"We'll also erect a large outdoor stage so we can have live bands playing regularly, I'm looking forward to that.

"Of course we'll have all the major fast food franchises, overall, it will provide a lot of much needed jobs for the area."

The group were dumb struck, one or two of them looked ready to explode. Miss mouth almighty spoke up again.

"You'll never get planning approval, we'll see to that, we won't settle for anything less than having Wigglesworth rebuilt to its former glory."

"Good luck with that, I don't see how that is going to happen, not unless the insurance company pay out. They've already rejected three independent quotations for the rebuilding of the house, they're now looking at a lump sum settlement and this I will use to develop 'Wigglesworth Wonders.'

"It should only take about two years to construct all the rides, about a quarter of the time it would take to rebuild the house."

By this stage, several of them had turned a nice shade of puce.

"It's never going to happen we won't allow it, we'll picket the site and stop any development taking place. This house is part of our national heritage, it must be preserved at all costs."

"Like I said, I can't be made to rebuild the house, there isn't a court in the land that can make that happen, so that's what I'm planning, before I sell up and move to Tasmania."

At this point it started to get ugly and voices became raised. Miss don't-get-your-knickers-in-a-twist stood about six inches from my face. Her breath smelt like a wrestler's jockstrap, her teeth a long overdue visit to the dentist. She looked ready to explode, the veins in her neck pulsing like beacons, her eyes like piss-holes in the snow.

"If you think you're going to do this, then swan off to bloody Tasmania, you're sadly mistaken. We're not a group to be taken lightly, we've friends in high places, so you'd better watch your back."

"I hope that's not a threat, because I also have friends in high places, as well as friends in low places, the kind that will do my bidding no questions asked, you know what I mean?"

I made a throat cutting gesture.

"So before you go making threats you can't follow up on, think of the consequences. Now if you don't mind I've more important things to do, than stand here discussing things that do not concern you or your militant knitting circle. Good day"

With that I ushered them to the door and told them not to come back. Then this bunch of tree-huggers stormed off, muttering threats about my well-being and making smart comments about my past.

That was fun, some people have no sense of humour, but I should've embellished it a bit more, like plans for having a gay and lesbian carnival parade each month. Starting in the grounds then parading out down through the main street in Bishop's Bluff culminating with a firework display back in the grounds.

That would have probably sent these straight-laced, wrinkled old farts into orbit. No doubt the press would get to hear of my nonexistent plans, it would be interesting to see how it would develop.

Of course, on a far more serious note, for me to lose Wigglesworth was a devastating loss but I was realistic, it would take years to complete the rebuild, so I concluded the site should be bulldozed.

Even if we decided to rebuild Wigglesworth, and that was a big if, because we would have to recruit skilled stonemasons that would be prepared to devote many years of their life to this project.

We'd also need skilled joiners and plasterers, as well as a lot of other trades, experienced in the different building techniques from this period.

Then what about the lost contents? They were irreplaceable, dating back hundreds of years in most cases. The value of these alone was insured for four million pounds. Even if we rebuilt the house it would have to be furnished, but it would be very difficult to source period items to suit.

Taking all this in account, I regrettably concluded that the house shouldn't be rebuilt. The reclaimed stone and roof slate would raise a couple of thousand pounds, other than that, there wouldn't be anything else that could be salvaged. The fire had been so intense that nothing else survived.

Chapter 27

It was springtime, Hazelhurst Manor looked resplendent, all the gardens were starting to bloom, I felt immense pride in what I'd achieved in rescuing this home from terminal decay. It wasn't finished by a long way, I was probably over ninety per cent there, but I tackled each room with the same enthusiasm and determination to return it to its former glory.

In the basement, I found several interesting items that had been hidden away behind a false wall, six intact suits of armour, several broad swords and about fourteen crossbows. All were in reasonable condition and had been coated in a form of wax to protect them from rust, a few of them I donated to the local museum.

Of course, there were the mandatory priest holes, I found three in total, it was great fun uncovering these time capsules of historical interest.

The Winchester Globe had heard about my restoration project, they asked if they could do a story on the revival of this Elizabethan home, so I agreed.

A reporter and a photographer came out, I told them how I had bought this derelict building and the work involved in restoring it to its former glory. I gave them a tour of the house during which time they took many photographs. I also gave them a number of photographs of the house before it was restored.

When the full-page article was published shortly afterwards, I was delighted with what was printed, it made me feel proud in what I'd achieved.

The day after the article appeared in the Globe, just after 7.00 p.m, there was a knock on the door

It was Megan. "Holy smoke I didn't expect to see you, please come inside. You're looking very well."

"Thanks, Luke, so are you. I didn't realise you were living back in the UK until I saw the article in the paper."

"After the death of Stephanie, I went back to America but couldn't settle. Chuck and I struggled to carry on it was hard for both of us so eventually, after much thought, I decided to come home."

"I'm glad you did, as soon as I saw your article, I felt I'd to come and see you. The house looks truly amazing."

"I appreciate that, still have quite a way to go before it's finished though, but I'm enjoying doing it, every day I'm uncovering things from its former life.

"Tell me, how was Tasmania?"

"You knew I was there, how come?"

"Your former housekeeper is Alistair's auntie, remember he was my apprentice, she hoped you'd come back soon."

"It was certainly enjoyable out there, the tea plantation was amazing, but the sheep farms were so vast they took my breath away. They covered two-hundred-thousand hectares, I toured some of it by helicopter, and some we rode out on horseback to inspect. It's all very impressive.

"Not sure what I'm going to do with them yet, whether to keep them or sell them, but I'll be deciding over the next few months. I could return and live there. It's a beautiful place, plus the weather is fantastic, such a change from here.

"With everything that's happened in the past, I think maybe I should make the change. If I do, the one big problem will be all my business interests here, it won't be easy to manage them from out there."

"Afraid I can't advise you on that Megan, business was never my strong point, but I'm sure you'll work something out. Would you care for a drink?"

"That would be nice, Chardonnay if you have one."

With drink in hand, she toured the house, "I'm impressed, with what you've done, Luke, you would've put some of the rooms at Wigglesworth to shame. Love the suits of armour, they really set the scene."

We toured the upstairs and eventually we came to the old nursery.

"I see you've the children's room ready, is there something I should know?"

"No, it was the only room on this floor that hadn't been worked on. It was originally the nursery, I decided to restore it so this level was complete, that's all, there's no woman on the horizon."

"Well, you'd be a good catch for someone. Anyway, Luke, I think it's time that I went home. Thanks for the drink, will talk soon, bye."

With that, she left in a hurry, her demeanour changed just as soon as she saw the nursery. What the hell was all that about?

The following day I received a phone call from Anita Gilmore, who was only twenty when she'd received Stephanie's heart. The NHS had erroneously passed on to her my details and after some detective work on her part she tracked me down. Since then she had been in touch on a regular basis.

She said she'd love to visit me the following Saturday, if it was convenient and if it was, could I book a hotel for one night? I told her that wasn't necessary as I'd several guest rooms and she was welcome to stay with me with as many of her friends as she wanted to bring along.

Saturday morning arrived. Just after 10.30, I saw a car turn in through the gates then head up the long winding driveway and park outside. I went out to great her.

She was about average height, slim with long black hair, and she was beautiful, with a lovely smile and looked a picture of health.

"Luke Clemson, great to meet you at long last."

"Anita, it's lovely to meet you, welcome to 'Hazelhurst Manor'. Let me take your bag. Please come inside and we'll have some coffee?"

"Wow, what a fantastic place you have."

"Thank you, it's taken me a long time to get it to this level, it was pretty derelict when I started. It hadn't been lived in for over thirty years, the roof had collapsed and some of the interior walls were so unsafe they had to come down and be rebuilt. I still have some way to go before it's finished, mostly in the grounds plus a couple of bedrooms to decorate."

"It looks amazing, like a hotel, it must've been hard work."

"Yes, it's been labour of love, but I've enjoyed doing it. How has your health been since the transplant?"

"Absolutely perfect, I'm very active, I play netball plus I'm a member of my local rowing club. You've no idea what it meant for me to get a new heart. I'd problems from an early age, I'd a valve replacement at the age of ten, but basically a poor quality of life. I could barely breathe and it was only a matter of time before it gave out. Now I'm as fit as fiddle, all the people who know me can't believe the change in me.

"I was fortunate that the new heart was a perfect tissue match, the surgeon who performed the transplant said he couldn't have wished for it to be any closer.

"I have six-monthly checkups purely as a precaution, and I'm on anti-rejection drugs, probably will be for the rest of my life, although there's been no sign of that. I'm so grateful to you for what you did in giving me a new life. I wonder, Luke, would it be possible to see a photograph of your wife?"

I'd no pictures of Stephanie on display, it was still quite painful even at this stage, so I took an album from a drawer.

"This is us sailing down to Florida on her boat, *Excalibur*, it was our first time together socially, that's her twin brother, Chuck."

"God she was a beautiful woman, it's hard to imagine I've got her heart beating inside of me."

When she said this, it knocked me for six, it was the last thing I expected her to say, I became quite emotional.

"I'm so sorry, Luke, I didn't mean to upset you, that was very insensitive, please forgive me."

"It's Ok, Anita, it's still a bit raw, we were married for less than a year and they were the happiest months of my life. It was an awful tragedy, but it's great to see you looking so well, I feel she lives on in you.

"I'll take your bag up to your room, then we'll go and have some lunch in the 'Hare and Hounds' my local pub, they do great food. You also picked a good weekend, it's the county fair and there'll be lots to see."

I saw Luke at the fair with a beautiful young woman, she was less than half his age. Oh my god, was she going to be the next Mrs Clemson? I'd been away for too long, perhaps she's the reason the nursery had been made ready? I needed to speak to him before he made a huge mistake.

We'd a great time at the fair, then in the evening, we'd dinner at the 'Bon Appetite' restaurant that was situated just by the side of Lowbridge Lake. Tony, the headwaiter seated us outside on the deck. It was a warm night, the smell of flowers and shrubs drifted in on the evening breeze. Yachts zigzagged across the lake in an attempt to get the last of the day's wind.

Anita was an absolute pleasure to be with, charming, full of life with an infectious laugh, at times it was almost like Stephanie was there. It was lovely to be in the company of a beautiful woman again, even though she was half my age, she was just so refreshing to be with.

"Luke, can I ask you something? My boyfriend, Brian, and I are getting married in November, we'd like it if you could be there. Would you be able to attend, you can also bring along a companion?"

"Of course, I'd be delighted to come, I look forward to it."

"Fantastic, you'll receive an official invite shortly, my mum will be thrilled, she's dying to meet you, she never stops talking about what you did for us, and what an unselfish thing it was. It was her idea to try and trace and thank you for what you did, although, it wasn't easy as the NHS wouldn't give us any information. It was only when we received by mistake internal documents intended for someone else giving your contact details that we got the ball rolling and managed to track you down. I hope you don't mind?"

"I'm glad you did, to see you in such good health with a zest for life, I know I made the right decision."

Just after lunch the next day, she thanked me for a wonderful weekend and returned to London.

The following day Megan arrived at my house.

"Hi Luke, did you enjoy your time at the fair?"

"Yes it was lovely, I didn't see you there."

"No, but I saw you with your new lady friend, she's a bit young for you isn't she?"

Did I detect an element of jealousy?

"You've got it wrong, she just wanted to visit me to say thank you. She's one of the organ recipients and received Stephanie's heart and just wanted to say how grateful she was and to see what she looked like, that's all. She also invited me to her wedding later this year."

"Sorry, I was afraid you might be taking the plunge again."

"Would that have concerned you?"

"Of course it would, I never stopped loving you despite what has happened in the past. I know I've been an absolute shit and done some awful things to you over the years, but I never ceased to have feelings for you."

"What are you saying, Megan?"

"Can we not try again? I know you still have a fondness for me."

"You can't be serious, after everything that has happened between us it would be suicidal, not sure I want to go down that path of mayhem again. I'm lonely and need female company, but preferably one that comes without a danger warning."

She had a hurt look on her face.

"Please let me explain, Luke? When you said you'd found someone else and moved on, I was devastated. I'm the one that normally ends relationships. I was insanely jealous, even though I'd never met her.

"All my life I'd got my own way, especially with men. I suppose I just got obsessed with the fact that someone had dumped me. When I did what I did, I never thought for one minute they'd find you guilty.

"Inspector Hyde said they'd proof I wasn't telling the truth when I said we were together all night. Another witness had come forward who'd seen me at Basil's house at that time. I suppose I panicked when he said this. He said they would overlook the fact that I'd lied if I became a witness for the prosecution. If I refused he would make sure I was jailed and he would see that Daddy had a hard time in prison.

"What was I to do? I'd no option but to comply, it wasn't that I wanted revenge, I'm not that evil, I was just so afraid of what

Hyde would do to Daddy who was already having a difficult time.

"When the foreman of the jury gave their verdicts, I couldn't believe it. From that moment on I couldn't forgive myself for what I'd done.

"I know I should've come forward and told them I lied about you leaving the house. But, I'm afraid I didn't have the courage, something I'll regret for the rest of my life.

"Since all this started, I've been lonely, like an outcast with very little contact with the opposite sex, a pariah would be a good description of how I feel.

"During all this time, Luke, never a day went by that I didn't think of you. You're the only person I've ever truly loved. Why don't I stay the night, no strings attached just as friends, then we can take it from there?"

I thought about it for a while, I still had strong feelings for her, despite everything she had inflicted on me over the years. She was still stunning looking and had kept her figure as well as looking as young as ever. She looked at me, her beautiful eyes studying me, willing an answer, I knew I couldn't resist her.

"Very well, Megan, I hope I don't regret it."

It was late the next morning before we both awoke from our sleep. We'd a night of passion that I'd never experienced in my life. She was truly a master in her craft at seduction. It'd been well over a year since I'd felt the warmth of a woman's body, and I'm afraid I made up for lost time. Our sweat-covered bodies were glued together like limpets.

We both had a shower then brunch.

"Thanks for a lovely night, Luke, it was truly enjoyable, I'll be in touch."

Over the next few weeks she would stop by and the odd night would stay over. It was all very casual but I felt there could be a sting in the tail, I wasn't wrong.

"Morning, Luke, can I have a word with you?"

"Sure Megan, come on in. What's up?"

"I'm pregnant!"

I just stood there in a state of shock, trying to take in what she'd just said.

"And yes, in case you are wondering, it's yours, I'm just six weeks gone. Confirmed by my GP."

I didn't know whether to laugh or cry, all the years I'd yearned for children, now to be hit with this.

"But I thought you were, and I hate to use the phrase, barren."

"When I was in Hobart, I got talking to one of my female staff about kids and regretted the fact I couldn't have children.

"She recommended I go and see her uncle who was a top man in his field. Anyway, after giving it some thought I went to see him, he was a consultant gynaecologist. After he'd examined me he said I was still young enough to bear children and he thought he could help me.

"I was admitted into their private hospital, where he performed an exploratory procedure. It was discovered my Fallopian tubes were partially blocked, so he operated on me to solve the problem.

"He felt that after everything had settled down I'd be able to get pregnant. That was just before Xmas, what do you think, are you happy?"

"Stunned, would be a better word, all the years we tried, yet in just a few weeks we've hit the jackpot, where do we go from here?"

"We could always get married."

"Then what, suppose in a couple of months you get bored and decide to start an affair?"

"Those days are all behind me, Luke, I promise."

"You're asking me to forget everything that you've done to me, not to mention help getting me jailed for something I didn't do?"

"Not forget, but forgive, I know you can, you've a big heart and I know you don't bear grudges.

"What I'll do is sign a prenuptial agreement, splitting my total wealth with you as a sign of my commitment to you. You can have it worded whatever way you want so that I won't repeat past indiscretions."

"Our relationship was never about money, Megan, I loved you more than anything in this world."

"I'm just trying to prove to you that I've changed, and the prenuptial is my way of convincing you that I mean what I say. My wealth is estimated at over two and a half billion pounds, not to mention my assets in Tasmania, which if I sell, should bring in another few hundred million. What do you say?"

"I'm still trying to get my head around this after everything that has happened between us."

I sat down in shock, this was a bolt out of the blue. Several minutes passed as I tried to come to terms with what Megan had just told me. A dad at last, children were something that I'd always yearned for, maybe this could be the turning point for both of us.

Megan was still very beautiful, she'd this magnetism that I found impossible to resist. She sat down beside me and held my hand.

"Well, Luke, what will it be?"

Eventually, I felt able to answer her, "It would have to be a civil service. I know there are a lot of people who'll think I'm raving mad, but the answer is yes.

"However, we'll live here, this is my home now and it'll be the perfect place to bring up children."

"I don't have the slightest problem with that, you've created something wonderful here and I look forward to spending the rest of my life with you."

We got married in the registry office in Winchester a month later, then waited for the birth of our twins, yes twins, a girl and a boy, we named them Stephanie and Chuck.

They were born at Hazelhurst Manor, After all that had happened, life had finally dealt me a decent hand.

However, it very soon became apparent that Megan wasn't the maternal type, everything was a major chore for her, she became stressed out over the least little thing.

Eventually, I recruited a live-in nanny to help take care of the twins.

Marina was originally from Estonia, she had a wonderful way with children, having come from a large family herself. She fitted into our family life perfectly.

Megan would spend many hours in the gym that I had created in the basement, getting her figure back in shape.

The twins were almost a year old, when an agreement was finally reached with the insurance company. They agreed to pay for the total rebuild of Wigglesworth, however due to the fact we'd reached the limit of our cover of £20 million there'd be a shortfall. This meant that part of refurnishing the house wouldn't be covered. I didn't see this as a major problem it's not as if we couldn't afford it, but it would be nigh on impossible to source all the items of furniture from this period, so I would make them myself, after all, that's what I'd been doing all my working life.

I decided that I'd be the project manager. We'd received three independent quotations and we selected one company that I was quite familiar with. They were excellent stonemasons, responsible for many of the government buildings in the county. They weren't the cheapest, but I knew they would do a good job. Part of the agreement was to give us a fixed quotation for the rebuild that eliminated any nasty surprises that could arise as the project moved forward. They were also able to commit staff to the project for the duration of the build, estimated at up to seven years.

Sadly, only about one percent of the Forest Marble stone from the original building could be recycled, the rest would be ground up and used as hardcore in the foundations and filler in the walls.

The original stone used in the building of Wigglesworth came from a quarry at the eastern end of the estate. It hadn't been used for that purpose for over 150 years, so we obtained permission from the local authorities to reopen it as a quarry.

We moved in drilling and blasting equipment, also heavy stone cutting machinery. There were a number of stonemasons employed there, cutting and dressing all the Forest Marble before transporting it to the site.

We had located the original drawings and plans for the house from her father's safety deposit box in Barclays Bank. Along with these, and numerous photographs of every part of the exterior, the architects were able to draw up detailed plans of every section of the house, even down to the size and shape of each block of stone and its position in the rebuild.

Of course, we'd got that anal group from English Heritage, breathing down our necks for every step of the way. After four years, we'd made significant progress and we were probably about two years ahead of schedule. All that remained was to fit the windows making the house watertight, we could then start on the interior.

During this period, Megan rarely visited the site, which surprised me, after all we were rebuilding her family home. She'd spend time visiting friends during the day, whilst Marina took care of the children. I'd then take over in the evenings to give her a break. They were great fun and I looked forward to that time of the day.

One day I drove out to Ringwood to see Dave Barber who was creating our stained glass windows. On the way back I thought I saw Megan's Jaguar pull into the car park of the 'White Swan' hotel, so I followed at a discrete distance.

It was her all right, as she climbed out of her car, I saw a tall familiar-looking guy walk over to her. Then I remembered where I'd seen him before, it was Charles Bambury, a freelance stonemason who did work for us at different stages of the build. They embraced and went into the hotel.

What the hell was all this about? Was it an innocent liaison or something more sinister? I mustered up the courage to go into the hotel. I searched the different lounges looked into the bar and restaurant but there was no sign of them, so the next stop was reception.

"Excuse me, do you have a Charles Bambury staying here?"

"One moment sir, I'll check...yes we do."

"Could I have his room number please, I need to speak to him urgently?"

"I'm sorry sir, we're not allowed to give out room numbers, but if you'd like to go into that cubicle under the stairs and pick up the phone, I'll put a call through to his room."

"Thank you."

After several seconds, a breathless Bambury answered, "Yes, what is it?"

I didn't answer, after several more seconds, "Is there anyone there?" I still didn't answer, then in the background I heard,

"Who is it, darling?" I would know that voice anywhere, it was Megan.

I had this gut wrenching feeling, all the past memories came flooding back. I raced home to Hazelhurst to contemplate my course of action.

I'd just put the twins to bed when Megan arrived home at 7.30 p.m.

"Hi, Luke, how was your day?"

"Good, took a ride out to Ringwood earlier today to see Dave Barber, he's making the stained glass windows for the east wing. They look fantastic as close as you could ever get to the original. How was your day?"

"Spent the afternoon with Penny Marston she's opened another boutique in Romsey. Then we went to the 'Silver Spoon' for an early bird dinner."

"You weren't near Ringwood were you?"

I could see the expression on her face change.

"No, why'd you ask?"

"I was just passing the White Swan and I thought I saw your car outside."

"Wasn't me, could have been anyone, there are lots of the new Jags around."

"Guess I was mistaken then."

"Yes you were, anyway, I'll just go up to see the twins."

Why would she lie unless she had a guilty secret. One thing was for sure, it'd be a different story this time around I wouldn't stand by and do nothing.

Chapter 28

By degrees the house had risen up from the ground, as had the scaffolding. New lengths of piping clamped together created an intricate web of metal that extended around the whole perimeter and reached well into the sky. However, great care must be taken with this system, the nuts and bolts must be checked regularly to ensure they don't become loose.

As each element of the build was finished, we'd the dreaded English Heritage to pass or reject it.

One thing they criticised was a flying buttress they felt was different to how it was originally. I couldn't see anything wrong with it, especially with it being so far from the ground, but they had to be obeyed.

I contacted the mason who'd worked on it to liaise with Mr Warburton from English Heritage. Charles Bambury arrived on site shortly afterwards. After a brief discussion, he climbed to the very top of scaffolding and started work on rectifying the problem.

It was late afternoon when apparently Mr Bambury did a backward somersault from 80 feet that would have earned him maximum points in the Olympic Games.

Sadly, his entry wouldn't have impressed the judges, Forest Marble is rather unforgiving and doesn't provide for a soft landing.

I was at the other end of the site when the accident happened. He was working on the flying buttress when a scaffolding pole gave way and he plummeted to the ground. His body was eventually removed to the county morgue.

When Megan became aware there'd been an incident on site, she came straight over.

"Just heard there's been accident, Luke, what happened?"

“This chap was doing an adjustment on one of the flying buttresses. English Heritage insisted it was changed and it would appear he lost his footing when the scaffolding gave way.”

“Who was it.”

“You probably don't know him, he was a freelancer, a chap called Charlie Bambury.”

The look on Megan's face said it all.

“Was he killed?”

“Oh yes, you don't fall from that height and survive.”

At this point she turned and as she walked away I could see her sobbing.

The accident had a profound effect on a number of people. Mr Warburton felt if he hadn't insisted on the change, Charlie Bambury would still be alive. They’d be helpful and a lot more accommodating in future.

Of course, Megan was in shock and obviously very upset but she couldn't acknowledge that she’d been having a relationship with him.

Let this be a lesson!

The local police and the Health & Safety Executive did a thorough investigation, but eventually they came to the conclusion it was an unfortunate accident.

After the funeral of Charlie Bambury, I gave myself a reality check. What the hell was I doing after promising Luke my cheating days were over? This would never happen again, how could I have been so stupid risking everything that I had, just because I was shown a bit of flattery by an oversexed stone humper?

The last of the stained-glass windows had been fitted in position, they looked spectacular. Dave Barber was a craftsman of the highest calibre, hopefully his creation would be around for several hundred years. I congratulated him on his outstanding work.

The building was now watertight and we could start on the interior.

Megan now spent more time with the twins, making sure they got to school on time then collecting them in the afternoon. The tragic death of Bambury, had an obvious effect on her, but slowly she came out of her shell.

I don't know if there were any more incidents of her infidelity. Maybe she suspected Bambury's demise was more than an accident, I don't really know but I think it did the trick.

It just proved the point that I'd been weak and if I'd taken a more assertive role sooner than when I did, Megan would have been a different person, not prone to wandering with all the deceit and infidelity that came with it.

I wouldn't have had to undertake the drastic action that I did and the likes of Thornwood, Wimpole and company would still be alive!

Made in the USA
Charleston, SC
07 December 2014